Twice Loved

Twice Loved

Lori Copeland

AVON
INSPIRE
An Imprint of HarperCollins*Publishers*

HarperCollins books may be purchased for educational, business, or sales promotional use. For information please write: Special Markets Department, HarperCollins Publishers, 10 East 53rd Street, New York, NY 10022.

FIRST EDITION

Library of Congress Cataloging-in-Publication Data
Copeland, Lori.
    Twice loved/Lori Copeland. — 1st ed.
      p. cm.   (Belles of Timber Creek)
    ISBN 978-0-06-136491-4 (pbk.)
    1. Women teachers—Fiction 2. Texas—Fiction. I. Title.
    813'.54—dc22

08 09 10 11 12   OV/RRD   10 9 8 7 6 5 4 3 2 1

Prologue

Willow Madison thought by the time she turned nineteen, she would have the spirit of a wild mustang racing across the Texas plains—free of entanglements, liberated of sorrow, racing free with the herd. Wind in her eyes, unencumbered mane . . .

Instead, her mare pulled her in a buckboard, trotting across the rutted Texas countryside, heart heavy with what she was about to perpetuate.

She spat out a bug, then worked the handkerchief up her neck and over her mouth. Dust flew from the mare's hooves and fogged her sight. Fear shaded her senses. The five barrels of kerosene in the wagon bed made her uneasy, but then, the whole sordid purpose of her journey was nerve-racking. If she had her say, she'd turn this rig around and head straight for home as fast as the horse could run. But she didn't have her say.

Although, after a year of war—living with death twenty-four hours a day, and then walking away last month with nothing more serious than a sprained ankle—fear should no longer be a part of her vocabulary.

She could do this. She had to do it. Copper and Audrey were counting on her.

Yet, deliberately setting her bonnet for a man wealthy beyond description and candidly in the market for a bride wasn't her idea of romance, or for that matter, integrity. She shook her head. Marriage was a sacred matter, and she planned to honor her vows. Love was highly overrated.

Money to the wealthy was a minute matter; two coins to Willow meant she and her friends would either eat or go hungry.

She lifted a hand to shield the late afternoon glare. Black clouds hung in the west, but the hot sun seared her back. Willow urged the horse to a faster gait. She'd spent two nights on the trail, and she didn't intend to waste a third. Her eyes fixed on the lowering clouds, charged with torrential rain—or were they? Uncle Wallace warned that it rarely rained in Thunder Ridge—only thundered and lightninged. Regardless, she was ready to be done with this godforsaken journey.

An hour later, Willow spotted a wooden sign at a crossroad. An arrow pointed west, and the crude lettering read: *Thunder Ridge 1/2 mile.*

Flicking the reins, she set off. The buckboard bounced through heavy ruts. Kerosene splashed against tightly sealed lids. Would five full barrels be enough? She mulled her uncle's letter over in her mind.

Don't forget to bring kerosene. The men are busy rebuilding the mill so they don't remember that cold winter winds will come again.

And her reply:

Dear Uncle Wallace,

Due to circumstances, I am accepting your invitation to stay with you. I will come immediately and bring kerosene.

She winced, picturing Copper and Audrey, fellow soldiers and schoolteachers. The women's expressions had paled when she told them that she had accepted Uncle Wallace's solution to everyone's problem.

"It isn't right, Willow." Copper shook fiery-colored tresses. "It isn't fair to take advantage of the rich in this disgraceful manner."

"Right or wrong, we have to eat."

Audrey frowned. "But marry a man for money instead of love? Do you really think that's what God would want for you?" Well, it wasn't Willow's first choice, but she could do it. When the Yanks had come and burned, pillaged, and killed, Timber Creek's surviving women had banded and fought back, formerly happy brides, and three single women. Willow and her friends had helped bitter husbandless women and mothers dig shallow graves and bury children before they took up arms. Then they had formed a small but formidable band, and they fought. Four had gone down fighting for what they believed, but the women had fought as hard and as determined as any man.

Had God intended for women to go to war? He hadn't built them for battle, but when threatened with all they held dear, females fought in self-defense. There wasn't much left of Timber Creek, but the women—with the help of eighty-five-year-old town drunk Asa Jeeters—had fought and driven off more than one band of Yankee soldiers.

Asa had gone to eternity, speeded by a Yankee bullet, but not before he had met the Lord, on his knees in a dark, damp root cellar. Willow was sure Asa walked with the angels now, but her imagination balked at picturing him in a white robe, strumming a harp. Saint Peter had his hands full with Asa.

News of Lee's Appomattox surrender hadn't reached Timber Creek when the last five women laid down their arms and walked away with their lives—Willow, Copper, Audrey, and two women old enough to be their mothers. The older women, Ester and Othel, drifted away, beaten, worn. Willow, Copper, and Audrey forged a bond, vowing they would care for each other, come what may. They were educated. All three had taught school before towns were burned; they could go on, with God's help. And each other's.

Uncle Wallace's letter, well-worn from rereading as she made her decision, crackled in Willow's pocket.

Dearest Willow,

The war is over, and I beg you to come now. Sunday past, Silas Sterling announced his intentions to take a bride by the end of the year. There are two available women in Thunder Ridge: the Widow Gleeson, far too old to bear children, and Lilly Forrester, fourteen but maturing rapidly. Silas is a kind man, moral, has good teeth and bone structure, and has a practical sense of humor. Marrying Silas will ensure you a comfortable life. I have spoken to the Reverend Cordell, and he has agreed that Thunder Ridge is long overdue to reopen school, so you will be able to put your knowledge to use while Silas properly courts you. I am extending an invitation to your friends Copper and Audrey to come with you. Neighboring areas will soon be looking for schoolteachers, and my house is large enough to accommodate you and many others. I cannot offer you financial security, since the house is my only asset, but you and your friends are welcome to its shelter. Very soon, I must sell my home and get something smaller, but until you're married and financially secure with Silas, I will retain the house.

I know the plan may not appeal to your spirited nature, Willow, but it is the only answer. I promised my dear brother and your mother I would look after you, and I fear I have neglected my word. It is nothing short of God's grace that you have survived the war. My prayers have been answered. I have not heard, nor has anyone else, of women fighting, but I suppose there is a first for everything. The war is over; your parents are dead. You have no one—I have no one. Come to Thunder Ridge and begin a new life, a life of privilege as Silas's wife. One glimpse of your hair, the color of a stormy Texas sunset, and those sapphire eyes, and the man will be smitten. Come, Willow. And don't forget to bring kerosene. The men are busy rebuilding the mill so they don't remember that cold winter winds will come again. Their thoughts are centered on getting the mill up and running so the town will again have revenue.

Rain scented the air as Willow spotted Thunder Ridge. Silhouetted against an angry sky, five buildings jutted up from ground that hadn't seen rain in a spell. The wagon rattled closer, and Willow focused on the sawmill located at the edge of town. A water wheel gently turned water. Row upon row of neatly stacked planks and shingles lined the east side of the work shed.

Thunder Ridge. Deep in the heart of the Texas Panhandle, and her new home.

Willow wasn't certain she'd make a proper rich man's wife. She wasn't all that refined, but she'd try. Though her feminine nature was a bit tarnished, she was naturally gifted with a quick mind, and her cooking was edible.

Not all was lost. Thunder Ridge would soon be Copper and Audrey's security too. Once Willow settled, she would send for her soul mates. Uncle Wallace said there were towns nearby, towns that would need schoolmarms, and the good Lord knew Copper and Audrey's families were long gone.

Poor Uncle. Aunt Claudine had died of a strange illness three years earlier, and he had later retired as county judge. He was alone now. His old house could shelter a lot of homeless women for the time being. Copper and Audrey would be cared for, and Willow would strive hard to make a good life for everyone.

Marrying a man solely to acquire financial sanctuary went against her grain, but realistically, the option was a sensible choice. Security—that's all a marriage required. Willow had met many a man on the battlefield but sparks had never flown—only lead bullets.

Timber Creek refugees had lost everything but their lives. God had spared Willow and her friends for a reason—what, she couldn't comprehend, but someday she would understand, and she'd have a few respectful questions for her Maker. The women had faced and conquered Armageddon. Willow could cope with a harmless old man, provide a temporary home for her friends, and look after Wallace . . . and Silas in his waning years. Perhaps this was her finest hour, her very reason for existence.

So be it, Father. I will do whatever I need to do.

Lightning forked, followed by a boom. The buckboard jarred. Willow struggled to control the rearing mare. The startled animal lunged, racing headlong into the gathering storm.

Willow shouted. A second clap of thunder vibrated the earth. Out of control, the horse galloped headlong for the mill.

Walt Sessions, a millworker, ambled out of the mill shack and lifted a lighted match to his rolled smoke. He glanced up, his eyes focusing on a buckboard and a screaming woman. The horse dragged the buckboard, heading straight for the mill. The match flamed between his fingers.

"Whoa!" the woman shouted. She stood, both heels braced against the wooden seat, sawing on the reins. "Whoa!"

Thunder shook the ground. Straight ahead of the runaway horse, a wagon stacked with newly planed lumber sat in the middle of the road.

"Out of the way! Coming through!" The buckboard bore down on the wagon.

"Move!" the woman shouted at a man standing beside the conveyance. Caleb Gray glanced up, then lunged aside as they rattled past. At the last moment, the horse veered, dragging the buckboard like a rag doll. The hitch snapped, flinging the cart a good thirty feet. Wheels skidded, barrels bounced. Wood planks split, contents spilling onto the mill-pond. The woman flew through the air and landed with a jarring thud. A slick rose on the water's surface, the volatile stench saturating the early June air.

Walt swore as the match seared his fingers. He flung the stick into the water.

The ensuing swoosh of igniting kerosene would later be compared to the Second Coming. Red-hot flames could easily have been mistaken for chariots of fire.

Walt was said to have never grown another hair or eyebrow until the day he died, but even more noteworthy, the stormy June evening the new schoolmarm came to town could very well be the talk of generations to come.

Chapter 1

Tucker Gray threw up an arm to shield his face. Dirt and rubble rained down, fiery fingers licked up timbered mill walls. He swayed, then regained his balance and vaulted forward to escape the sudden firestorm.

Bursting through the wooden door, he bolted to freedom. Lightning ripped the sky. Thunder detonated.

He groaned. The weeks of hammering and nailing, hours, days of backbreaking work wiped out with one lightning strike. He brushed trailing remnants of fire off his smoldering shoulders. Sometimes he wondered if God even liked him. Five years of a hell-torn war. Starting all over . . . now this.

His eyes focused on the blazing pond, then switched to his cousin Caleb. What the . . . ?

"Over here!" Caleb shouted. He was some distance away, bending over an object on the ground.

Tucker began to move, one foot in front of the other, away from the burning building. He absently batted the front of his sizzling shirt. Why would a buckboard be in the pond? A blistered section of the millwheel dropped into the dingy water, sending up a sheet of liquid and steam like a geyser. From the looks of things, the fire must have started near the wheel. He frowned. Nothing made sense in the chaos surrounding him. War hadn't been this confusing.

Eli Gray raced to help Caleb, who was carrying what Tucker could now see was a body. A female body. Tucker met the two cousins halfway and relieved Caleb of the slight weight.

"What happened?" A heavy oily stench filled his nostrils.

Caleb turned to look at the shooting flames. "From the smell of it, I'd guess the buckboard was full of kerosene."

Kerosene. Tucker sniffed. That was the source of the loud *swoosh* he'd heard. Minutes later he'd been battling flames, barely escaping with his life. Lucky he'd been in the office alone.

"Kerosene!" Eli repeated, shaking his head. "Why would a woman be hauling kerosene?"

Tucker shifted the woman's slight weight and carried her to a level spot away from the flames. "She must be the judge's niece—the new schoolmarm—from Timber Creek. Judge mentioned his niece would bring kerosene when she came."

Caleb turned and focused on the blazing shack and pond. "She brought it, all right."

Tucker's eyes traced Caleb as his cousin knelt beside the young woman, searching for a pulse.

Judge Wallace Madison rushed through the veil of smoke hovering over the mill yard.

"Willow! Is she all right?"

Caleb looked up with a sober expression. "She's got a pulse. I think the impact knocked her cold."

"Bring her to the house," Wallace ordered. "Quick, man! She could be seriously injured."

Tucker glanced at the hectic scene. Every able-bodied man in town had responded to the fire. Most worked for the mill, but others must have seen the fire and come running. He turned and followed his cousins as Eli carried Willow to the Madison house. High-stepping up the incline, Wallace led the way.

Judge Madison's house sat atop the hill—a narrow, bizarre construction consisting of three stories jutting straight up, plain as the nose on your face. Rumor was that Claudine Madison must have been in her cups when she designed the atrocity, and Wallace, a liberal soul, had allowed her free rein.

"Inside," Wallace ordered. "Third-floor bedroom."

Third floor. Eli was breathing hard by now, so Tucker hefted Willow's slight weight and calculated the winding stairway. *There must be twenty stairs on each landing.* "What about a downstairs room?"

"None," Wallace confided. "Poor planning, but nevertheless, I've learned to cope."

The young woman lay limp in Tucker's arms. Shifting her weight, he began the climb.

"Careful now—Eli, fetch the doctor."

"He's in Beeder's Cove this week, sir. I couldn't get back in over an hour."

"Go!"

Eli turned and descended the stairs, stepping around Caleb. "You better send for Jolie, Caleb. By the time I get back . . ."

Caleb shook his dark head. "You know Wallace don't hold with that Acadian woman's voodoo."

"Me either, but she might be able to save the young lady's life."

Caleb frowned. "Her pulse was mighty uneven."

Tucker spoke over his shoulder. "Just go get her. And get back with the doctor as soon as you can."

Tucker reached the first landing with Wallace way ahead of him.

The judge continued up the second flight, and Tucker trailed him. "Thank goodness you're strong men. I don't know what I would do without you. Poor Willow—the thunder must have spooked the horse."

Winded, Tucker paused, and hitched up the young woman, readjusting her weight. He'd carried many a wounded man off the battlefield, but never up three flights of stairs. The lady was light as a feather, but a wet feather, reeking of kerosene.

Wallace continued. "Saw the mill was burning. So sorry—I know you boys have worked hard to get it up and running again. Those years you were off fighting left a real hole in this town. Glad you're back—and we'll rebuild that mill, you have my word."

Tucker wasn't sure what part Wallace played in "we" other than standing on the sidelines day after day postulating un-invited instructions, but he was a good soul.

Peculiar, but likable.

Reaching the third landing, Wallace turned and walked past seven closed doorways before he paused and opened one. Thunder shook the old house as Tucker followed him into the room and gently laid the young woman on the quilted spread. The room was massive with a four-poster bed, chiffonier, and two cane-bottomed, slat-backed rocking chairs sitting in a window alcove.

"Claudine's favorite room in the house," Wallace explained, standing back to admire the view. "You can see the whole town from up here."

Indeed. Tucker focused on red flames swallowing up the mill's wood shingle roof.

"Now, now." Wallace crooned, bending close to his niece. "Her breathing appears even. I believe it's only a thump on the head. She's a tough one."

Tucker wasn't so certain she'd escaped with just a thump. Landing on her head could have caused serious injury. Maybe Jolie could help when she got here. He had a hunch Caleb would be back shortly, whether Wallace wanted Jolie or not.

Wallace stood back, beaming. "Quite lovely, wouldn't you say?"

Tucker focused on the small woman lying death-like on the bedspread. Her muddy clothing soiled the spread, a dark bruise formed on one side of her forehead, and her kerosene-saturated hair lay loose on the pillow. Still, it was easy to see she was comely—in a disheveled sort of way. He took a closer look. Strawberry blond hair, long dark lashes against fair skin.

The judge stage-whispered. "She fought in the war, you know—with several other women."

"No . . . I didn't know." Tucker had spent almost five years on the battlefield and never once encountered a woman.

"Oh, I know it's quite unusual, but she fought all right, as scrappy as any man." Wallace filled Tucker in on the remarkable circumstances.

Curiosity piqued, Tucker asked. "What happened to the other women?"

"Willow wrote me and said that only five survived the battles. She and her two friends, and two older ladies. I can't recall what the older women decided to do once word finally reached Timber Creek that the war was over. It's taken so long to get the news out to the battlegrounds." Wallace *tsk*ed, eyes fixed on his niece. "She looks a might peaked."

Peaked. Hauling a load of kerosene all the way from Timber Creek should have taken years off her life. It was a wonder she had made it this far, and Tucker was surprised the judge didn't have any more sense than to ask her to bring it with her. Wonder she hadn't set fire to something long before she reached Thunder Ridge.

Tucker bent and touched Willow's pulse. He wasn't a doctor, but her injuries didn't appear to be life threatening. No jutting bones. No ragged gasping for breath or visible blood. Outside the window, men raced back and forth from the river above the mill and the burning kerosene slick, toting buckets of water to douse flames. Their efforts were in vain. The mill was gone. Only the loaded wagon and stacks of planed lumber and shingles piled to the side of the road escaped the inferno.

Caleb returned with Jolie, the Acadian woman who lived just outside of town with her husband and five children.

Wallace blocked Willow. "Don't touch her! I don't want any voodoo hands on my niece."

The woman shrugged and turned to leave. Tucker stopped her. "I don't hold with concoctions or spells, but do you have an herb—anything to revive her?"

The woman nodded.

Tucker glanced to Wallace. "Would you agree to an herb? We need to bring her around and see how badly she's hurt."

"Eli's gone for the doctor."

"Her injuries could worsen, but it's your decision."

The judge's teeth worried his bottom lip.

Caleb addressed the Acadian. "What do you have?"

The woman opened her bag, and took out a small vial. Wallace's eyes evaluated the worrisome contents.

"Judge?" Tucker inquired. Outside, shouts and confusion rose. Thunder cracked, vibrating the third floor.

"What's in the bottle?" Judge ventured.

The woman shrugged.

Wallace fished a handkerchief out of his vest pocket. "I suppose I have no recourse . . . but be careful."

Uncapping the bottle, Jolie lightly ran the open vial back and forth beneath Willow's nose.

"Careful." Wallace crept closer. "Not too much. If anything happens to her you'll answer to Silas Sterling!"

Tucker looked up. "Silas? I thought she's your niece—the new schoolmarm." The committee had voted and agreed that Wallace's niece should be hired to reopen school this fall. Silas was on the committee, but the whole town had a stake in the young woman's health.

"She is. She is my niece." Wallace's head bobbed. "But she is also to be Silas's new bride."

Caleb frowned. "Sterling's going to marry this woman?"

Tucker couldn't picture it. Silas and this . . . Didn't make sense.

The healer gently waved the bottle beneath Willow's nose again. The young woman stirred and coughed.

A relieved smile surfaced to the judge's lined features. "Ah, she's coming around." He pushed the vial aside when the dark-eyed Acadian was about to administer another whiff.

Tucker stepped back, eyes focused on the young beauty. Her eyes opened wide, the color of blue sapphires. Confusion waited in their depths.

"What . . . ? Where . . . ?"

"Lie back, dear. You've had a small accident, but nothing appears to be broken." The judge hovered above his niece.

"Accident?"

Tucker joined Caleb at the doorway as Jolie swiftly ran her hands over Willow, apparently probing for broken bones.

"Looks like she's going to be okay," Caleb remarked.

"Yeah." Tucker studied the woman on the bed. He hadn't been around one this comely in years. Maybe that explained the unfamiliar jolt of female recognition that rattled male instincts. "I wasn't aware Silas had chosen a bride . . . didn't he just announce his decision to take a wife last month?"

His cousin nodded. "Seems to me he did."

Wallace spoke a word to Willow before lifting his head. "Gentlemen, thank you for your assistance."

Tucker nodded. "You say your niece is going to marry Sterling?"

"Ah, yes." Wallace focused on the dazed girl lying on the bed. "After a proper courtship, of course. Meanwhile, she'll prepare the new school for fall attendance. Of course, the committee will be notified in plenty of time to find a school-marm replacement when the marriage takes place."

He bent toward his niece again. "Willow, love, you rest. I'll show the gentlemen out, and be back momentarily."

"Uncle Wallace . . . ?"

"Rest, dear."

He hurriedly shooed the men into the hallway, motioning for the Acadian to go away.

Recapping the vial, the woman slipped the bottle into her satchel.

Caleb lowered his voice. "Do you get the idea that maybe Silas doesn't know he's about to marry Wallace's niece?"

Tucker nodded. "Sounds that way." Wallace had decided to move fast, set his cap for Sterling's money, and used his pretty niece for bait. Or was it the other way around? Had the weary "soldier" set her bonnet for Silas Sterling, using the judge for bait? The latter, he decided. News traveled fast, and every available woman who'd heard of Silas's intention to marry and produce an heir to his vast fortune would be swarming Thunder Ridge like a hive of hornets. Greedy hornets.

Wallace joined the men at the doorway. "What sort of witchcraft, hoodoo, poison is in that vial? Frog lips and mosquito ears?" His aversion to the woman's medicine bled through his salty observations.

"Smelling salts," Tucker supplied.

"Really. Smelling salts."

Tucker and Caleb followed Wallace and Jolie downstairs.

The fragrance of fried chicken drifted from the kitchen. No sign of Betsy Pike, the judge's housekeeper. For one moment Tucker wondered what it would be like to come home to chicken frying and a loving face to greet him at the door. He'd been a bachelor for too long, and the war had destroyed any marriage prospects he might have harbored. Since coming home, every waking moment and every dollar he owned or could borrow had gone into the mill, and getting it back in working order. Now it had been destroyed, and someone had to pay for damages.

Wallace smiled dismissively at Tucker. "I appreciate your help with my niece. The poor girl has been through so much. I do hope the events of this ghastly night don't overly traumatize her."

"She was real lucky," Caleb agreed. "It could have been a tragedy if she had remained in that buckboard." He shook his head. "God had his eye on her, for sure."

"Can't deny that," the judge agreed. "I'll need to put a handsome offering in the plate come Sunday."

"Doubt that God's concerned about money." Tucker knew his voice was as dry as the dust blanketing Thunder Ridge, but he didn't care. His livelihood had been ruined tonight, and the income of half the able-bodied men in town. Had the judge given that any thought? Because of his niece, the town was in a real bind.

As if Wallace read his mind, he spoke up, "I'm sorry about the sawmill, Tucker. As I said, we'll help rebuild. The town can't survive without it."

Help rebuild? The judge or his niece would assume full responsibility for the accident. The war had eaten up years of prosperity, and Thunder Ridge had come so close to a new start. Now he had to start over, and he knew how much help he could expect from the judge. Wallace was a good man, but he didn't have a cent to his name. He was approaching old age, and he'd barely gotten by the past few years. Silas Sterling held the purse strings in Thunder Ridge. Was he willing to uphold the judge's responsibilities?

He glanced at Caleb. "We've got to get that fire under control."

"Now gentlemen, there's nothing to worry about," Judge reassured. "It appeared earlier there was plenty of manpower. Your services shouldn't be needed."

Tucker swallowed back anger. Statements like that made it hard to be charitable. What woman with a lick of sense would bring a wagon full of kerosene into town during a thunderstorm?

Wallace trailed the men to the door. "I'll be down to help directly. I'll settle up with that woman."

"Jolie?"

"Yes. That woman."

Jolie had stood to the side quietly, seemingly aware of her place in the judge's eye.

Tucker nodded. At least he didn't plan to burn her at the stake.

Tucker and Caleb left the Madison house and strode to the fire. Now that he was sure the woman was conscious, Tucker's thoughts centered on the mill. Every able-bodied man in town was down there carrying water from the nearby river. They could be thankful the fire hadn't spread to the outer buildings, and the horses and mules were safe. Men had led the animals outside and corralled them in pens away from the fire. The bunkhouses were seared by burning embers, but diligent workers had spotted the fires and doused them in time.

Now Tucker and Caleb grabbed hoes and rakes to fight random blazes set from windblown sparks. Wind was their enemy tonight. As soon as one fire was mastered, another sprang up. Tucker glanced in frustration at the sky. Thunder exploded overhead, lightning cracked, but not one drop of rain fell.

It was as if God had abandoned Thunder Ridge.

Chapter 2

Caleb loomed out of the darkness. "We're making progress."

"Are we? Seems like everywhere I look, another fire springs up. The wind is killing us."

"I know, but we're on top of it. Won't be long until we have it under control, and besides, the storm's moving out. The wind will die soon."

Tucker glanced up and had to grin, though there wasn't a humorous thing about his situation. "Always the optimist, aren't you?"

"Like I always tell you, Tuck, it's as easy to see the good as the bad."

"Maybe." Tucker whirled to rake dust over a clump of grass that suddenly ignited. He'd stop and look for the blessing once the fire was under control, before it burned half the town. If the wind shifted to the south, they'd be fighting house fires in another hour. Frame homes with wood-shingled roofs would go up like tinder. Even the judge's fancy house would go—and why couldn't the man have painted that monstrosity a halfway normal color? That ugly green stuck out like a sore thumb.

Mrs. Tompkins approached, water bucket and dipper in hand. "You boys look like you're parched." She reached in and brought up a dipperful and handed it to Caleb.

He drank it down and handed the dipper back to her. "Much obliged, Mrs. Tompkins. That hit the spot."

"I know water's real scarce, but a man's got to have it to live. As long as we can carry it from the river, we'll be fine. There's coffee and sandwiches in the bunkhouse. We women want to do our part. We know how much the sawmill means to the town, and to you folks."

Tucker took the water, relishing the way it relieved his parched throat. "I appreciate it, ma'am."

"Yes," she mused, eyes fastened on the firefighting efforts. "If we didn't have the river, law, we'd plain burn up. Think it will rain soon?"

"Can't say, ma'am. I'm not God." If he were, he'd never let Thunder Ridge get this dry. War would never mar the land again, and he sure wouldn't set wild women bearing kegs of kerosene loose on the town.

His gaze followed his neighbor as she walked away, carrying her bucket of water to a group of men using sacks wet with river water to beat out the flames. Caleb was right—the wind had calmed some and that would help.

He focused on the scene of destruction, anger building in his chest.

All that hard work for nothing. He'd have a hard time forgiving the judge's niece, accident or not.

He'd said as much to Caleb, but his cousin upheld the new schoolmarm. "The woman didn't intend to set fire to the mill. It wasn't planned."

Tucker grunted. "I'd hate to think of how much damage she'd have done if she'd set her mind to it."

Caleb's chuckle didn't improve Tucker's mood. Occasionally the wind whipped across the rubble, stirring up miniature flames that danced for a few minutes before dying away.

Tucker sighed. "Be a couple of days before it cools enough to start clearing it off."

"Yeah." Caleb took off his hat and wiped sweat. "Won't be much left to worry about. But we can probably get it ready to start building in two, three days."

"Build it with what? It'll take a while to get lumber and materials. We don't have anything to build with, and no saw to cut boards." The saw went with the tool shed.

"At least she missed the wagon." Caleb grinned. "All those boards are cut and ready for delivery. We won't lose that order."

Tucker grunted. "All of our records went up in flame. We don't have any idea who ordered lumber, or how much."

"I can recall most—over in Blackberry Hill and Beeder's Cove. I know Lakeys ordered some. It'll take a few weeks, but we'll get it sorted out."

Tucker couldn't buy the confidence. "It's going to get worse before it gets better."

"You're in some mood tonight. Cheer up." Caleb thumped Tucker on the shoulder. "We're alive, aren't we? This time last year, we wouldn't have bet a plugged nickel on it, but here we are—safe, and still got our arms and legs. Nobody got hurt in the accident. We can always rebuild."

Thunder rumbled in the west, and Caleb jerked his head in that direction. "Another storm building."

"Yeah. Pity we can't eat thunder. We wouldn't have so much to worry about."

"No reason to be bitter. Won't help anything." Caleb swung a pick over his shoulder. "You comin'?"

Tucker paused. "You really want to do it?"

"Do what?"

"Build back. We've spent the last several weeks working ourselves to death, and it's been destroyed in a few hours."

"We have to rebuild."

Tucker shuffled his boots. "There's no law that says we have to. But we can . . . if we want."

"Well now, although there might be a disagreement over who foots the bill, I don't plan to quit, and I'm bettin' when Eli comes back, he'll say the same. We're family, and family doesn't walk away from family. I'm in it for the long haul. Eli too. The fire is a setback, but we're Grays. Grays don't quit."

Tucker settled his hat. He would have agreed yesterday; today, he wasn't so sure.

An abrupt gust of wind stirred the embers and sent sparks flying. In a few minutes, a dozen new fires flared. He glanced at the brooding clouds. "Lord, I wish it would rain."

Caleb respectfully covered his heart with his hat. "I second that, Lord."

Caleb strode off, heading for a patch of burning grass while Tucker turned his attention to a stand of brush that stood in the way of the creeping flames. He had to stop the fire before it reached dry twigs and shriveled leaves.

He spotted the judge, standing well back out of the way, watching the activity. What sort of man would help his niece marry a man she didn't know and didn't love, just because he had money? And Silas did have money. Lots of it. Less if he assumed Miss Madison's bill.

He gave a vicious slash with the rake at a creeping line of fire. Where was the rain?

Willow lay between musty-smelling sheets, her gaze wandering the room. Where was she? She remembered Uncle Wallace bending over her. A small, silent woman. And there were others. She wasn't sure how many. Men, she thought, but from where, she had no idea.

Her temple throbbed when she moved, and the room occasionally went fuzzy. She reached up and rubbed her forehead, her probing fingers locating a knot that felt as big as a wild turkey egg. She remembered approaching town—the thunder booming overhead, confusion—but she couldn't remember how she got in this room.

Darkness had fallen. A red glow danced against the opposite wall. Fire. She shoved herself to a sitting position. She could hear voices—a crowd of people. Easing off the bed, her shoes touched hard wood. Her head was killing her. Had she hit a cow? A buffalo?

She eased to the double window, shaky, head reeling. The room tilted, and she grabbed for the sill to support her weight. The scene outside slowly came into focus. Where the sawmill had once stood was now a smoldering pile of angry coals. Men scurried around the blaze, fighting random fires popping up here and there. Something catastrophic had occurred in Thunder Ridge, and she had a sinking feeling the disarray had something to do with her. But what? Her brain refused to register.

Holding onto the sill, then a chair, and then making a lunge for the bed, she fell across the mattress, energy depleted.

Suddenly she lifted her head. Kerosene. She smelled kerosene. Bringing her fingers to her nose, she sniffed. They were covered in an oily substance. She tried to focus on the smut and grime. She lifted the other hand. Both were covered in the dark, greasy matter.

Dropping her head back to the mattress, she closed her eyes. Whatever had happened, she needed to assist. She couldn't remain here in this room, while others fought a town fire. Too dry. The buildings would go up like dried chaff. Willow Madison didn't hide. She had to get up, go out there, and help. Do what she could . . . to help. The bed swayed.

A loaded lumber wagon flashed through her haze. Shouts. Smells.

Fire.

Dear Lord. Sheets of rolling flames, catching the water wheel and leaping to the mill's shingled roof.

She rolled off the bed, her aching feet striking hard wood. Carefully pulling herself up, she straightened.

Those five barrels of kerosene. What happened to the fuel? She lifted her left hand and sniffed, a sense of dread settling over her.

Where was that kerosene?

It was her last rational thought before the fog swallowed her.

Chapter 3

The following morning, Willow bent close to the oval mirror while inspecting the angry knot on her forehead. She'd had less injury on the battlefield. Her cheeks bloomed when she thought about her unsettling entrance to Thunder Ridge. Had Silas Sterling been present to observe her unorthodox arrival? Had the man she planned to marry witnessed the humiliating debacle?

Well, Mr. Sterling would realize soon enough that the bride Wallace intended for him was not genteel in manner or spirit, though Willow had never found herself in such a pickle.

Picking up a brush, she ran it through her ravaged hair. All things considered, she had fared well with her explosive entry. She could have been lying on an undertaker's slab this morning.

What moron had left a lumber wagon sitting directly in the main road?

Horror rose to the back of her throat. The buckboard. Had it burned too? Pitching the brush aside, she reached for her dress and shimmied into the soiled cotton. That buckboard was all she had—her sole possession, that, her personal belongings, and the mare . . .

The mare? Had her horse perished in the accident?

Cognizant of the dull throb at her temple, she slipped on her boots and left the room to creep down the three-story staircase.

All was quiet. When she reached the kitchen she saw a note propped against a plate of crispy brown fried chicken written in Wallace's familiar scrawl.

Gone for my morning stroll. If you waken before I return, here's your breakfast, and there's lemonade in the icehouse. I'll be back shortly.

Your loving uncle,
Wallace

Laying the note aside, Willow eyed the chicken. Did the judge have something against eggs and bacon? No matter, she wasn't hungry. She'd skip breakfast. The worry of losing the buckboard and mare was more immediate.

The thunderstorm had passed. Apparently the front had been nothing but bluster and fury, because Willow's boots kicked up dry dust when she stepped off the porch. She turned to study the strange house, always a source of fascination. She'd visited here twice, once as a small child and another when Claudine went to be with the Lord. The structure had always been a well of curiosity with its stovepipe shape and musty-smelling rooms. In earlier years, Claudine had insisted the house be painted blue to blend with the sky. When she passed, Uncle had changed the color to a putrid green, now matching the dying grass. The prior color reminded him of Claudine, and the memory was too painful. Claudine had never cared for green.

Both the judge and Claudine had lived on the odd side of life, but Willow had never heard a harsh word spoken about them. Wallace was a community fixture. For over fifty years, his horse-drawn buggy had traveled the back roads and administered justice, married folks, and took care of whatever needed his attention. He was known to brag that he loved his work, and his work loved him.

Willow returned to her newest worry—the buckboard. Where was it? It wasn't hard to spot the mill. Smoke filled the early morning air. Some men still worked to douse the last of the persistent flames.

Please, God, let the mare and the buckboard be safe.

Hopes were dashed when she rounded a corner and spotted the shell of the burned vehicle. Her stomach hit the ground. She was destitute. Where was the horse? She skimmed the ground for a carcass, but there was none.

She and the other women had come upon the riderless mare one day in a field. They quickly claimed the animal and put her to good use. The horse and buckboard hauled water and supplies to town, relieving the women of the arduous task. After the battles, the women had been left with virtually nothing. Oh, a few homes remained standing, among them Audrey's boarding room, but most had been leveled.

The women managed to fashion enough shelter to keep them dry. They foraged for food, and took baths in the river.

Willow's gaze traced the seared ground, pausing to focus on a tall, dark-haired man putting out a fire patch.

Lifting her hands, she cupped her mouth. "You there!"

The man slowly turned to focus on her. Her stomach leaped to her chest. She'd seen many a man on the battlefield, but this one was different. Heavily muscled, dark, penetrating eyes. Acadian? Indian? A blend? Whatever, he was easily a handsome man.

She approached and realized that she would probably have to look up at him, but barely. She gathered her composure and continued. "Could you point me to the mill owner?"

Surely if anyone knew about the mare's fate, the owner could tell her.

Moving the rake aside, the man rested on the handle. "That would be Tucker Gray."

He wasn't French, but she had made the correct assumption. She did have to look up at him. "May I speak with him?"

"Free country."

She stepped back. Well, how rude. No doubt it was all over town that she was the—for want of a better term—idiot who had set the pond on fire and burned the mill to the ground. Townsfolk couldn't be too happy with her. Her chin rose. Ordinarily she wouldn't pursue a fight, but she needed that mare. "Can you tell me where I might find him?"

His gaze skimmed her lightly. "I could."

She waited, then blurted. "Well? Where is he?" Was the man dim-witted?

"Standing right in front of you."

Marvelous. Dim-witted and a buffoon. Her temple throbbed. "Is there a foreman—a man in charge—an overseer?"

He shifted his stance. "That would be me."

She feared her strained smile was anything but tolerant. "My horse. Where is it?"

He slowly turned to stare at the smoldering heap upturned beside the road, and her heart sank. Her worst fear was about to be realized. She hadn't cried in years; she wasn't a crying woman, but a huge lump rose to her throat and she swallowed. "There's nothing left?"

"The mare. She's stabled at your uncle's. Other than spooked, she came through the incident without a scratch."

Swift relief filled Willow. She slumped, and a strong arm shot out to catch her. "Miss Madison. Should you be out of bed?"

He knew her name? Willow touched her aching temple. "Yes. I'm fine, thank you." She straightened, leaving the comfort of his support. "I'm sorry . . . I didn't catch your name."

"Tucker Gray. I own the mill, and my cousins help me run it." He turned to focus on translucent smoke. "Drove the last nail yesterday—we'd just rebuilt, you know. Been off fighting in the war." He shifted, leaning on the shovel, talking to himself more than her. "Yeah, drove the last nail late yesterday afternoon." He turned back. "About an hour before you arrived."

It wasn't what he had said; it was his tone that suddenly piqued her. *Before you arrived*. He made it sound like Black Death had blown into town.

"Mr. . . ." She searched for a last name, though she was certain he'd given one.

"Gray."

"Mr. Gray. I deeply apologize for the tragedy, but surely whoever left that lumber wagon sitting in the middle of the road doesn't have the brains God gave a goose."

He shifted again, gripping the rake handle so tightly blood rose to the surface. "That also would be me—or I told Caleb to leave it sit while he checked the hitch."

Heat flooded her cheeks. The man was making her look like the fool. "That was plain irresponsible." Calm. The situation called for calm assurance. When her horse veered, the hitch broke and threw the buckboard into the pond. How the fuel ignited was still a source of puzzlement. Of course Mr. Gray was upset. He'd lost his business.

She cleared her throat. "Thunder spooked the horse. I tried to control the reins, but the animal ran straight down the road. Had she not had to veer so sharply to avoid hitting the lumber wagon, the hitch would have held. There would have been no spilled kerosene in the water, and the accident would have never happened. The accident is clearly not my fault."

What if he insisted that she pay for damages? She couldn't, and Uncle Wallace could barely support his needs. Her heart hammered and Gray's face swam before her.

He fixed dark eyes on her. "Are you going to faint?"

"No, I am not." Now he was getting on her nerves. She removed a hanky from her pocket and wiped the perspiration on her forehead. Then again, she might faint, but not in front of him. The building heat was insufferable for June.

"Go back to bed, Miss Madison. Tomorrow morning, please stop by my office, and we'll hash this out. Your horse is fine." He walked off, leaving her standing.

She held the hanky to her splitting forehead. "Office? What office? Didn't it burn?"

He turned with a cool look. "I stand corrected. It did. Well, I guess I'll set a desk up outside the ruins. That should do nicely." He pivoted, grasping the rake, and walked on.

Rude. That's what he was. Just plain rude. Well, she'd dealt with rude men before, and she wasn't a wilting pansy.

"Fine." She called. "But this is your fault. Not mine." She wanted that made clear before morning.

Spinning on one boot heel, he confronted her. Suddenly he wasn't so strikingly handsome. He looked plain mad—mad enough to eat a burned stick. "My fault?"

"Your fault. If you hadn't left that wagon in the middle of the road, the horse wouldn't have had to swerve, and if she didn't have to swerve, the buckboard wouldn't have broken loose and . . ." She'd said this before. "Your fault."

He leaned on the rake, matching her determined stance.

When it was apparent he wasn't going to do anything but stare, she prompted, "It's true. Why would anyone with half a brain leave a lumber wagon in the middle of a main thoroughfare? Well, sir, if you ask me—"

"I didn't ask you."

"I told you anyway." She could see this conversation was going nowhere. The man was pig-headed, stubborn, and completely lacking in logic.

He whirled and stalked off but suddenly stopped and turned back. "Just for the record, I had a man moving that stack of freshly planed lumber when you came riding into town on the hounds from hell and set my pond on fire, and the water wheel, which then burned down my mill office."

A faint image of a startled figure near the stack of lumber flashed through her mind. The shape did have to lunge for his life . . .

But then that didn't excuse Mr. Know-it-All from responsibility. That lumber wagon should not have been there in the first place.

She turned around and walked off. Her first impression of Tucker Gray was correct. He was a buffoon.

A stubborn, completely irrational, irresponsible buffoon.

Chapter 4

Tucker watched her stalk off. It wasn't enough that he'd lost his livelihood, and everything inside the sawmill; he had an unreasonable, irresponsible female to contend with. If this woman thought she could do this kind of damage, and then just walk away, she had another thing coming. She was going to accept responsibility whether she liked it or not.

John Franklin, owner of the blacksmith shop, approached. "Hey, Tucker. You doing all right?"

"As good as I can be, considering the circumstances."

"Yep. Sure is a shame about the mill. People here depended on it bringing new life to the town." He hesitated. "You planning to build back?"

"We hope to, John. It's going to take a while."

"No doubt. Well, when you're ready, you can count on me. I can swing a hammer with the best of them."

"I'll remember that. Need all the men I can get."

"I hear the new schoolmarm isn't hurt. That's good."

"Yeah, she's fine. She just happened to have five barrels of kerosene with her."

John shook his head. "So I heard—well, that was real unfortunate. You reckon she's too flighty to be a schoolmarm?"

Tucker frowned. "Thunder spooked the horse. Guess it could have happened to anyone."

John smiled. "That's awfully good of you, Tucker. A lot of people would be downright mad if this had happened to them. Takes a real man to have an attitude like that when all he owns is lying in ruins around him."

Tucker colored at John's praise. It had only been minutes ago that he was breathing fire and brimstone at Willow Madison. Now he was defending her?

A gust of wind sent sparks flying. A shout behind the men signaled a fresh batch of fires. Tucker walked on, rake in hand.

Wallace approached from the opposite trail. "Looks like we've about got it under control."

Tucker eyed him sourly.

Judge smiled. "Good people here in Thunder Ridge. We help our own."

Tucker nodded and was about to walk on when Wallace called out. "I'm sorry I can't do more of the physical work. Bad back, you know. But I'm praying for you."

Now what? Willow stood at her bedroom window, staring out. What a mess. She'd come to Thunder Ridge to begin a new life; instead, she'd been partly responsible for calamity. But the larger blame lay with Tucker Gray. The lumber wagon shouldn't have been blocking the road, but in retrospect, she should have handled the mare more efficiently. She wasn't a ninny. She could handle a horse or a team with the best of men, but that troublesome thunder had caught her off guard. She moved from the window and sank to the bed.

Her earlier encounter with Tucker Gray threatened to resurrect her head pain. She was going to sit in this room until she calmed down. Maybe all evening, if necessary. Judge was out for another of his strolls, and she simply couldn't go out and face the stares again. Folks had been nice, but seemed a bit leery. Why would they trust her? Fear blocked her throat. What if they changed their minds and refused to let her teach? *What then, Willow Madison?* As expected, a headache bloomed.

Her eyes roamed the room. Uncle Wallace's home. She'd had a blurred impression of the remainder of the house, but this room seemed quite nice. Besides the chiffonier, there was a scratched bedside table holding a boudoir lamp with a Portsmouth Pairpoint Roses shade. A dressing table with a beveled mirror, two rocking chairs, and a couple of occasional tables completed the furnishings. A braided, woolen rug covered the floor beside the bed. Yes indeed, a very comfortable room, and evidently a lot of thought had gone into the furnishings.

Perhaps tomorrow she would venture out, meet with the school board. Her shoulders slumped. No doubt her future pupils knew about their new teacher's unorthodox arrival. Many fathers worked at the mill, relied on the income. What would the families do until the mill was rebuilt—if it were rebuilt? Where would all that money come from? Silas Sterling, no doubt, but she couldn't begin a relationship with him based on debt, even an innocuous one. If she could be of service, she would be justified in the relationship, but if she was a freeloader, that was different. She'd work for all she'd acquired.

A light tap sounded at the door. She sat up straighter. "Yes? Uncle Wallace?" The Judge hovered around her like a mother hen. She wasn't accustomed to such fuss.

The door opened and a short, gray-haired woman, round and plump as an apple, edged in, clutching a loaded tray. "Good evening. I'm Betsy Pike, Judge's housekeeper. He hired me on a few months ago when he decided he didn't know how to cook and clean." She grinned. "I've brought your supper."

The judge had a housekeeper? She must have taken a terrific knock to the head because she was totally unaware of the woman. "You didn't need to go to all that trouble. I could come downstairs . . . "I'm Willow."

"I know who you are, dear. Wish I'd have been here yesterday during all the fuss, but it was my day off. Are you feeling better now?"

"I'm fine." Other than a bass drum pounding in her head.

Betsy set a tray on a small table, and drew up a chair. "You just sit down here and eat something. I saw the plate of chicken. Judge cook you breakfast this morning?"

Willow smiled and nodded.

"That man is going to grow feathers one of these days. How many times do I have to tell him you don't eat chicken for breakfast?"

Willow obediently lowered herself into the chair, and

spread the cloth napkin on her lap. Betsy lifted covers from the dishes, revealing three pieces of chicken, fried potatoes, and a slab of chocolate cake. A pot of steaming tea rounded out the repast. Willow's stomach growled, and she realized she hadn't eaten in nearly twenty-four hours. No wonder she felt faint.

Betsy settled back, apparently planning to sit and visit. She couldn't imagine Claudine putting up with such familiarity if she were alive, though Willow welcomed the company. Aunt Claudine had been a strange choice for Uncle Wallace. It wasn't that he was all that strict, but he had been a sharp contrast to his flamboyant wife. Willow knew her Aunt Claudine loved sherry and used it for more than cooking purposes. Sherry had been one of those family secrets everyone knew, but no one talked about. Willow had met Claudine once when Willow was a child, and again when Wallace and his wife paid a visit to Timber Creek when Willow's parents were alive.

She remembered the occasion well. Claudine had tickled Willow under the chin, told her she was a pretty filly, and demanded to know where her mother kept the "spirits." Willow assumed Claudine was asking about ghostly things until Willow's mother had drawn her aside and whispered the secret. From that moment on, Willow had watched Claudine like a hawk for signs of drunkenness, but all she ever noticed was a nice older lady with a few black hairs sprouting on her chin, who told amusing stories.

Willow smiled at the memory. Uncle Wallace had been devastated when his wife died. The ways of love had always been a mystery to Willow. She believed in love, even if she'd never been in that happy state of confusion, but she did think people should be a little more sensible about the matter.

Copper claimed, according to the romantic stories she used to read in the women's magazines, folks heard bells ringing and saw stars whirling overhead. It all sounded very irregular to Willow. She preferred a more practical approach to life. Tucker Gray's image surfaced, and she grimly banished all thoughts of the man. She pitied his wife, if he had one.

"That's right, eat it all," Betsy said, breaking into her thoughts. "I like to see a woman with a good appetite."

Willow glanced in surprise at her plate. How had she managed to eat all that food and not realize it? She quickly laid her fork aside. "I must have been hungrier than I thought."

Betsy laughed. "You've been through enough to give you an appetite. That accident could have been deadly. You're lucky to be alive."

"I suppose so." She tried not to think about the brush with death. If she hadn't jumped from the wagon when she did, she would have been on board when the kerosene ignited and burned everything in sight. She might have burned, too. She said as much to Betsy.

The housekeeper frowned. "Wasn't your time, young'un. Lord still has plans for you."

Yes. To marry Silas Sterling.

Betsy chattered on, barely stopping for breath, keeping up a running commentary on the town and its occupants.

"And the school?" Willow asked. "Is it close by?" Without her buckboard, she might face a long walk during the school term.

"It's at the north end, sets off to itself a ways. Nothing

fancy, just a one-room building, little more than a shack, but don't you worry, the men of this town will get it in shape for you. We're all excited to think a new teacher has come."

Still, Willow sensed something evasive in Betsy's manner. It concerned her somewhat, but she supposed she'd find out more for herself tomorrow. What Betsy might find unsuitable could very well be something with which Willow could make do. She wasn't used to fancy.

"I trust the children are excited."

Worry lines creased the older woman's brow. "Well, as to that, I couldn't say. I remember from my own school days it was a lot more fun to be able to run free instead of being cooped up in school."

Willowed stiffened. "I hope to make it an enjoyable experience."

"I'm sure you will. The thing is, the older boys and girls can be a handful. They're not always on their best behavior, if you know what I mean."

"You're saying they will be hard to control?"

"You could say that, yes."

"Well, I've handled worrisome children before." She'd faced Yankee guns without running, and a handful of troublemakers wouldn't beat her, either. She was here to teach, and they would learn. Like it or not.

Willow viewed the empty tray. "We're on the third floor. It was a long way for you to carry my supper up all those stairs. I'm sorry. I could have come downstairs."

Betsy sighed. "I'll tell you what, Miss Claudine was a good enough woman in her way, but she didn't know beans about designing houses. This one reminds me of a knight's castle you read about in them fancy books. Not nearly as big, but Judge should have put his foot down. It was 'yes, dear,' to anything Claudine wanted. Should have said no once in a while."

Willow understood her concerns. "I understand all of my personal belongings burned with the wagon."

Betsy nodded. "I'm afraid so. Miss Claudine's clothes are still here, but she would have made two of you. They wouldn't begin to fit."

"Oh . . . I'm sorry." She would feel strange wearing them anyway.

Willow insisted on carrying the tray downstairs. The journey would give her a chance to see more of the house. It was big, even bigger than she remembered. Plenty of room for Audrey and Copper, but the décor was decidedly overdone. Accustomed to sparser surroundings, Willow was overwhelmed by the horde of knickknacks.

In the parlor, a statue of a woman, fully clothed, thank goodness—although the stone draping of her gown seemed rather lacking in virtue—held a brass lamp with an amber shade. A bust of Shakespeare perched on top of a mahogany cabinet filled with porcelain figurines. Ruffled cushions in varying shades of blue and green were piled on couches and chairs. The cluttered fireplace mantel held a clock, vases, candleholders, and a large porcelain eagle.

Betsy shook her head. "Takes me all day to dust this stuff. It'll be the death of me, but the judge won't get rid of a single item because they belonged to Claudine. He really loved her, he did."

She set the tray down on the round oak table. "Thank you for supper, Betsy. What time is breakfast?"

"Mr. Wallace eats at six, but I can fix yours earlier, if you like."

Willow shook her head. "I don't expect special treatment. I won't have any trouble adapting to your routine."

Betsy smiled. "I can tell we're going to get along just fine. Anything I can do to make your stay here more pleasant, you just tell me."

"I will, and no more hauling trays up to the third floor. I can come down here."

Willow decided to return to her room. In the foyer, she bumped into the judge, who was just coming in from his stroll. He paused for a moment, assessing her. "Oh, my dear Willow. I thought you'd be in bed. You must rest, dear."

"I'm fine, Uncle. I just brought my tray downstairs. Betsy was kind enough to carry it up to me."

"Yes, Betsy is as good as they come. Claudine"—he choked over the name—"Claudine . . . would approve."

She reached out to lay a hand on his shoulder. "Oh, I know how much you must miss her."

"I do. She was a wonderful woman. The townspeople never really understood her." The faraway look in his eyes faded, and he focused on Willow. "My dear, you are even more beautiful than I remembered. Silas will be enchanted."

Silas. How had she forgotten him? What would he be like? According to Uncle Wallace, he had good teeth and bone structure. But she'd heard horses described the same way.

Wallace patted her shoulder. "Run along, dear niece. You need your rest."

She smiled. "Yes, I am rather tired. I believe I'll turn in."

"Of course, my dear. I'll see you in the morning. I hope you rest well."

"I'm sure I will." She started the tedious climb to her third-floor room.

Later, Willow stood in the darkened bedroom, staring out the window at what remained of the mill. Thunder blasted overhead, and lightning crackled as another storm moved through. Suddenly, the enormity of her plan struck with the force of a blow. Could she do this? She had to. Like it or not, she'd set her course.

Flames had died to a smoldering pile of rubble. The wind calmed, and most of the overpowering smoke had blown away. Tucker leaned on his rake. The bunkhouse suffered minor damage, but it was still standing.

Pete Peevy paused and took off his hat. He'd worked twenty feet from Tucker the past half hour. "Guess that about does it, boss. Me and the boys drew straws to see who would take the first watch tonight."

"No need for that, Pete. I'd planned to watch for new fires myself. You men need your rest. You've done enough."

"So have you, and there's more of us. We figure no one will have to be on patrol over an hour at the most. It won't hurt us."

Tucker reached out and shook the man's hand. "Thanks, Pete. Tell the men I appreciate it."

Pete nodded. "We won't leave you, Tuck. You can count on most of us staying through thick and thin. See you in the morning."

Singly, or in small groups, the townspeople filed by, shaking his hand and expressing their sympathy at his loss. As the last of them trailed up the path to seek much needed rest, or hitched horses to buckboards, Tucker put out another small fire.

Caleb joined him. "Pete says they've got it under control."

"After two days, I'd hope." Tucker was dog-tired, but he wouldn't sleep without worrying, so he might as well stand watch for flash fires tonight. His men had worked without stopping. They needed to go home to their families.

"We had good help. We could have lost a lot more than just the sawmill."

Tucker agreed. "Could have lost the town, I guess."

Caleb stretched weary muscles. "How you figure we're going to meet wages and buy the materials we need to rebuild?"

"Don't know. It's going to be tight. Maybe we can take a second loan at the bank. Surely Horace will understand. Thunder Ridge is his home."

Caleb snorted. "Using what for collateral? You've mortgaged everything you own and then some."

"Guess I'll have to come up with more. The bunkhouses, a couple of outbuildings—it's all we have left."

Caleb climbed the path toward home. Morning would be soon enough to assess the overall damage, and he had a meeting scheduled with Willow Madison. Might be once she cooled, she'd agree to damages, and he wouldn't have to ask Horace for more money.

The possibility was about as likely as a pig trying to pass as a pack mule.

Chapter 5

E arly morning sunshine streamed through the narrow bedroom pane when someone tapped softly on the guest bedroom door.

Willow stiffly pushed to sit up on the side of the bed. She'd been awake and dressed for hours, but she wasn't sure Wallace had risen so she'd lain down again. Every bone in her body cried for mercy. The hard fall had been more damaging than she had expected. She was fortunate she could get out of bed.

"Come in, Uncle Wallace."

The heavy door swung open, and her smiling uncle set a small brown leather valise inside the doorway. "The Widow Gleeson sent a few gowns and personal items. So thoughtful of her."

Willow covered her face with her hands. Her head beat like a war drum. "Very thoughtful. I'll send a note of appreciation immediately." She owned two gowns—the one she was wearing, and the one that had burned with the buckboard. Widow Gleeson's generosity was a godsend.

The judge pulled a timepiece from his pocket and consulted it. "Dear me, it is late. Hurry then, change your dress. We have a meeting with the Reverend Cordell at nine, and then I'll want to introduce you to Silas Sterling. He's on the school committee and most eager to meet you, my dear."

The reverend's name rang a bell. Wallace had written that he headed the newly formed school board. Willow was anxious to meet the man, and even more eager to begin her new duties. Less eager to meet Silas Sterling, but she couldn't avoid the inevitable.

Judge sobered. "My dear, are you certain you're up to this visit? That was a nasty spill you took."

She scratched her dust-saturated hair. "Is there warm water on the stove?"

"Most certainly. As long as the supply holds out. You'll have to carry it up to the bathing alcove. . . ." Faded blue eyes lightly brushed her appearance. "My, my, you could use a good scrub."

Indeed she could. She studied the oily grime beneath her fingernails, and remembered trying to block her catapult from the wagon. Dust hemmed the bottom of her gown, and in general she looked like a hooligan. "I promise to hurry."

Wallace closed the door, and she slid off the bed and eased to the doorway. Unlatching the lock on the leather valise, she removed a gown and held it to her breastbone for inspection. She was thought to be petite, but the Widow Gleeson apparently was even smaller. Well, she'd have to compress her additional size into the clean gown, because she had nothing else.

An hour later she accompanied Wallace out the front door. The clean gown and unmentionables restored her spirits, but Willow sympathized with a Christmas goose. She feared if she took one good breath and released it, buttons would fly.

The smell of smoke hung in stagnant air. Willow's eyes sought the smoldering mill ruins, and her footsteps paused. *The buffoon.* She'd been *ordered* to meet with him this morning in regard to the accident.

Wallace glanced up. "Something wrong, dear? If you're not feeling well I can reschedule the meeting."

"No need. I just remembered that I'm supposed to meet Mr. Gray this morning to discuss the accident."

"Ah, yes, most unfortunate about your buckboard, but soon you'll have no need for the conveyance." He winked, and reminded her so of her father, Willow indulged his optimism. She'd not met Mr. Sterling, and at this juncture there was no reason to think he would take a fancy to her. Just because she was accessible didn't mean that he would be smitten by her. A man of his social position didn't fall for the first available woman who crossed his path—of this she was quite confident.

"Silas has a fine livery full of handsome carriages," the judge noted. "He's a most fascinating individual. Instead of living close to his investments, he's chosen to come home, far from the open seas, and run his empire."

Willow didn't give a fig about fine carriages. The buckboard was her source of independence, and now it was gone.

"Come along dear, the reverend is waiting."

"What about Mr. Gray?"

"I'll stop by the mill on my way home. The accident is men's business. You're not to worry your pretty head. Mr. Gray will be compensated for his losses."

"He shouldn't be compensated one cent! The accident was clearly an act of insensitive negligence on Mr. Gray's part. And even if it were my fault, how would I pay for all that damage?" Building a mill would take more money than she'd ever seen.

"How?" Wallace paused and turned to face her. "Willow, are you not aware of Mr. Sterling's vast worth? Why, it's measureless. He owns fleets of cargo ships that carry silk and other goods back and forth from the Orient. When you're married, you'll want for nothing."

Speculation didn't pay bills, and she thought it highly arrogant to be spending his wealth. "I didn't cause the accident, Uncle Wallace. Mr. Gray set a load of lumber in the roadway. Thunder frightened my mare, and she bolted, heading straight down the road. She was forced to veer sharply to avoid careening headlong into that lumber wagon, which caused the hitch to snap, thus spilling the kerosene into the pond." She drew a deep breath. "And don't let him convince you otherwise."

"My . . . well, how did the fire start?"

"That I can't say, but I didn't have a match." Of that she was confident. She'd eaten cold beans two nights in a row because she had forgotten the means for lighting a fire. "Perhaps a lightning strike—it was thundering something awful at the time."

"Yes, you know it thunders and lightnings a lot around

here. Very peculiar. And never seems to rain." He shook his head. "Go on."

"I don't know how the fire started, but it spread across the pond like—" she snapped her thumb and forefinger "—that." She did have a vague recollection of a brief flare of light before the kerosene ignited, but in retrospect she'd decided that her memory of the whole humiliating incident was too vague to commit to anything solid, much less lay proper blame.

"Most unfortunate."

"Most. If the wagon hadn't been blocking the road, none of this would have happened." Willow adjusted her too-tight bodice. And she would have arrived in Thunder Ridge with a bit more decorum.

They fell into stride, and Willow's thoughts turned to the previous subject.

"Suppose Mr. Sterling doesn't find me suitable."

Her uncle laughed. "Preposterous. You're a rose among thorns. Highly educated, refined—"

She interrupted. "Until a few weeks ago, I was crawling on the ground shooting men." She hardly considered her conduct genteel.

"Fighting in defense of your country, young lady! And that's all behind you. Now you will prepare the school for fall attendance, work on your appearance, and allow Silas a proper courting time."

Work on what appearance? She glanced down. What was wrong with her appearance?

Judge continued. "Of course. there are wedding plans to consider, and the parties and various soirées involved with the excitement. Thunder Ridge is small, but our neighboring communities are close, so the turnout should be extravagant and quite worthy of Silas's standing."

By now, they had reached the small glistening white church. A freshly painted bell hung beside a garden of dead pansies. A white picket fence lined the cobblestone walk, leading to two vertical doors that met in the middle.

"Pretty, isn't it?" Wallace remarked. "This is where you'll wed. Late fall, perhaps. When the trees are luminous with color and the air has a bit of a bite to it."

Willow mentally shook her head. He had the date set, and she had yet to meet her husband-to-be. Would he be old and decrepit? Short? Fat? Bald? Breath smelling of wild onions and strong drink? She shuddered. "What happened to the pansies?"

"The reverend won't give up. Every year he plants pansies in hopes rain will come, but it hasn't rained in two years. Not a sizable rain, leastways. Only a few random showers have blown through, but enough to give the reverend hope each spring."

When they entered the church foyer, Reverend Cordell turned from the altar where he'd been kneeling and came to greet them. Grasping Willow's hand, he smiled, sincere warmth radiating from the man with a crop of snow-white hair and ruddy features. "My dear. How good it is to see you looking so fit. I feared after the terrible accident you might be abed a few days."

"Thank you. I'm a bit sore this morning, but no real harm done."

Reverend Cordell briefly closed his eyes. "Praise God. Now. Shall we get down to business? There's much to talk about and see. Silas will be joining us later. He is most anxious to meet you."

He led the way to a small study on the right side of the altar. For more than an hour, Willow listened to plans for reopening the school—perhaps as many as three reopenings in the area.

"Once Thunder Ridge is running smoothly, Beeder's Cove and Blackberry Hill will open again, good Lord willing." *Audrey and Copper.* Willow's pulse hammered. Her friends would, indeed, have a place to teach, and if they couldn't live together, at least the women would be close enough to visit back and forth on a regular basis. This could soften the blow of marriage to a man she didn't love.

"Of course we'll need to find new teachers. Most have left or retired."

"I believe I can help in that area," Willow said.

The reverend lifted a brow.

"I have two close friends who are teachers."

"Oh? Are they presently employed?"

"No. They're living in my hometown—Timber Creek— though because of the war, there is no longer a town, just a few inhabitable dwellings." The image of her lovely childhood home flashed through her mind. Flowers, green grass. Porches and rose-covered balconies. All black rubble now. And a handful of residents.

"I'm sorry."

Wallace interceded. "Terrible, terrible thing, the war. The Yankees burned Timber Creek and . . . well, it was simply terrible."

"Yes. Terrible," Willow echoed. "My friends are there now,

but they are actively seeking work, and I am quite certain they would love to speak to you about the possible positions."

"Excellent! Then perhaps we can move ahead with plans far quicker than anticipated, but of course our first order of business will be Thunder Ridge. Are you eager to see the school—or what will soon be the school? The old one burned to the ground."

Willow eased slowly to her feet. The ill-fitting unmentionables Widow Gleeson had so graciously provided were creeping. "Most eager, Reverend."

A knock sounded at the door. "That must be Silas." Reverend Cordell called, "Come in!"

The door swung open and Willow turned to get her first look at her intended husband. Silas Sterling stood in the doorway, resplendent in a dark green suit, complemented by a lighter green shirt. Rings glittered from his fingers, and his nails were neatly trimmed and polished. He smiled, and suddenly Willow's reservations tempered when his smile reminded her of her father's.

"Miss Madison?"

Willow stepped forward. "Mr. Sterling."

He reached for her hand, holding it lightly. "So very good to meet you. I've been anticipating our meeting."

She returned his smile. "Thank you. As have I."

The wealthy suitor barely stayed long enough to make her acquaintance, and Willow was grateful. He chatted briefly with the judge, inquired of the reverend's continuing robust health, and then excused himself, saying he had business elsewhere.

Before he left, he turned back to Willow. "I trust that once you're settled, you'll join me for tea?"

"Yes. I'd like that, Mr. Sterling."

Merry blue eyes caught hers. "Good day, Miss Madison."

When the study door closed, Willow sank back to her chair. Silence covered the small study.

"Well, that went nicely!" the judge praised.

"Most cordial," Reverend Cordell agreed.

And he didn't mention a word of my disastrous arrival. Drawing a deep breath, Willow grinned. "Yes, Mr. Sterling seemed rather delightful."

Years older than Willow expected, but captivating. The dreaded meeting was rather like removing a worrisome stone from one's shoe.

Relief felt so good.

Chapter 6

Tucker didn't know what time Willow Madison planned to make her appearance, but he was ready for her. Outside the mill office ruins, he carefully arranged a small table and two chairs for their meeting, and then sat down in one, legs crossed and arms folded.

Caleb approached from the north. "Can I ask you something?"

"Shoot."

"Why are these chairs and table out here, and why are you sitting out here by yourself?

"I have an appointment with the Madison woman."

"And you think she'll show?" Caleb shook his head. "Come on, Tuck, you know that accident wasn't entirely her fault. That's a flatland horse. She's not used to the kind of thunder we have around here. She spooked. Shucks, that thunder spooks everyone who ventures near here. We hardly notice it anymore, but it can be real jarring to a new-comer."

Tucker set his lips in a tight line. "She should have driven around that lumber wagon. Around it, over it, beside it—through it, if necessary. Anything other than let the horse have its head."

"Driven around it? She was fighting the horse. I saw her. Seems to me she didn't have much choice but to let it run wild. That mare was so shook up it probably didn't see the wagon until it was right on top of it. I doubt if Miss Madison had enough strength to pull her up in time."

"Then she shouldn't have been hauling five barrels of kerosene. Only the judge would come up with an idea like that."

Caleb frowned. "Bad-mouthing the judge? You are in a temper. Wallace is a good man, and you know it. Don't blame him for the accident."

Tucker recognized the truth when he heard it, but still, the truth wasn't much help in rebuilding that mill. If he were in a bad mood, it was Willow Madison's fault. Days of fighting to save his livelihood. What man worth his salt would be agreeable?

Caleb squinted at the sky. "Gonna be hot. Not a cloud in the sky."

Tucker shifted. "Where's Eli?"

"Home. Ate breakfast and went to bed for a couple of hours. Said fighting fire for a couple of days wore him out."

"Doc come yet?"

"Can't. There's an outbreak of influenza in the foothills. Said he'd be back in a few days. But Willow seems to be faring okay."

"That woman doesn't need anything but a head doctor. She was up and about the next day, down here harassing me. I saw her leave the house with the judge earlier this morning. She's doing just fine."

"I wouldn't have bet a plugged nickel she could get out of bed for days, let alone get down all those stairs. I'd never been inside Wallace's monstrosity, and now that I have, I'm not in a hurry to go back. That house is downright strange. What did she want?"

"Who?"

"The Madison woman. You said you saw her earlier this morning?"

"I've seen her. I didn't say she came this way, but I figure she'll be sashaying down here pretty soon."

Caleb shoved his hat back on his head and released a long breath. "I can see this is going to get worse before it gets better."

Tucker eyed him from beneath the brim of his hat. "Whose side you on?"

"Yours, but Tuck, you can get pretty muleheaded at times. You know that."

"Muleheaded? Miss Madison seems to think I have half a brain." Tucker didn't miss Caleb's half–smile, quickly reined.

"That a fact?"

"If I'd had half a brain, the lumber wagon wouldn't have been sitting in the middle of the road. If I'd been taking care of business, her horse wouldn't have swerved, the mill wouldn't have burned, and life would be just dandy."

Caleb grinned. "Said it in a nice ladylike manner, did she?"

The twinkle in Caleb's eyes irked Tucker. There wasn't

anything funny about this situation. "Said it like a high-handed spitfire. I pity Silas if he ends up with that one, which is evidently what she and Wallace have in mind."

"Silas can take care of himself. No woman will hook him unless he's willing to be hooked. Besides, he's looking for a wife, and she's a pretty little thing, you have to admit."

"I didn't notice."

Now that was a lie, and they both knew it. There wasn't a man alive who wouldn't notice Willow Madison, but noticing her wasn't the same thing as finding her attractive.

"When do you think we can start cleaning up that mess?" Caleb asked, indicating the rubble covering the mill site. Vagrant spirals of smoke rose, hanging in the air.

"A day or two, I suppose. It's still hot. We can't do much until it cools down."

"I thought we'd lost the whole shebang, but we've got that big stack of lumber out back of the bunkhouse. The fire didn't touch it. Enough to make a start, I guess."

Tucker shook his head. "Not near enough, and we can't cut more without a saw blade."

Caleb absently took a seat. "I have an idea."

His cousin wasn't one to babble. If he had a plan, then it was probably something he'd thought seriously about. Tucker raised an eyebrow. "I'm listening."

"We can't do much without a saw, so how about we telegraph that big sawmill company we passed on our way home from the war, explain our situation, and ask if they've got a used blade they'll sell. Remember, they were switching over to those new circular saws, so they might have a muley saw they don't need anymore."

Tucker considered the thought. "Might work. You want to take care of it?"

Caleb grinned. "I'll get right on it. We need to get up and running as soon as we can. People are depending on us. A closed mill hurts the whole town." He vacated the chair and left, striding purposefully toward the mercantile.

Tucker fumbled for his pocket watch. One full hour he'd been sitting here waiting for that woman. She wasn't coming. He stuck the timepiece back in his trousers. All right, if that was the way she wanted it, he'd find her. She couldn't ignore him or her responsibilities, and it was high time someone told her.

Chapter 7

⤸

Uncle Wallace paused before a small, tin-covered building at the edge of town. The shack had two windows, both with broken panes, and a door on each end. The ground outside was covered with chicken feathers. Rustic was too kind a word for this dilapidated hovel. Willow knew a chicken pen when she saw it.

Judge waved a hand at the gaping doorway facing them. The wooden door dangled on a broken hinge, also covered in chicken feathers and white droppings.

"Well, there it is."

Willow's eyes skimmed the shack. "There what is?"

"The new schoolhouse."

Her jaw dropped. That—whatever it was—was the schoolhouse? She offered him a chance to backtrack. "You're not serious."

He shifted, his apologetic features betraying his feigned

enthusiasm. "It's not much now, but soon . . . soon it will be most suitable."

Willow reeled from the news. She hadn't expected much, but this couldn't be considered anything. The chickens had moved out, so she could have it for a school?

She stepped up to peer inside the gaping dark hole. When her eyes adjusted to the dim light, words failed her. A row of nesting boxes ran along one side. A roost built of wooden poles filled the other. The piles of accumulated droppings under the perch made it very clear that she had once again assumed incorrectly—the chickens had yet to move. She shot the judge a reproachful glare. "This is not a school. It's a henhouse."

"Well, yes," he admitted. "It used to be. However, it's not been in use for some time."

"Since when?" Everything looked—she sidestepped a white blob—too fresh.

"Yes, well, admittedly not long, and a few old laying hens have refused to give it up, but only a few and we're working on them." Willow's eyes traveled the hovel. "Do you seriously intend to put children in here? There's no room for children. Or desks, for that matter. Whatever made you pick this old henhouse?"

She realized she was lashing out. He might not be responsible for the location, but she was so disappointed she could cry. She hadn't harbored great expectations concerning the schoolhouse—after all, they had been through a war—but a henhouse? Outrageous.

"I realize this is a bit of a shock—we'd hoped to be farther along with renovation before you arrived, but time ran out." He cleared his throat, clearly uncomfortable with her response. "Tucker has volunteered to oversee the work. The old school burned last year."

Willow's stomach soured. "Tucker Gray."

"Yes." The judge smiled. "You've met—oh dear, yes, of course, you've met. Well, never you mind, Tucker Gray and his men are quite efficient. I'm sure you'll be thrilled with their work."

She shifted. She was supposed to put up with that man on a daily basis? The knot on her temple throbbed. "Can I at least request a decent door?"

"A door. Yes indeed, my dear. I'll personally see to it." Relief dripped from his brow.

"And those nesting boxes removed. And the roost taken away." She wrinkled her nose. "I assume I'm not expected to shovel out those dried droppings under the roost."

"Oh, no. Dear me, no. Perish the thought. You needn't concern yourself with a thing. The men will do it all. It wouldn't be proper for Silas's intended to do anything so menial."

Willow planned to hold him to the decree. As far as being Silas's intended, that was the last thing on her mind. A decent schoolhouse. And less—much less—of the white stuff. That's all she asked.

Wallace whipped out a handkerchief and mopped his brow. "We need to get back to the house. The heat is beastly and things to do, you know."

Her eyes swept the site. Perhaps it did have possibilities. The setting was nice, tall trees and cool shade. The war had taught her to appreciate the small things. When one didn't have what one needed, then the next best thing would be to use what was available.

She turned back to the judge. "Why don't you go on back? I'll look around here a little more, and then I'd like to have a look around town, maybe get acquainted with the towns-folk?" Soon she would be shaping their young children's minds; she wanted to know all about her pupils' back-ground—the kind of homes they came from, the problems they faced. Her pupils weren't just students. She knew she would come to love them like family.

"Yes, well, don't stay out too long." Wallace scurried away.

Rat deserting the ship. Willow hoped he remembered to stop by and set Tucker Gray straight about the accident.

She turned back to the henhouse. She would be surprised if the town did warm to her easily after the fire incident. Not a single soul knew it was entirely Tucker Gray's fault. Town loyalty and all that stuff. But she'd eventually win their hearts, and if Gray were a man, he'd make it very clear he'd left the wagon of lumber in the middle of the road.

She'd had the intellect and foresight to avoid a real tragedy by *not* plowing straight through that load of lumber and pos-sibly killing the mare and herself in the process. Her blood ran hot just thinking about it. She doubted if he'd do her any favors. Well, he'd have no choice. The children needed an education, and the school board had hired her. Whether Mr. High-and-Mighty Gray liked it or not, she was here to stay.

Now that she had a chance to examine the building, she could see that while certainly not all she had hoped, with work it could be suitable. At least it had a wood plank floor, instead of packed dirt. The floor was littered with straw from the nests and scattered droppings. Hens weren't very particular about where they made their messes.

Scattered here and there were those watering dishes that looked like glass saucers screwed onto a quart canning jar, along with a couple of long wooden feeding troughs.

Take out the nests and the roost, clean the floor, and the room was usable. They'd need heat for winter—a stove and stovepipe, a chimney too. Oh, it needed a lot of work, but it wasn't completely impractical. *I can do all things through Him who strengthens me.*

She could do this. She'd done many things she'd once thought out of the question—killed men, somebody's brother or father or husband—but never allowed herself to think of those desperate acts. When there was nothing to fill her belly, she'd eaten grubs, and she'd held dying children in her arms after a battle. She'd helped women bury their families, dug graves with nothing more than a rusty pick, and she'd cried enough tears to fill two sizeable buckets.

Teaching school in a henhouse would be a picnic.

She wandered outside, eyes scanning the grounds. The schoolyard would have to be cleared. Flowers would be nice but scarce as hen's teeth in this town. A big bell. . . . Suddenly, she wanted a school bell.

Silas Sterling. If he was so rich, perhaps she could coax him into buying a school bell. One with a sound that could be heard for miles.

Chapter 8

Eli's heavy boots hit the ground like a man with something on his mind. Tucker discarded his earlier thought of personally tracking down the Madison girl, and waited for him to get there. His cousin's eyes were red-rimmed and weary.

"Morning, Tucker."

"Morning, Eli."

"How's Miss Madison today?"

Tucker shrugged. "Haven't talked to her. She was supposed to be here this morning but she hasn't shown up yet."

"She seems pleasant enough."

Tucker met his cousin's gaze. The remark took him aback. Eli didn't comment on women. Eli didn't like women. He'd loved one woman, and they hadn't been married a year when the war claimed him for the battlefront. The wife died a few months later in childbirth. Tucker's gaze shifted to the small cemetery that lay below in the valley. There Eli's life rested.

He turned to pick up a shovel. "You need something?"

"I'm thinking this is real bad, but we'll have more help rebuilding this time. Most men are back from the war."

"Yeah, men needing a paycheck. Where am I going to find men who'll work and delay their pay until the mill is up and running again?"

Eli shrugged, his dark looks pensive. "It won't be easy, but there's no point in being bitter about it. Everything will work eventually."

"Sometimes I wonder." Eli and Caleb failed to see what a mess this was, and how long it would take to replace what they'd lost. It would take time—a lot of time—to recover. Tucker glanced toward the Madison house. Where *was* that female? He needed answers. Money. Time. Patience.

Cool down and think rationally. The good Lord had never once let him down, and it wasn't likely He'd start now.

He nodded at Eli. "I suppose you have things to do. I've got business up the hill."

Eli apparently took the hint. "Thought I'd drop by the bunkhouse and make a few repairs."

Tucker didn't like to cut Eli short, but they couldn't waste time talking about the situation; they had to do something about it. He dropped the shovel and strode toward the Madison house.

Betsy answered the door at his insistent rap. "Well, Tucker, what a surprise. Don't just stand there holding the door open, letting flies in. What brings you this way? I'd have thought you'd have your hands full today."

He stepped inside and struggled with the urge to fold his elbows to his side so he wouldn't knock over one of Claudine's knickknacks. She had a lot of money tied up in gilded swans and china butterflies. Judge never refused her anything.

Betsy grinned. "Willow's not home, but you come on back to the kitchen. I just baked sugar cookies, and I've got a fresh pot of coffee."

He trailed her, smarting from her observation. Why would she assume he came to see Willow? He had—but not the way Betsy thought. The two had business to discuss. And that was all. If he ever felt attracted to a woman, it wouldn't be someone like Willow Madison. Not even close.

Sitting down at the round kitchen table, he thanked Betsy when she placed a cup of steaming coffee and a plate of warm sugar cookies in front of him. He bit into one. "Betsy, your husband's the luckiest man on earth."

She grinned again, flashing large white teeth. "You go on, now, Tucker Gray. You could have any woman you wanted. Truth is, you're too picky."

"Think so." He reached for another cookie. "But they just don't make them like you anymore."

She laughed. "You sweet talker. Save your blarney for someone who can chase after you. Now what do you want with Willow?"

"Who said I wanted anything with her?"

"Well, you're not in the habit of dropping by, so I just figured she was the draw."

"I need to talk to her about the damage she did to the mill."

Betsy shook her head, forehead pensive. "Now, Tucker, Willow didn't intend to set fire to the sawmill. You ought to know better than that."

What was it about that woman that had the town's loyalty without half of them ever setting eyes on her? He was tired of people telling him Willow wasn't to blame. Before you know it, they'd start blaming him! He glowered. "You noticed the mill this morning? It isn't there."

The housekeeper sent a reproachful look. "Now that's just plain petty of you. If anything's to blame, it's the thunder. Spooked that poor mare into bolting, and you had that lumber wagon in the way."

"Now you stop right there. I own a sawmill." Or at least, he did until Miss "Runaway" Madison hit town. "I have a right to load lumber and unload it on that very spot. That accident was not my fault, and you can't say it was."

"I didn't say it was, I merely reminded you that the lumber wagon was in the way, which it was. You didn't know the mare would spook, but neither did the judge's niece. It was one of them natural catastrophes. No one's fault, really."

"Says you. She didn't have to hit the pond. A man would have driven around the wagon and avoided the disaster. That's all I'm saying."

Betsy turned from the stove. "Are you saying the accident happened because Willow is a woman? You don't think women should be allowed to drive a wagon? Maybe you think we should just stay in the house and wait on you men."

"Now, Betsy, I didn't say that."

"You might as well have, and I'll not hear that kind of talk in my kitchen. Now off with you, Tucker Gray. If you want to argue, go find Willow. She and the judge are out there somewhere. The two left together 'bout an hour ago, so they shouldn't be far off."

He stood up and stacked a handful of cookies in his palm. "She plans to marry Silas."

"Who does?"

"Willow. Judge said so. She's here to set her cap for Silas. A man she's never met before. Now what do you think of the sweet little niece?"

Betsy's lips drew in in a thoughtful manner. "Oh, I don't know. Love don't always last. A woman needs to be giving some thought to security. And Silas is a very secure man when it comes to money. Nice, too."

Tucker chuckled. "You're saying love isn't important in a marriage? You're forgetting that the Bible says love is important. It knows all, bears all?"

She swatted him with a dishtowel. "Silas is male, and Willow is surely female. Can't argue with that, and I don't see a problem with it. He wants a wife, she wants security. They both get what they want, and everyone's happy."

Except Tucker. He was a long way from being happy, and it didn't have anything to do with Willow Madison. Why would it? She could marry whomever she wanted, and as long as she paid damages, he couldn't care less. It was none of his business what Willow Madison did, and he planned to keep it that way. His Bible said the only real security comes from God. Someone ought to tell the Madison woman that.

John Franklin was working in front of his blacksmith shop when Tucker passed.

"Hey there, Tuck. Guess who I saw out this morning taking a walk with her uncle? That feisty new schoolteacher."

"I need a word with her. You see where they went?"

"They were heading for the church last I saw. You know,

Tucker, the judge's niece is sure a looker. Can't understand why she isn't married."

"Yeah. A real puzzle."

Most men probably had too much common sense to get hitched to a firebrand like Willow Madison. A man's sense of survival had to kick in sometime.

John firmed his lips. "You know, I don't believe that accident was her fault. A fine little woman like that wouldn't do anything wrong. Got the sweetest smile." He winked at Tucker. "If I was a young buck like you, I'd be trying to get better acquainted. Competition for her favors is bound to be intense."

"Sorry, not interested." Tucker lifted a finger to his hat. "Take care, John."

He walked away, marveling at the effect Willow had, particularly on the men. Caleb and Eli were both ready to forgive her for burning their business to the ground. John talking foolishness about her smile. It didn't make sense. Was the town so desperate for a schoolteacher it'd take a moron?

She didn't affect him. Not a bit. His only interest was trying to recoup some of his financial losses.

He stopped at the church, where Reverend Cordell was busy dusting the pews. "Tucker, what brings you here today?"

"I'm looking for Wallace and his niece. John told me they were coming here."

Reverend Cordell brightened. "Yes, indeed. They were here. Lovely young lady. A privilege to meet her. I believe Wallace went home to rest, and she remained at the proposed school site. She'll make a wonderful teacher. I have to say I was very impressed. Very."

Tucker nodded. Apparently every man in town had lost his sanity.

Chapter 9

"Miss Madison." Willow glanced up when she heard her name. Engrossed with thoughts of the new school, she hadn't heard anyone approach. The familiar excitement had taken root, the exhilaration of educating young minds coursed through her veins once she'd toured the school . . . or what would soon become the school. Granted, it was a dismal chicken coop now, but it would be rewarding to watch the project take shape. She could hardly wait to write Audrey and Copper and . . .

"Miss Madison." Drawn back, she turned to seek the source of summons and her heart sank when she saw Tucker Gray. What did he want?

"Yes?"

He approached, sunlight highlighting his expansive shoulders. Sunshine and outdoors lent him a rugged look. The man was impossibly striking . . . and Willow had no doubt he knew it. Tucker Gray's expression was anything but cordial this morning.

"Correct me if I'm wrong, but didn't we have an appointment?"

"Oh, yes. That." She snapped open a parasol the Widow Gleeson had supplied. The sun was merciless today. "Uncle Wallace said he'd be by to speak to you."

A muscle flexed in the mill owner's left jaw. "My appointment wasn't with the judge."

"True, but we have nothing to discuss. My uncle will be around shortly." She was about to continue on her way when he blocked her path. She stepped back, her hand tightening around the mother-of-pearl parasol handle. His eyes locked with hers.

How *dare* he block her route?

Stepping to the right, she attempted to avoid him, but he immediately stopped her.

She stepped. He blocked.

Biting her lower lip, she drew an impatient breath. "I have been occupied this morning, Mr. Gray. Now will you kindly step out of my way?"

"So have I, but I keep my commitments."

"And I keep mine. I have been hired to reopen the school in Thunder Ridge. I have been inspecting the property." She abhorred her clipped, ridged tone . . . her schoolmarm tone, but there it was. This man brought out the defiance in her.

He shifted stances, stubbornness written all over him. "You've been inspecting the henhouse."

"It may be a henhouse now, but men will change that shortly."

His gaze held hers. "That was the plan until yesterday."

She shrugged. "Obviously, you are misinformed. I just left Reverend Cordell, and he assured me the new school would be ready for occupancy early August, which will allow me ample time to prepare for the coming school year."

His stance relaxed, and a slow grin spread across his captivating features. "Obviously, *you're* misinformed, Miss Madison. I'm in charge of remodeling that henhouse, and in view of the mill burning down, the school might have to be put on hold."

"On hold?" Willow flared. Oh yes, *he* was in charge of the renovation process. She would be forced to put up with this . . . this jester every day until the refurbishing was completed.

Lord, this isn't fair.

He reached over and gently tapped her dropped jaw closed.

Of all the . . . How boorish! She snapped the parasol shut.

"On hold," he repeated, way too cheerfully, she decided.

"That's impossible. Area children are expecting to begin school September first. You'll have to appoint someone else to the project."

"Miss Madison, do you know what it takes to rebuild a mill?"

She didn't, but that was beside the issue. "The school should warrant importance over the mill."

"The mill provides the town income. The workers earn a dollar and a half a day. That goes a long way toward feeding a family. If it comes down to a choice, which do you think they'll choose? Besides, you'll be gone shortly after the school opens, so why are you getting your bustle in a bunch?"

His nerve was shocking, and disgraceful. Lifting her nose, she met his egotistical stare. "I don't know what you're talking about."

"Your mission."

"I have no mission."

"Not true. Your uncle said you were here to marry Silas Sterling."

She gasped. Why would Uncle Wallace tell him such sensitive issues?

"My uncle may have mentioned Mr. Sterling is seeking a wife . . . but that doesn't mean . . ." He left her speechless. She recovered.

"I am here to reopen a school." She shot him a scathing glower and popped open the parasol. "But what if I were interested in Mr. Sterling? Has he not publicly announced his intent to take a wife?"

"And produce an heir."

She briefly nodded. "The latter would be a logical assumption."

"Are you aware that the man is thirty years your senior?"

"I am." Not. She didn't know his exact years, but Uncle Wallace had said "older"—he hadn't mentioned the man had one foot in the grave. Forty-nine years old? Practically ancient! Yet he'd looked spry and energetic.

"And you will do this?" His tone resonated disdain.

She snapped the umbrella closed and bonked the top of his head.

He stepped back, and she lifted her skirt and whisked around him. "Good morning, Mr. Gray."

"Don't think this excuses you from your responsibility."

"I have no responsibility other than the school," she called over her shoulder.

"We'll see about that," he called back. "Someone's paying for these damages and it won't be me."

He was correct. It couldn't be him. Willow's chin lifted higher. Judge said he didn't own anything but the clothes on his back. The thought brought her up short. If he were that poor, how could he possibly rebuild the sawmill? She hadn't considered that snag. The town's survival hinged on the business, and the accident had taken away its livelihood. Suddenly her independence drooped.

"Heard you fought in the war," he taunted as she proceeded on her way.

"Congratulations. Your reasoning is faulty, but your hearing is excellent."

He rubbed the top of his head. "I should consider myself lucky. You could have shot me."

Squelching a grin, she focused on the path before her. "Indeed, I could have, Mr. Gray."

Indeed, she could have. And if circumstances forced them to work together in the coming weeks, he'd best watch his behavior.

Chapter 10

That afternoon Tucker entered the bank and removed his hat. He'd known Horace Padget most of his life. The banker had helped many citizens of Thunder Ridge, for a price of course. Horace never missed a penny interest. He was so tightfisted he could pinch a nickel until the buffalo bucked. The man had a dollar sign for a heart.

Who am I fooling? Horace wouldn't be loaning Tucker more money—his present note with the bank was already staggering. And then what would he do? He needed cash to meet his payroll, and pay for that saw Caleb was going to order. It took money to operate a business, and they hadn't been up and running long enough to build up a cash flow.

Nellie Crawford, bank teller and Horace's personal secretary, peered at him over her glasses. Her husband, Sam, worked at the mill. She'd know how important it was that he keep up with the payroll. She smiled at him. "Tucker. What can I do for you?"

"I need to see Horace. He in a good mood today?"

Nellie frowned at the levity. "As good as he ever is, I suppose."

Well, now he knew not to expect too much. "Is he busy? I won't take a lot of his time."

"I'll see. You wait right here and I'll be back in a minute.

Tucker eyed her retreating back, wondering what she thought he would do if he moved from this spot. Lift a couple of twenties from the cash drawer? He shook his head ruefully. For an ex-soldier and a business owner, he didn't command the sort of respect he deserved. Nellie gave him orders like he was a kid. She opened the door to Horace's office and motioned for him to come, and he ambled toward her.

Horace sat behind a big walnut desk, waiting for him, and from his expression, Tucker didn't expect this to be a happy experience. If it wasn't for Caleb and Eli and the men who worked at the mill, he'd just say forget it. He'd never been in debt in his life—until he rebuilt the sawmill the first time, but if he wanted to rebuild it again, he had to take the dreaded step right now. He shook Horace's hand, pulled out a chair, and sat down across the desk from the pudgy banker.

Horace nodded. "Tucker. Good to see you. What can I do for you?"

Now that the moment had come, the words stuck in his throat. He didn't like asking anyone for favors unless he could do something in return, and Horace didn't need one thing from him. He cleared his throat. "I was thinking about enlarging my bank loan to rebuild."

"I figured as much. What did you have in mind for collateral?"

"Well, there's the land. Outbuildings and the bunkhouse. That ought to be worth something."

"Land values around here are in the cellar. Not much need for land that never gets rain."

"Now, that's not fair, Horace. We do get rain once in a while. Otherwise, we couldn't keep going."

"Very seldom. And we keep going because several creeks run into the river upstream, and it drifts down to us. The land here isn't good for growing anything, and you can't raise cattle or horses without water. Unless you have river frontage, you can't raise enough grass to feed a goat."

Tucker realized the truth in that. "Yes, well, back to the loan. I need some operating cash and enough to meet the payroll until I can get the mill up and running again."

Horace shook his head. "How do you plan to get the lumber to rebuild? There's no other sawmill in twenty miles of here. I suppose you could get the logs and float them into the mill site, but you have no way to cut them into boards. No saw, no nothing."

Tucker stiffened at this downright heresy. No matter that he had said the same things himself—no outsider was going to speak in a derogatory manner about his sawmill. "The mill does a lot of good in the community."

Horace nodded. "That it does. Been a blessing in more ways than one."

"So how about that loan?"

The banker leaned back in his chair, placing the tips of his fingers together. "I'm wondering why you want to build back. Be a lot of work and expense. Can't understand a young man like you taking on that kind of task."

"I know all of that, but Caleb and Eli will be in this with me. It's a family-run business, and we're not in the mood to quit."

Horace pursed his lips. "Do you have any plans you can tell me about?"

Well, no, he didn't. Just a determination that was growing stronger every minute. He should have given this a little more thought. Should've had a comprehensive plan about how he would accomplish the task facing him. As usual, he jumped before looking. Now he had to convince Horace he knew what he was doing. Kind of hard when you didn't have any idea.

Tucker cleared his throat again. "Well, we've got the loggers out felling trees. The strippers are busy, and we've got men hauling in the logs ready to get started working."

"And how do you plan on sawing those logs into boards?"

He nodded. "Caleb is in the market for a new saw. New to us, anyway. A big sawmill we passed on our way home from the war is switching over from muley to the circular. We plan to buy a used one from them, put it under a makeshift roof, and get back in business."

The banker pushed his lips out as if thinking. "You don't have the saw yet."

"Not yet. However, like I told you, we're in the market for one. Probably have it in a few days." At least he hoped so. If not, he didn't have any idea how they'd get those boards sawed.

Horace grimaced, as if he'd just made up his mind. "Tucker, I know you need the money, and I'd like to help you out."

Tucker sat a little straighter. Now they were getting somewhere.

"I'd honestly like to help you, Tucker, but I have to show good stewardship. Take care of the bank's money as if it were my own. Tell you what. You come back to see me when you have the saw, and we'll talk."

"When I have the saw?"

"Yes. You get the saw, and then we'll talk about money."

He opened his mouth to tell Horace what he thought about his way of doing business, but he closed it before the words could come hurtling out. He'd get the saw, all right, and then Horace would loan him that money or he'd . . . well, he didn't know what he'd do, but whatever he decided on, he'd get it done.

Tucker left the bank wanting to kick something. Or someone. He didn't have a guarantee that Caleb would get the saw, and if he did, Horace would probably come up with a new reason not to hand over the money. Some folks were just downright contrary.

Chapter 11

Thunder shattered the stillness of Wallace Madison's parlor. Willow jumped as if shot and caught her teacup. Silas Sterling sat across from her, smiling.

"The weather here takes a bit of getting used to," he remarked. The house vibrated on its foundation.

"Is there a reason why it thunders and lightnings and never rains?" She steadied the thin china, brushing spilled tea off her gown.

"Oh, it rains occasionally. The town hired some sort of weather 'expert' once, but he could never sufficiently explain the strange phenomenon." Silas sipped from his cup.

Willow studied him. He wasn't the sort of man who would ordinarily interest her, but he wasn't repugnant, either—quite organized in appearance, hair carefully pulled back in a neat graying queue. He dressed fancier than most, mostly the fashionable excesses of London, and wore rings on most every finger. She focused on a particularly large turquoise on the third finger of his right hand. She didn't care for turquoise. Too showy. She tried to concentrate on the conversation.

"Willow briefly fought in the war," Uncle Wallace said, "but it has in no way detracted from her womanliness. Tell him, Willow."

She glanced up. "Tell him what?"

"That fighting in the war has in no way detracted from your womanliness."

Willow smiled. "I hardly think Mr. Sterling would consider one's patriotic duty a worrisome issue."

Silas leaned forward. "On the contrary, it's fascinating. You actually fought?"

"We didn't have a choice, Mr. Sterling." She set her cup and saucer on the side table. "The Yankees kept coming, destroying, looting, and committing unspeakable acts. Word of Lee's surrender to Grant at Appomattox didn't reach our area until many weeks after it happened."

Silas pensively stroked his chin. "Then you were unaware that Lincoln was shot on the fourteenth, five days later."

"I only learned of Lincoln's death recently. A great tragedy."

"Sitting in Ford's Theatre," Silas mused. "One never knows, does one?"

"No, one doesn't." Willow could have never imagined sitting in a parlor with a man thirty years her senior, contemplating matrimony.

Moses's word to the heads of the tribes concerning the children of Israel came to mind. *This is the thing which the Lord has commanded. If a man makes a vow to the Lord, or swears an oath to bind himself by some agreement, he shall not break his word; he shall do according to all that proceeds out of his mouth.*

Her father had been a stickler for memorizing scripture. "You'll need it someday," he had contended, and Willow had dutifully studied the Old and New Testament. God's word was God's word. If she committed to matrimony—if she stood before God and took a solemn vow—it would be for life. A vise tightened somewhere deep in her stomach.

She looked up. "How did you come to settle in Thunder Ridge, Mr. Sterling?"

"My family was here, my parents and a sister. They're all gone now. I left for many years to, shall we say, make my mark on the world, but then returned some two years ago when my sister died of the pox. It was time the black sheep settled down." He offered a warm smile, so gracious, so unlike Tucker Gray. She shook the thought aside when her guest changed the subject.

"Pity about the mill. Tucker and his cousins had just finished building it. You know they fought in the war some five years."

"I didn't know," Willow admitted.

"Yes, pity about the fire," Wallace said.

"Uncle Wallace. Have you spoken with Mr. Gray yet?"

"Not yet, Willow, but I plan to later today."

"I believe he is most anxious to settle the matter."

"I'll go over shortly. He need not worry."

"Rebuilding will be costly," Silas observed. "Might I be of assistance?"

"No," Wallace refused, and Willow choked on the tea she'd just picked up. "That will all be taken care of."

When you and Willow marry, he might have well added. Willow thought it better to be up front and candid.

"Mr. Sterling— "

Wallace interrupted. "Tell us more about your life away from Thunder Ridge. You own many ships. That must be fascinating."

Thunder and lightning raged outside the parlor window as Silas regaled them with adventure after adventure. Around two o'clock, Mr. Sterling rose and announced that it was time for his afternoon nap.

"Oh, yes . . . mine too," Wallace concurred. Willow walked to the door with the shipping tycoon. When he took her hand and gently kissed it, she felt nothing. No sudden leap of pulse, no quickened heartbeat, yet neither did she feel disgust. Perhaps given the summer months, she would fall in love with this kind man. The good Lord knew she'd done more difficult things.

Thunder cracked, disquieting her. The hairs on her arms stood with charged electricity. A sign—a sign from God. This could be good. Right?

Behind Silas a lightning bolt struck a tree and split the top. *More likely a dire warning straight from the Throne to tread lightly with God's sovereignty.*

Willow pulled out a chair at the kitchen table and sat down. Betsy bustled around the room, while a spicy fragrance permeated the air. Willow sniffed appreciatively. "Gingerbread? I haven't had gingerbread in a long time." Not since the Yankees invaded the town and stole everything. There had been precious little left to eat, and nothing at all for luxuries.

"Thought it might make a satisfying dessert with some canned peaches." Betsy ran a damp cloth over the table, removing a smudge of flour. "So how do you like our little town?"

Willow shrugged. "It seems friendly enough. I was afraid people would be angry over the mill, but if they are, they're not saying so." At least no one was except Tucker Gray. The man couldn't be nice if he tried.

Betsy didn't reply, and the silence stretched out until Willow brought up what she really wanted to talk about.

"Silas seems like a nice man."

"That he is. Rich too."

Willow stiffened. "I would never marry a man just for his money."

A flush stained her cheeks, as she remembered that was exactly what she planned to do. It wasn't just greed motivating her. She was doing this for Audrey and Copper. And she would be a good wife. While it would be a marriage of convenience on her part, she would make sure Silas had no reason to complain. Betsy removed the pan of gingerbread from the oven and carefully placed it on a hot mat. "Wait until it cools a bit, and you can have a piece."

Willow inhaled the fragrance. "It smells wonderful."

The older woman got a couple of saucers from the cabinets and carried them to the table. "Back to Silas. He's a good, decent man. Always thought he was a bit dull, but if a woman wanted security and someone dependable, she couldn't beat Silas."

"I see." And she did. That was what she wanted to know, but somehow it didn't make her feel any better. If he was all that great, why hadn't someone snapped him up before now?

She decided to change the subject. "Betsy, have you seen the schoolhouse?"

Betsy nodded, her expression a bit wary. "Yes, I know where it is."

"It's a henhouse."

The housekeeper slid a square of gingerbread onto a saucer and set it in front of Willow. "I'll get you a glass of cold buttermilk to go with that. I know the schoolhouse isn't what you expected, but it can be fixed."

"I suppose. But I expected something a bit more . . . presentable."

Wallace entered the kitchen. "Do I smell gingerbread? What a wonderful idea, Betsy." He cut himself a large chunk. "So, Willow. I believe Silas was reasonably impressed with you, my dear. That was to be expected, of course."

Caught unaware, Willow struggled to find something to say that didn't sound either proud or simple.

"And why wouldn't he be?" Betsy demanded. "Any man would appreciate a woman like Willow."

Wallace spoke around a bite of gingerbread. "And what did you think of Silas? An outstanding suitor, I believe."

Willow paused to think. "Well, he's polite and considerate. I suppose I have no complaints." She felt uncomfortable discussing the man this way. It didn't seem like the Christian thing to do.

The judge polished off the gingerbread. "Someday I'd like to get a carriage from the livery stable and drive you by his house. Let you see where you'll be living."

Betsy raised an eyebrow. "Has Silas proposed to her yet?"

"No, but he will. Why wouldn't he? My niece is far above every woman in Thunder Ridge."

Willow frowned. "You said there were just two available women in town."

"You did?" Betsy turned to face Wallace.

Willow spoke up before he could answer. "I believe one was the Widow Gleeson and other was a fourteen-year-old girl, much too young for Silas. Right, Uncle Wallace?"

Wallace looked flustered. "I meant eligible women, of course."

Betsy shot him a glance. "Did you forget we're just miles from Blackberry Hill or Beeder's Cove? There are plenty of women there who aren't hitched."

Wallace opened his mouth and then shut it. Without saying another word, he beat a hasty retreat.

Betsy shook her head. "I declare, Wallace is a nice enough man, but a bit flighty sometimes."

Willow figured it was time to change the subject. "He seems to miss Aunt Claudine."

"He does. They were about the best-matched couple I knew. Seems like he just hasn't been the same since Claudine died. That kind of love doesn't come around very often."

"Do you think a marriage of convenience can be a good marriage?"

Betsy pursed her lips, her expression thoughtful. "It can be a good thing, I guess."

Willow felt a tickle of apprehension. "Can't two strangers come to love each other?"

"You and Silas?"

Willow nodded.

"I don't know. We'll just have to hope for the best."

"That doesn't sound very promising." Not that it mattered. She had promised the others, and they were depending on her. She could make the sacrifice if she must.

Chapter 12

The town doctor had finally returned, but after Willow's brief visit, he assured her that she had no lasting effects from the accident.

That afternoon, Willow wrote Copper and Audrey.

And so my dear friends, I invite you to prayerfully consider moving to Thunder Ridge. And may I remind you again that Uncle welcomes you into his home. There is plenty of room for all of us in his big old house. Discounting a certain mill owner, the people are friendly and most helpful. Once Thunder Ridge School is running smoothly, the adjoining communities have expressed a wish to reopen schools. Though I have not personally visited Beeder's Cove and Blackberry Hill, I hear nothing but good things about these communities.

A tide of loneliness swept Willow, and she ceased writing. How she missed Copper and Audrey. For the last few years, they had been constant companions, fighting to stay alive. Audrey's practical sense had probably saved their lives more than once. Copper's infectious laugh made life easier. She loved the finer things of life and didn't care to admit it. She was generous, yet cautious, and never fell for a hard-luck story. Foreign locations fascinated her; she read books upon books about England, Scotland, and Germany. She and Silas would be more perfectly suited to each other. . . .

Her pen began to move.

I miss you more than I can express in mere words. Soon, I pray, you will come, and we will be reunited.

She paused. Now that the buckboard was gone, she couldn't visit them, and the trip would be unnecessary. Nothing of value remained in Timber Creek except her friends, and an occasional family passing through the area. And Uncle Wallace had no means of conveyance. When Aunt Claudine passed, he'd sold the horse and carriage, stating that he could walk wherever he intended, and he had no intention of going any farther than his feet would take him in his declining years. Willow had seen no evidence of a stage line and hadn't thought to ask about one. Pushing the letter aside, she stood up and stretched. Outside, heat simmered off dry yellow grass. Without rain, the landscape was parched, even this early in the season.

The large rooms echoed with silence this morning. Wallace had gone early to pay a friend a visit. That left Willow to fill the day with meaningless activities. Betsy kept the house so well there was little left for anyone else to do. Perhaps she would clean the church and make a favorable impression on the reverend.

Changing into her old cotton print, she carefully lay the

Widow Gleeson's gown aside, happy to do so. The dress was two sizes too small, and the front buttons presented an ungainly sight. She must remember to sew the buttons on more securely or she would be faced with a most unpleasant experience. The widow had been less endowed, while Willow . . .

She shook her head. She'd sew those buttons on more firmly before she left the house.

Midmorning, she stepped out onto the stoop, and carefully locked the door. Swinging into a walk, she covered the brief distance to the church. Her eye caught the dead flowerbed, and she hurried to draw water from the well at the side of the church in hopes of resurrecting the plants. Releasing the long rope, she waited for the familiar splash. And waited. Standing on tiptoes, she peered into the incalculable depths.

"Looking for a match, Miss Madison?"

She froze. *Tucker Gray*. And the lout had caught her with her backside in the air, peering into a black hole.

Stepping back, she straightened her bodice and whirled to face the sawmill owner. "Is there no end to your jocularity?"

"Unlimited," he confessed, "when I'm in such inspiring company."

Willow seared him with what she hoped was an impervious—actually snitty—look.

He cocked a dark brow. "Did you lose something in the well?"

"No." He had no need to know her business, and she had no need to inform him.

"Do you stare into wells frequently without a purpose?"

"No." She refused to match his verbal sparring. She had far more important matters than squabbling with him.

"If you had in mind to resurrect those pansies in the front, you can forget it. That well's been dry for years."

She turned to glance at the small rock formation.

"Hasn't Wallace mentioned that we live in drought conditions?"

The judge hadn't, but the reverend had mentioned it. The news didn't surprise her. Everything looked dead or gasping for its last breath. Shrubbery, trees. No wonder the mill had caught fire so easily.

She turned back. "Then why plant flowers?"

Tucker shrugged.

Willow's eyes fastened briefly on his heavily muscled forearms. Years of swinging a maul, manning a whipsaw, splitting logs, and wielding a wedge had produced a hearty specimen. How had Tucker Gray escaped matrimony? Single women might be scarce as water in these parts, but surely not oblivious to this man. She realized he was attempting to answer her question.

"This dry spell's hard on the town's women. They try, but water for nonessential plants like flowers is prohibited." He turned to point to a vegetable garden at the house next door to the church. Willow had seen better plants, but considering the lack of rain, the garden wasn't that bad. In the center, flowers bloomed.

"That's Suzy Walker's garden. She hauls water from the river. Carries buckets every day, so her family can eat during the winter. Since her vegetables can't survive without water, the flowers get the water, too."

Willow's eyes scanned the vegetable patch—cabbage, onions, and potatoes, fairly hardy cucumber vines, tomato plants, rows of corn just starting to thrust out of the ground.

"What about the others? What do they do for fresh vegetables?"

"They depend on the mercantile for canned goods."

Willow thought about the huge vegetable garden her family had planted each spring. Water had been plentiful, as had good sunshine and adequate rain. They'd grown everything they consumed, and made preserves and pies from the peach and apple orchards at the back of their property.

Tucker's voice dropped. "Some in Thunder Ridge go hungry if the winter is particularly long."

Willow knew about hunger, too. Before the war, she'd led a sheltered life, but that was before the Yankees rode in and burned her home—destroyed her naiveté. She had gone to sleep hungry many a night. Dark days flashed. . . . She closed her mind, aware that he was talking again.

"Your uncle stopped by a few minutes ago."

"I trust you had a satisfactory visit." Judge had put it off as long as he could, but over breakfast Willow had insisted that he settle the matter. She couldn't bear to think the town would suffer from her insistence that Mr. Gray make arrangements for a loan with the bank.

"We agreed to disagree how the fire originated, but for the time being, I'm starting construction on the new mill. The town has been without adequate income for years now."

How would he rebuild without the money?

"Yes . . . I understand that you and your cousins fought in the war?"

He nodded. "Five years. I was at Manassas and Bull Run, among others."

"I fought a year—defending what little the Yankees left of Timber Creek, my home."

He nodded a second time, eyes dark with warning. "Conserve on water, Miss Madison. It may not rain for months."

"The school . . . ?" she asked as he proceeded on his way. If he was planning to begin reconstruction, there would be little time to work on a school.

Without breaking stride, he returned. "We'll work on the henhouse at night."

"School," she corrected, lest he forget they were talking about educating young minds, not pullets.

"Whatever, Miss Madison."

At night? She sank to the low well wall. Work from sunup to sundown at the sawmill, and then work nights at the school? What was he? Goliath?

She bounded to her feet. "When will I see you again?" Her face burned. She'd meant to say, when did he plan to start the remodeling project?

He turned around to face her. "Sunday morning."

"Sunday? That's the Lord's Day. You don't plan to work on the Lord's Day?"

"No, Miss Madison, I don't plan to work on the Lord's Day. I sing in the choir." He broke into a deep throaty chuckle.

"Oh, fine." She sank back against the rock wall. Not only would she have to contend with him Monday through Saturday, she'd also be confined with him Sunday morning.

The matter was starting to be just plain wearisome.

Chapter 13

Tucker lifted a charred beam and manhandled it to the wagon. A brassy sun beat down from overhead, turning the sawmill site into a furnace. A faltering breeze barely stirred the powdery ashes. He paused to wipe sweat from his forehead. Eli stopped beside him. "We're making progress."

"Yeah. At least we're getting the mess cleared away. Do you realize we're starting with less than we had in the beginning?" When that Madison woman did something, she did it well.

Eli lowered his voice. "How did you get along with Horace?"

"He told me to come back when we had a saw. I figured he didn't think we had a chance of coming up with one."

"Well, he's wrong. Caleb is sure we'll receive the saw in a couple of weeks."

Tucker looked around at the men straining to clear the

debris from the site. Two weeks? The men would expect regular paychecks, and they had earned them. Even the ones who weren't loggers and trimmers went to the woods every day to help fell trees. They had to go quite a way upstream to reach forests where there had been enough rain to grow trees big enough to use for lumber.

He wondered, not for the first time, why people continued to live in Thunder Ridge when it received so little rainfall. Just an hour's ride in either direction would bring a friendlier atmosphere. He suspected sheer stubbornness held them here. The citizens of Thunder Ridge were a varied and cantankerous lot. They wouldn't consider moving away, just because it might be easier somewhere else. Their religious beliefs reflected that attitude, too. Living too easy a life might lead one into sin, but it wasn't likely people would take to living a life of sin just because they had rain. He thought about forgetting the whole business of owning a sawmill. Just saddle up and ride out to where life would be simpler, and there wouldn't be a woman like Willow Madison to keep him awake nights.

Tucker's fists clenched involuntarily. That bull-headed female was still insisting the fire wasn't her fault. And now she was trying to duck out on her responsibility. Well, he intended to see that she paid for her mistakes. It wasn't that he was vindictive; he just needed the money to rebuild.

"Who's watching Tate?"

Eli's six-year-old son was a handful. Eli worked the farm when he wasn't helping with the sawmill. He'd built a nice little carpentry shop, too, where he did repair work for the neighbors. Not enough to live on, to be sure, but it would help. And Eli had promised that if the work was distributed a little more evenly, he would spend more time with Tate. Tucker heartily approved. A man and his son needed to be around each other as much as possible. By the time Eli had gotten the news of his wife's death, she had been gone a year. Ma had stepped in and raised little Tate, but the problem was, she thought he was so blamed cute she didn't bother to correct him. The kid was as ornery as all get-out and bound to get worse if Eli didn't get himself a good wife and settle down to spend a little time raising his son.

He realized Eli was staring at him strangely.

"You okay, Tucker? I said he's with Ma."

"Yeah. I'm fine. I was just thinking about Tate. You should take off early and go spend some time with him."

"He's fine with Ma. She's doing a good job with him, and sometimes it seems like I'm just in the way. Think about it. The child has lived with his grandma for as long as he can remember. I show up one day and tell him that I'm his daddy, and he's supposed to just accept it and be happy?"

"He's a smart boy. Give him a little more time, and he'll come around."

"I'm not a patient man." Eli took off his hat and knocked the dust off. "What if he doesn't?"

"He will. What you're seeing now is just a boy being a boy, not rebellion. You have to expect that and be glad he's healthy."

"I am." Eli sighed. "Well, the sooner we get this mess cleaned up, the sooner we can get back to real work."

He wandered off to join Caleb, who was working on the far side of the sawmill site. Tucker watched them for a while, wondering how they were going to rebuild the mill if Horace refused to lend them the money. He supposed he could ask Silas for a loan, and he had every expectation the man would come through. The problem lay with Tucker. He couldn't bring himself to accept help—not from Silas. It wasn't unusual for a single man to look for a wife with an eye to obtaining an heir, but a man didn't have good sense if he didn't realize there was more to marriage than kids and housework. Love factored in there somewhere—at least in his book. But nothing made a man more attractive to a woman than a healthy bank account.

Chapter 14

Willow opened the door of the church and peered inside, looking for Reverend Cordell. However, the small, one-room building was vacant. It was a pretty little church—white with a short steeple, and a simple wooden cross on the wall behind the pulpit. The pews were made of oak. The persistent drought made cleanliness impossible. One would have to dust every day to keep up. She walked down the aisle to the front of the church. It had a piano but no organ. An unaffordable luxury, she supposed. The town didn't have an air of prosperity. They'd had an organ in Timber Creek, but the Yankee raiders had burned the church. The destruction of the small building had been hard to take. Seemed like it had even hit harder than losing her home.

She located a broom. Surely no one would care if she did some cleaning. She craved something to do. She got busy, sweeping between the pews and straightening the hymnals.

She supposed, from the unkind thoughts she had been harboring toward Tucker Gray, that perhaps it was time she did something for the Lord, even if it was just tidying the church. She found someone's spit cup, half filled with nauseating sludge from tobacco juice.

Willow sighed and cleaned up the mess.

She put the broom away and used a cloth to dust the pews. The door open and Silas entered, looking a little taken aback to see her. "Willow? What are you doing here?"

"I didn't have anything to do, so I decided to clean the church. I hope that's all right."

"Of course it is, but it's not necessary. We have others who do that."

"I enjoyed it. Frankly it seemed little enough to compensate the town for the way they have accepted me. The few people I've met are much friendlier than I expected after the accident that burned down the mill."

Silas smiled. "I'm sure they understand that such a sweet, lovely lady like you would never have done anything like that on purpose."

"Of course I wouldn't. It was an accident, made worse by that lumber wagon parked in the way." She still did a slow burn every time she thought of it and *that man* who insisted it was all her fault. How unfair of him.

Silas indicated one of the pews. "It's a stroke of good fortune I didn't expect, finding you here. We have a chance to get better acquainted without having someone interrupting us. May we sit down and talk for a while?"

That was what she wanted, wasn't it? Still, Willow couldn't ignore a feeling of discomfort, as if she were masquerading under false pretensions. She tried to ignore the thought that she was attempting to lure Silas into marriage. It was his idea to find a wife. She was just helping in his search.

They sat down, and Willow demurely clasped her hands in her lap, waiting for him to start the conversation. Silas leaned against the pew, turning to face her while resting one arm along the back of the seat. "So what do you think of Thunder Ridge?"

"The town is fine, but the barrage of thunder is most disconcerting. I suppose one gets used to it after a while."

"I believe one does. I barely notice it anymore." He shifted, smiling at her. "Soon I will have you and Wallace for dinner. My entertainment skills are a bit rusty, but I intend to make some changes in my social life. I've become too much of a recluse."

Willow sought a way to change the conversation before it turned personal. She glanced around the church, looking for inspiration. "The church doesn't have an organ. Is that from religious convictions?"

"No, not at all. In fact, I've mentioned it a few times, but we never seem to get anything done. Mainly because we don't have anyone to play it, I suppose."

"No one to play an organ? How sad."

"Yes— do you play?"

"I occasionally played during services in Timber Creek. Then the Yankees came. . . ." She cleared her throat. "I miss playing very much. It was an important part of my life before the war."

"Then you must have it again. I'll purchase an organ. One is long overdue. It can replace the small choir."

"Replace the choir? Why would the church need to do that?"

"Trust me, it would be a blessing. With the exception of the Gray cousins, the rest of the men can't sing a decent note. I'm sure the congregation would be grateful, and it will do wonders for our worship service."

Willow had a strong image of how the Gray cousins—especially that Tucker—would accept having their choir dismantled so that she could play the organ. "Perhaps that's not such a good idea. I would be willing to work with the choir to try to . . ." She cleared her throat a second time. " . . . improve the quality."

"Oh, nonsense. The men can't sing a lick. The congregation will welcome the change."

"But still, don't you think you should give them a choice?"

Silas lifted a tolerant brow. "If you wish, but I fear if I ask, the inquiry will only result in a long-winded discussion that will ultimately retain the choir."

"At least discuss it with Reverend Cordell."

"As you wish."

Willow reflected uneasily that Silas, like a lot of men with money, was used to doing things his own way.

Tucker strode toward the mill, his mind on his work. He glanced up and spotted the judge coming from the opposite direction. "Morning, Wallace. You doing all right?"

"Tolerable," Wallace replied. "I was wondering how you were coming with replacing the sawmill."

"It's slow. We're working on clearing the ground. We should

be ready to start building in a few days, but it's a slow process."

"Were you able to salvage anything to work with?"

"The lumber that was stacked behind the bunkhouse, a few shingles, but everything else is gone. We're hauling new logs and getting ready to start cutting boards as soon as we get the new saw we're expecting."

"Ah, I was wondering if there would be materials to repair the henhouse. Er . . . I mean, the schoolhouse."

"I know what you meant." Tucker said. "And I'm not sure. We're going to have to scrounge for the supplies. Take those windows, for instance. You know where we can get window glass? It's scarce around here."

"I realize that, but a schoolroom must have windows. You can't expect to shut those children up in the dark."

"I've been asking around, and I located a couple of frames with most of the glass. We're missing a few panes, though, and I'm not sure we can find any that have all the glass in place."

"What about the doors?"

"I've got Eli busy making a couple, and knowing the kind of work he does, they'll be prime."

"Eli does fine work. But we need desks, and a teacher's desk. Books, all kinds of supplies. A very large task, indeed."

"I'll check with Tom at the mercantile and see what he has that we can use. We'll have to make do with what we have, Wallace. Unless you want to talk Silas into footing the bill for necessary supplies "

Wallace brightened. "I'll have Willow ask him. They're getting along famously. I understand he wants to purchase an organ for the church so Willow can play it. Isn't that a blessing?"

"An organ? Why is he doing that, and when did he ask if we wanted one?"

"Surely no one would object to such a generous gift. Why, it will add tremendously to the service."

Tucker didn't agree. They'd been getting by without one. What right did Willow Madison have to come to town and change church services? One more example of the woman's arrogance. He was developing a real antipathy to Miss Madison.

"Back to the schoolhouse," Wallace said. "You might talk to Willow. I'm sure she would have some ideas about those windows."

"No doubt." Tucker noticed how dry his voice was, but he didn't care. Miss Madison would have lots of ideas, but none that interested him. Someone needed to put that young woman in her place. It would take a firm hand to keep her in line. He liked his women a tad more feminine and a lot less aggressive.

The Widow Gleeson approached. "Oh, there you are, Tucker. I wanted to see you." She nodded at Wallace. "Hello, Judge."

"Yes, ma'am. What can I do for you?" Tucker had always liked the widow. She was tiny and well-put-together, almost doll-like in appearance, and generous to a fault. He understood she had given Willow Madison clothing to help her out, although everyone knew the she had little enough of her own. A good woman and quiet—well mannered, the way a lady ought to be. She could teach that Madison female a thing or two.

Now she smiled up at him. "I've been meaning to tell you that I have a piece of blackboard and some chalk you're welcome to use for the new schoolhouse."

"Well, that's mighty nice of you, ma'am. I know it will come in handy."

"Yes, indeed," Wallace added.

"And I have a water bucket and a dipper they can use, too. It's an extra one, and I don't need two, so you're welcome to it."

"Thank you, Mrs. Gleeson."

"Those children will get thirsty sitting in school all day. Of course, someone will have to volunteer to keep it filled. Miss Madison is too slight to carry water that far."

"I believe we can take care of that." Tucker smiled at her. "Anything else?"

"Well, yes. I just thought that perhaps we could make a list of all the things we need and post it at the mercantile and ask people to donate what they could."

"Splendid idea!" Wallace beamed. "Now, why didn't I think of that?"

Tucker glanced up the street in time to see Willow approaching. Quickly, he touched one finger to his hat in a goodbye salute. "Why don't you work on it? Now if you'll excuse me, I have pressing business."

He turned on his heel and strode off in the opposite direction. There was no way he was going to get in a confrontation with Willow Madison today. Be just his luck if she did marry Silas and decide to stay in Thunder Ridge.

Chapter 15

Willow leaned against the dresser, her gaze wandering the peculiar bedroom. The room was indeed nice enough, but an entire week had passed and she had yet to feel comfortable. Would Thunder Ridge ever feel like home?

Her slippers whispered across the floor, and she sat down in one of the slat-backed rocking chairs and folded her hands in her lap. Uncle Wallace had taken her to the mercantile and bought enough calico to make a new dress. She'd yearned for the pale blue muslin sprigged with pink and yellow flowers, but practicality prevailed. She settled for a dark blue solid that wouldn't show dirt. The unfinished dress hung on the closet door, ready to be hemmed, but she wasn't in a hemming mood. Frankly, she was plain bored. Accustomed to a busier life, this enforced inactivity was hard to accept. Surely Betsy would have something she could do.

She left the rocker and descended the flights of stairs to

the ground level. She was still trying to adjust to sleeping on the third floor. Her home in Timber Creek had no stairs, but Uncle Wallace's house was taller than a rugged pine tree. She could see the mill clearly from her window, which meant she saw more of Tucker Gray than she cared to.

Workers had cleared away the debris, and a pile of logs awaited the new saw. The town had watched for the arrival with anticipation. If she'd had any doubts about the importance of the mill's significance to Thunder Ridge, she understood clearly now. There weren't many ways a man could make a living in a town like this. The sawmill was a blessing to the community. And she had destroyed it. It was becoming less important to assess blame and more imperative to accept her part in the fiasco.

She found Betsy in the kitchen, kneading bread dough. When she entered, the housekeeper paused, smiling. "There you are. I wondered where you had gotten off to."

"I've been in my room. Is there anything I can do to help you? I've run out of work."

Betsy laughed. "Goodness, girl. You've cleaned this house until it shines. We're caught up on the washing and ironing. Not much left to do."

"I'd like to work on the schoolhouse, but since I can't do that, I need something to occupy my time. Surely you have a task I can do?"

Betsy placed the lump of dough in a greased bowl, and flipped it over a couple of times, making sure all sides came in contact with the shortening. "Well, there is the vegetable patch, such as it is. I guess you could hoe it out. I was planning to do that later, if I got around to it."

"I'll be glad to hoe." Willow reached for an apron. "What about water?"

"Just get the weeds out, and remember, you can empty the wash water on the garden." Betsy moved to the stove. "Be careful. It's hot as a smoking pistol out there. Must be a hundred in the shade, and there isn't much shade. Maybe you shouldn't do this. I don't want you to overdo. Judge will have my skin if you have a heat stroke."

"Don't worry. I'll be careful." Willow grabbed a battered hat off the rack by the back door and followed Betsy outside to a small shed, where she located the hoe.

A few minutes later, Willow stood in the middle of a small patch of plowed earth and not much else. Judge had planted potatoes. There were a couple of withered tomato plants, and a handful of onions attempting to put up shoots in the hot, humid weather. Plants didn't flourish without water. She cast a weary glance at the sky, focusing on the rolling clouds.

Within an hour, she had hoed the patch and emptied the wash water on the rows. If it ever rained, the little plot would yield a few fresh vegetables—enough to give the judge variety in his diet. She noticed that the man ate like a sparrow, picking at his food.

Her father, Wallace's brother, had been a giant of a man, with coal-black hair, and was strong as a wild horse. Wallace, with his thin, graying wisps of hair and small bones, shrunken with age, took after Grandma Madison. Betsy drove a buggy from Blackberry Hill during the day and cared for him and his house, but she went home at night, to her husband, whom she called Mr. Pike. Willow had yet to meet this paragon of male superiority, although she had heard enough about him to give her a good sense of the man. It was Mr. Pike this and Mr. Pike that. The man could do no wrong in his wife's eyes. It was evident Betsy had married for love.

Willow sighed. Well, it couldn't be that way for everyone. She'd like to hold out for some romantic dream, but she had obligations to meet, and as far as she could see, Silas Sterling was the answer to her problems. It wasn't as if she was deceiving him, yet guilt nagged her. Silas hadn't said anything about love, but wouldn't he eventually expect it? He wanted a wife and heir. The arrangement would be more business than personal, so why should she feel bad if he settled for less than love?

She returned the hoe to the shed and paused for a moment to listen to the chatter of men's voices coming from the sawmill site. She wasn't close enough to make out words and decided it was just the normal sound of men visiting while they worked.

Rumors flew that Horace Padget had caved and enlarged Tucker's bank note. The gossips must be true—yet one never knew. Bank officials did not loan money without sufficient collateral unless confidence was so high in the customer that Horace had gone out on a limb for Tucker Gray. By whatever means the stubborn mill owner had managed to start the rebuilding process, the project was coming along.

Weary from the heat and hoeing the rock-hard ground, she shut the shed door and went inside to see if Betsy needed anything.

The woman was down on her hands and knees scrubbing the floor when Willow walked in. The dough rested in pans, almost doubled in bulk. Soon the house would be filled with the fragrance of yeast and baking bread. She couldn't think of anything that smelled better, and, as her mother used to say, "too bad we can't smell butter." Maybe she could have a heel off a loaf when it was done, slathered with sweet, fresh-churned butter.

Betsy rinsed the cloth and hung it up to dry. "We're through for awhile. Why don't you take a walk and visit with the neighbors? Maybe check on the Widow Gleeson, and see if she'd like a loaf of fresh bread for her supper."

"I'd be happy to check on her." Willow climbed the stairs to her room and changed into the Widow's dress. At least the woman would see how thoughtful her gesture was. A few minutes later, she emerged from the house, eager to make new acquaintances.

Who should be coming down the path but the Widow Gleeson, smiling broadly and extending her hands. "My dear, how lovely that dress looks on you. I'm sure it never looked that fine on me."

Willow grasped the tiny fingers, withered with age. "I was on my way to visit you, Mrs. Gleeson. I wanted to thank you for the personal items you sent me. I don't know what I would have done without them."

The widow brushed the praise aside. "I'm just happy you could use them. Tell me, how do you like our little town so far?"

"It seems very . . ." She cast an eye to the sky. *Thunderous* was on the tip of her tongue, but she caught the careless observation. " . . . nice."

"Well, I know the thunder can be intimidating, especially to newcomers," the widow conceded.

"Indeed." It was like living with an unruly cannon.

"You'll adjust to it in time. I seldom notice it anymore." The widow patted her arm. "I know we're all delighted to have you with us, and we're looking forward to fall when the new school opens. Children need a worthy education."

"No argument there." Willow smiled. "And I'm delighted to have the opportunity to meet you, and thank you in person for your generosity."

"Oh, *pshaw*. It wasn't all that much. You'd have done the same." She glanced at the small watch pinned to her bosom. "Dear me. I'm late. I promised to sit with Paula Wiengarten this morning. She's delicate and in the family way. Her husband doesn't like to leave her alone. It's close to her time, you know, and he'll need someone to look after her until the midwife comes. Full moon soon. You know what that means."

Willow shook her head. She didn't—unless it meant it was easier to see better at night.

"Lots of babies born during a full moon. I'll drop by the judge's house sometime soon, and we'll have a lovely chat."

"I'll look forward to your visit. I'll make tea—and Betsy wants to know if you'd like a loaf of fresh-baked bread for supper."

"I'd love one! Tell Betsy thank you. There's nothing better than her bread."

Willow watched the Widow Gleeson scurry off. She seemed like a very kind soul.

Willow wandered past the blacksmith shop, where a large man with black bushy eyebrows like briar patches stood in the doorway. "Hey, there, Miss Willow Madison. Mighty hot day."

Sighing her assent, she paused to visit. "It is at that."

His eyes skimmed her. "I'm John—I own the place. You're looking mighty fit for the fall you took."

"I'm very well, thank you. Just a few aches and pains."

He took out a handkerchief and swiped it across his bald head, shiny with sweat. The heat of the forge reached Willow at this distance. How did the man bear working in such conditions? No wonder he was standing in the doorway, trying to get a breath of fresh air.

He nodded in the direction of the red-hot oven. "I'd best get back to work, before the fire dies down. I and the missus want to have you to supper one night. I'll let her pick the day. A word of advice, Miss Madison. Don't let the old biddies in town give you a hard time. Their bark's meaner than their bite."

With that, he turned and walked back inside, leaving Willow with a smile of confusion. What biddies? Weren't the town women pleased to have a new teacher? She made a mental note to ask Betsy.

She ambled toward the mercantile, but before reaching it, two women bore down on her. She paused in apprehension.

"Miss Madison, I presume?" the older of the two inquired. She wore a dress of violet silk, with a lace fichu at the neck. Her dark hair showed streaks of gray and she'd pulled it into a tidy roll on the back of her neck.

"Yes, and you are?"

"Mrs. Cordelia Padget. My husband is bank president."

Willow extended her hand. "Willow Madison."

"Pansy Henderson," the other woman announced. "My daughter will be a student in your school."

"And my son," Cordelia added. "Horace Padget, the third."

"I'm always delighted to meet my students' parents."

Cordelia came straight to the point. "We have a few questions, if you don't mind?"

"Certainly. How may I help?"

"I assume you begin every school day with the Lord's Prayer."

Pansy followed on her heels. "And you never let the boys and girls sit on the same side of the room? I strongly disapprove of mingling of the sexes." She raised her kohl-blackened brows cynically. "I'm certain that as a woman of high virtue you will agree that the common practice is morally unhealthy."

"Yes—no, I haven't determined seating, but I will keep your concerns in mind—"

"Are you proficient in mathematics?" Cordelia interrupted. "That's so important for boys. I want my son to be able to add a column satisfactorily, just like his father. Of course, there will be a position for him in the bank when he's older."

Willow nodded, trying to keep up with the women's steady stream of inquiries. Finally she nodded. "Yes, well, I'm so glad we've had this talk. I'll address all of your concerns when I hold open house." She hurried off, leaving the two women to gawk after her. It wasn't wise to make enemies before school even started, but these two were going to be troublesome.

At noon, Betsy served up ham and potatoes and rejected Willow's offer to help with the dishes. "You go on and relax. Once school starts, you'll have plenty to do. Enjoy your freedom while you can."

Willow remained at the table, her mind on the earlier conversation. "I met a couple of the students' mothers today."

Betsy, in the process of adding hot water to the dishpan, stopped and turned to look at her. "Oh dear, I hope it wasn't Cordelia and Pansy. I was hoping to prepare you in advance for those two."

"Yes, it was. How did you know?"

"Land, those two are as thick as bread and molasses. What did they have to gripe about today?"

Willow repeated the conversation. "If all the families are like those two, I'll have my work cut out for me."

"Don't give those harpies another thought. Those two are always looking for a complaint. If they give you any trouble, you tell me. I'll straighten them out in no time at all. I suppose they mean well but just have an exaggerated sense of their own importance."

"They had varied concerns regarding how I intend to run my schoolroom, and I have a feeling that no matter what I do, they won't be satisfied. Even John, the blacksmith, warned me not to be concerned about the townswomen's opinions. Should I be?"

"No, most are thrilled to have you here."

"With the exception of Cordelia and Pansy."

"No one can please those two, not even their husbands. Why do you think Horace spends so much time at the bank? Man's so henpecked he can't blow his nose unless she holds the hanky." Betsy patted Willow's shoulder. "You'll do fine, honey. Now put it aside, and ask the Good Lord to help you. You're going to do better than you think."

Willow got up from the table. "I may take a walk down by the river. It looked so lovely and cool earlier."

"About the only cool place in town." Betsy shooed her out of the kitchen. "Go. Relax and enjoy yourself. I'll have supper ready when you get back."

Willow welcomed the chance to orient her thoughts. It was imperative that she make a good impression on the town and its families. So far, she wasn't sure she had conveyed her teaching abilities. If they judged her by the sawmill fiasco, she had some fences to mend.

She dawdled away most of the afternoon in the cool, shaded overhang of the riverbank. She needed time to sit and listen; her father had taught her that. Even the Lord had needed time away, privacy. Sometimes life overwhelmed her to the point that she neglected to talk to Him.

The sun had begun to slide toward the horizon when she stood up and shook out her skirts. The reprieve had been a relaxing, peaceful one of solitude, exactly what she needed.

She wandered slowly back to the town, having chosen to visit the river above the town site, instead of the stream closest to the mill. The river curved around the community like a watery cradle. Without the blessing of the swiftly flowing water, the town would have been in dangerous straits, indeed.

As she drew closer to the church, she heard men's voices blended in harmony—or somewhat harmony. She approached carefully, not wanting to be noticed. Giving a quick glance around, she eased open the double door and quickly slipped into the dim foyer, listening to the men practice the morning invocation. Baritones harmoniously blended with deep bass. She did rather favor men's voices lifted in praise. Often, she'd heard Johnny Reb sing from the camps, praising the Lord.

"Praise God from whom all blessings flow . . ."

. The rich, sweet lyrical notes flowed like thick honey over Willow's mind. With the exception of two elderly men, the voices blended in delightful accord. She knew why Tucker was upset about Silas's plans to purchase a new organ and disband the choir. Somehow, the news had gotten out, although she was sure Silas hadn't said a thing, and she certainly hadn't. She suspected Uncle Wallace might be the innocent culprit.

The choir did lend a sweet reverence to the worship service. Switching to an organ would nullify a valued tradition. She wished she had been more forceful in convincing Silas to bring the idea of purchasing an organ before the church. Now it was too late. The instrument had been ordered and was due to arrive by mule train by late fall. She'd stop it if she could, but it wasn't her choice to make. Perhaps something could be worked out so the choir remained, in addition to the organ.

She closed her eyes and allowed the richness of tones to wash over her. She smiled, easily able to distinguish Tucker's baritone above the others. Rich and resonant, the praise flowed like spiritual water.

When the mill owner caught her eye, she quickly ducked. How embarrassing to be caught gaping. And with Tucker Gray's temperament, he'd be sure to let her know he'd seen her.

The man lived to humiliate her.

Chapter 16

Sunday morning, Willow and Judge Madison strolled to the church. Tucker Gray stood in the churchyard and nodded. "Wallace. Miss Madison."

Judge returned the greeting as Willow strode past. Gray's voice stopped her.

"We plan to start work on the schoolhouse tomorrow. I want to get as much done as possible before the saw gets here."

"That's good to hear." Willow fought back a grin. "Is there anything I can do to help?" She could outwork any man when it came to hauling and building and hoped he knew that.

"I think not." He smiled. "My men can handle it. A woman would get in the way."

Steam roiled inside, but she forfeited the occasion to publicly correct him. His male ego would suffer.

"I'm certain you're correct. We women should just stay home and dust furniture."

He grinned. "Whatever."

Still seething, Willow followed the judge inside. Several of the townspeople nodded and smiled. Betsy and a medium-sized man with a few sprinkles of gray amidst fiery red hair sat across from them. He leaned forward and grinned, presenting a good view of a generous gap between his front teeth. Freckles dusted his ruddy cheeks. "I brought the missus to services this morning. She wanted me to meet you."

Willow nodded, extending her hand, and they shook. "Pleased to make your acquaintance."

Betsy grinned. "He's my man."

Willow grinned. *This was the famous Mr. Pike.* He looked amazingly ordinary, but evidently not to his wife. Pride stood out like a scarlet coat on Betsy's features. Willow's smile widened. Not everyone had the luxury of marrying for true love, but she was glad Betsy had found her Prince Charming.

Willow emerged from services to find Silas Sterling waiting at the foot of the steps. "Willow, I have my chaise here. It would be my pleasure to offer you and the judge a ride home. "

Before she could refuse, Uncle Wallace accepted the invitation. "Willow would be happy to ride with you, but I'm having a bit of trouble with my leg, and the walk will be good for me. And Silas, we'd be happy to have you join us for dinner. Betsy always leaves more food than two of us can eat."

Willow feared Silas would be offended by the judge's blatant efforts to throw them together, but he readily accepted. She breathed a sigh of relief that Betsy had left a beef roast, potatoes, and carrots in the springhouse. One of her fine frosted chocolate fudge cakes sat on the dining room buffet. In a moment's time, Willow could whip up a batch of buttermilk biscuits to suit the men's taste.

Stepping into the fancy carriage, Willow settled her skirt. She felt very special indeed as the surrey rolled out of the churchyard. A lovely blue-and-white-striped top shaded the hot sun.

"I'm delighted you invited me to dinner." Silas masterfully handled the high-stepping bay.

"I'm delighted you could come." At the moment, she was delighted. After all, if things worked out, she would be accompanying this man home from church the rest of her life.

"Have I mentioned that you look quite lovely today?"

She knew he had to be reaching for conversation. She wore the same dress she'd worn for days now.

"Thank you, kind sir. And you look most handsome." Ordinary chatter between two about to become affianced. Still, the moments felt stilted, and Willow would be glad when the newness of it all evaporated.

Later, Uncle Wallace asked the blessing, then passed the meat platter. "Glad to have you with us today, Silas. Should do it more often."

The bachelor buttered a biscuit. "Always a pleasure, Judge. I eat well at home, but no one can match Willow's cooking. Everything is delicious."

Willow smiled. "The praise goes to Betsy. She manages to leave the Sunday meal on Saturday before she goes home. I can cook, but nothing to brag about."

He glanced up. "You don't cook?"

"I cook. But not nearly as well as Betsy." She'd learned at

her mother's knee, and it had served her well once she was on her own, but rarely did she prepare such a feast. She reached for a butter knife. "The choir sounded fine today."

Silas shook his head. "Surely you jest. If we could discourage a couple of the members from singing, it would help, but Reverend Cordell is determined not to hurt the men's feelings."

"I believe the Gray boys sing well enough," the judge said. "But when the new organ arrives, the service will improve enormously."

"Yet it seems heartless to dismiss the choir," Willow argued. "Perhaps when the organ arrives the combination will vastly improve the quality— "

"Nothing short of parting the Red Sea could improve those men's voices," Silas said. "An organ will greatly enrich the worship service, but if you insist, the choir will remain."

"Thank you. I do insist. It seems cold to disband the choir. I actually find their voices soothing."

Silas nodded his consent. "The instrument should arrive by the end of summer." He cut a bite of roast beef and chewed with a blissful air. "Best beef I've had in months. Could you get Betsy to share her secret with my cooks? Theirs tastes like highly seasoned shoe leather."

"Wait until you taste the fudge cake," Uncle Wallace crowed. "My favorite." Willow realized the judge and Silas got along superbly.

After dinner, Silas and Wallace visited in the parlor while Willow cleaned up the kitchen. When she joined the men later, Silas smiled. "Could I coax you into an afternoon walk? It's a pleasant day. Not a cloud in the sky."

Willow conceded. "If you promise there won't be any thunder."

Silas shook his head. "Of course I can't promise, but you'll be safe with me."

She knew he spoke the truth. She'd never met a less threatening man. Kind, approachable.

"If it appears thunder will be an issue, we'll take shelter posthaste," he promised. "And the minute a storm moves in, we'll start back."

Nodding, she accepted. "I'll get my parasol." Willow climbed the stairs to her room, thinking she would like nothing better than a brief nap and a good book this afternoon. Courting was wearisome.

Silas waited by the front door when she returned. "Ah, ready to go?"

"All ready." She glanced up, wishing for a rain cloud, but only fluffy white clouds skittered across the sky.

They set off down the narrow dirt road leading out of town. Dust, hot and powdery, puffed from beneath their shoe soles with every step. Willow searched for something to talk about. Audrey's practical advice came to mind: *"Get him to talk about himself."*

All right, she'd proceed with the strategy. "Uncle Wallace says you have a fleet of ships. You send them all over the world?"

"I do. Occasionally I even go along for the journey. It's fascinating to be out on the open sea, with nothing around except water and sky. Perhaps someday, you will accompany me."

From the twinkle in his eyes, and the coaxing tone in

his voice, his meaning was quite clear. Apparently, she had swiftly become the leading applicant for the position of Mrs. Silas Sterling. She wondered why the thought didn't give her a sense of reprieve.

Silas began to talk about his fleet of ships, of the treasures he brought back from foreign shores. As he spoke, weaving a picture of a life she could barely imagine, she realized that the affluent bachelor was an amiable and knowledgeable man. He reached for her hand, seizing it gently as they shared a compatible calm along the dusty road.

He smiled down at her. "I'm delighted to have this opportunity to get acquainted with you, Willow. You're a very accomplished and charming young lady."

"The walk has been most enjoyable, Mr. Sterling. I feel we're becoming friends."

"Silas. Please call me Silas."

"Silas," she complied. Earlier, she would have thought this moment unattainable, but she could grow to love this man, serve him as a dutiful wife. The past hour had shown her that all things were probable. He was comfortable to be with, undemanding, and an excellent conversationalist, painting a vivid picture of worlds she'd never experienced—bustling marketplaces, foreign lands with delicate silks and rare perfumes.

A buggy approached, pulled by a flashy bay with a white blaze and four white feet. Willow caught a glimpse of the occupants and sighed. Couldn't she ever escape the man? Tucker Gray held the reins, and a very pretty young woman sat beside him.

Drive on, Willow mentally challenged. *Don't ruin a perfectly lovely afternoon where all things seem possible.*

The wretched man pulled back on the reins, bringing the buggy to a halt beside the strolling couple. "Silas. Miss Madison. Beautiful afternoon for a stroll."

"It is at that." Silas removed his hat and bowed to the young woman. "I don't believe I've met your companion."

"Miss Meredith Johnson, Silas Sterling and Miss Willow Madison. Miss Johnson hails from Blackberry Hill."

Tucker made the introductions, but his eyes caught and held Willow's. For an instant, his expression turned dour, but then he smiled.

Willow gave him a momentary glance. She didn't have any trouble reading Mr. Tucker Gray. He abhorred her intentions to marry Silas for profit. Well, he might be surprised to learn that she enjoyed Mr. Sterling's company. He was an absolute gentleman, a trait Tucker obviously knew nothing about.

The couples briefly visited before Tucker picked up the reins, and off the buggy flew down the road, Miss Meredith's lyrical laugh floating over the summer countryside.

Suddenly it was hotter than Hades. Willow removed a handkerchief and rapidly fanned her flushed features.

"Oh, it is getting warm," Silas noted. "We'll start back, and I'll get you a cool glass of buttermilk."

Willow didn't want buttermilk. Truth be, she didn't know what she wanted.

Chapter 17

Musty air saturated the quiet vestibule when Willow entered the church. She paused, wrinkling her nose; a good scrub would alleviate the stale air. Why hadn't she noticed the distasteful odor earlier? Now that she was more familiar with the church, she could see that the pews were in need of varnish. Metal wall brackets holding gasoline lanterns were tarnished and moldy.

"Pity, isn't it?"

Willow turned to find Revered Cordell approaching. His placid manner reminded her of a tired old tomcat, loyal but worn out. "When Rosa Parker passed, there was no one to take her place. The other women help out, but cleaning is rather hit-and-miss these days. Rosa's dedication can't be matched." His eyes lightened. "Over thirty years she cleaned and polished the church. My, how this old house glistened." The smile faded. "I miss Rosa and her chatter. It made my

Tuesday." He looked up as if suddenly aware of Willow. "May I help you, Miss Madison?"

"I swept and dusted the church last week, Reverend Cordell, and now I'd like to do more. I should be able to come every week if you have no objections."

"Objections? Why, that's answered prayer!"

"If you could show me where you keep the lemon oil and the rest of the cleaning goods?"

"Yes, of course!" Willow trailed the short figure to the back closet where she had earlier located the broom and dust cloths.

After a bit of rummaging, he produced a nearly empty bottle of ammonia and the metal dustpan she hadn't been able to find earlier. "I'm sure there was more at one time, but . . . oh, dear. I'm afraid cleaning isn't my expertise."

"These will do nicely, and if I need anything more I'll see if I can borrow the item."

"Don't hesitate to disturb me if you need anything." The smile flashed. "I'll be in my study working on Sunday's message."

"Thank you—and Reverend, if you don't mind, after I clean I'd like to practice a bit on the piano. " She dreaded the thought of mastering the organ again after so many years of not playing.

"Practice all you like, my dear. I shall enjoy the music. However, I'm sure the instrument is sadly out of tune. An itinerant piano tuner comes through every year, and we have him look at it, but a month or two later, it's out again. Nonetheless, tone hasn't mattered since we haven't anyone to play it, but very soon, we'll have an organ."

She nodded. Yes, an organ would be an improvement, and used along with the choir, the music should be quite pleasing. She finished her chores late afternoon and paused before the old instrument, wondering if she had enough time to practice. She hadn't been home all day, and she didn't know if Uncle Wallace expected her to eat supper with him. Normally, he didn't, but often he mentioned that he enjoyed her company during meals.

Sliding behind the keyboard, she perched on the bench, positioning her hands on the ivory. Oh bliss! She gave middle C a cautious hit and winced at the result. *Oh, my. So out of tune.* Shameful, shameful neglect. Why hadn't church members taken better care of the lovely instrument? Rich, dark oak and keys made of the highest-quality ivory. Scooting back on the bench, she hit middle C again, her right foot lightly pressing the pedal. The note didn't sound much better. Still, she couldn't resist the desire to play.

She began "Amazing Grace." Her fingers tripped over the keys and she marveled how the years had failed to diminish her playing skills. God had given her the gift of playing by ear, yet she could read notes as well as any accomplished pianist. She played, eyes closed, letting the sweet but off-key music drench her weary soul. How she had missed this through all those years of war! Nights, lying beneath the stars, she would talk to the Lord, praying for mercy and guidance. Always running through her mind were the words, "Amazing Grace, how sweet the sound . . ." Even though some of the keys gave off discordant notes, she took pleasure in the message they conveyed.

Hot tears rolled down her cheeks as the last notes faded slowly into worshipful silence. She sat quietly, head bowed.

Then, soft applause.

She glanced up to see Silas Sterling in the doorway, hat held deferentially against his breast. "Stunning. Simply splendid."

Color stained her cheeks. She hadn't been aware that she had an audience. "I polished the instrument, and I couldn't resist."

Silas approached the altar, his tone articulate with appreciation. "My dear Willow, what a talent the good Lord has given you. Please say that you will share your ability very soon with the residents of Thunder Ridge."

Her face burned hot. "Thank you ever so kindly, Silas, but it's been years since I've played, and the instrument is out of tune."

"But your presentation was flawless!"

She laughed. "Oh, the piano desperately needs tuning." She gently closed the lid. "In a few weeks, I'll be happy to play, if we can get the instrument to hold a pitch."

"I shall hold you to your promise." He supplied his arm, and she slid off the bench. "I was passing by when I heard the music. I could not resist eavesdropping. This makes the wait for the organ all that much longer."

"The piano is lovely."

"Ah yes. It is, isn't it? And the new organ will be even nicer."

She wanted to ask if he had gifted the piano, too, but she sensed that he was a man who would not tout his benevolence. "What will happen to the piano once the new organ arrives?"

"I suppose someone might take it—"

"Can I have it?"

"You?" He chuckled. "Willow, you'll have no need for old pianos. Name your desires, and you shall have them."

All she wanted was this piano, but perhaps someone needier could use it.

He gazed down on her. "May I walk you home?"

"Thank you. I'll finish up and be with you in a moment."

Afternoon shadows lengthened as the couple strolled the homeward path. With each passing day, Willow sensed her reservations about the town and this man easing. Perhaps she could be happy here, with Silas Sterling. His touch was light, and he didn't smell of sweat and pomade.

Silas tucked her hand in the bend of his elbow. "I learn more about you every day, and I'm surprised at your versatility. Is there anything you can't do?"

Marry a man I don't love? "Quite a few things. Actually I'm a woman of limited talents."

He chuckled. "Let's see. You fought in the war; you drove a buckboard all the way from Timber Creek, the wagon loaded with flammable material. You're a teacher, and accomplished conversationalist, an excellent pianist, and I can only look forward to your organ-playing skills. As far as I'm concerned, that's quite a handsome list."

She looked up, her cheeks warm from his obvious sincerity. A woman could do worse in a choice of mates. "I set fire to the mill. I believe you overlooked that accomplishment."

He brushed the incident aside. "An accident. No one could or does blame you."

Willow sniffed. "Mr. Gray does."

Silas smiled. "I do believe you'll have to forgive him for his attitude. The good man has experienced a painful loss. The Gray cousins had worked day and night on the mill—just finished it, I believe—and then in a few minutes, the work proved to be in vain. Discouragement causes many a man to lose heart and temper."

Lose heart. Had Tucker lost heart because of her incompetence? She prayed not. She might not care for the man, but she wished him no ill will. Not once had she considered his losses more than in brief, angry passing.

Silas helped her skirt a plank in the walkway. "We men hate to admit our failures. It's much easier to pass along the blame to someone else than it is to admit our own culpability."

Remorse hung heavy in her heart. Was she guilty of passing the blame? True, she had had a part in destroying the mill, but it was completely unintentional. However, in retrospect, Tucker Gray hadn't left that lumber wagon in the way in a reckless endeavor to burn down his mill. Perhaps she was being a bit inflexible. She thought of his deliberate taunting and decided that whatever grief she'd dealt to the man, he had returned threefold. Still, losing one's spirit was not a small problem.

Silas squeezed her hand. "You're suddenly very quiet."

"Just enjoying the walk."

"And I, the company."

"Oh yes, me too," she said. "Enjoying the company." She wasn't good at wooing a man, pure and simple. The rules felt tight on her, like the Widow's unmentionables, and anyone with a lick of sense would have to agree that she was more efficient on the battlefield than in romance. "It's a lovely day. Not one clap of thunder," she marveled.

"Merely a pleasant interlude, I'm afraid. We seldom go more than three or four days at the most without thunder and lightning."

"Why would the settlers establish a town here? A few miles in either direction would be more favorable terrain."

"And that's why Beeder's Cove and Blackberry Hill were established, but the original settlers decided to stay. Thunder Ridge is quite pleasant in fair weather, and it's possible our forefathers assumed, with all the thunder, that there must be rain on occasion. But alas, they were sadly mistaken. However, there've been a few years when we do get enough moisture to see us through."

"Do you plan to remain here?" With his means and influence, he could live anywhere he wanted.

"Oh yes. I've experienced my share of the world. Thunder Ridge is my home, will be my earthly home until the Lord deems otherwise."

The Madison house was in sight. Silas paused. "I enjoyed our time together, Willow. You brighten my life. I'm delighted you came to Thunder Ridge, and my prayer is that you like it well enough to make it your home."

Oddly enough, she wanted to make that promise. She wanted to make his smile ever wider, but she couldn't. Not yet.

"Thank you, Silas. It's been a lovely walk."

At the door, he lifted her hand lightly to his lips. "Hearing you today enhanced my life. Perhaps you'll play for me again soon."

Willow smiled. "I'll play whenever you like. And Silas, I'm glad you agreed to keep the choir, too. The men so enjoy their service to the Lord, and does it really matter to the Almighty if they're singing perfectly? The Good Book says, 'Make a joyful noise,' but it doesn't mention anything about only pleasant or on-key noise. I've witnessed many an off-tune praise on the battlefield as men lay drawing their last breath."

His smile indulged her. "Let's allow the men to make that decision. Once the organ arrives, they may feel differently about their service." He chuckled. "You're most tender-hearted, my lady, especially in view of your and Tucker's persistent clash of wills. I find your mind-set most refreshing."

Oh dear. Silas had noticed her and Tucker's ongoing feud. And he still thought her refreshing?

She sighed. The judge was right. Silas had few, if any, flaws.

Chapter 18

⁓

Supper dishes squared away, Willow untied her apron and called, "Uncle Wallace? I'm going for a walk."

Her uncle's voice filtered back from somewhere deep in the house. "Quite all right, my dear. I'll be here when you return."

Fireflies lazily drifted on warm evening air when she stepped out of the house and paused. Which direction should she go? She wasn't in the mood to walk to the river. On a whim, she turned in the direction of the future schoolhouse. The distinct whack of hammers reached her ears as soon as she passed the church. Tucker Gray was making good on his promise. For a second, concern filled her.

She'd seen him at work early this morning, head bent low over a makeshift table, so deep in thought she hadn't bothered to offer a polite hello—not that he expected her to speak.

The lowering sun slid behind a bank of clouds. Varying shades of pink, rose, and amber tempered the fearsome heat.

When she approached the schoolhouse, she paused, rethinking her intent. Actually, she was looking forward to bothering him; he was rather—oh, for want of a better word—*engaging* when he scowled. A dark, nicely shaped brow would lift, and brown, penetrating eyes would focus on her. She knew he thought her to be scatterbrained and impulsive, a woman who would burn down a man's mill with reckless regard. She straightened the bodice on the Widow Gleeson's tight dress and approached the door. Knocking lightly, she waited for a response. Inside the sounds of hammering kept a fixed beat.

Willow rapped, then doubled her fist and pounded. The door flew open, knocking against two leaning two-by-fours. The boards fell, striking Tucker across the back of his head and shoulder. He went to his knees and hammering ceased.

A man working in the right-hand corner dropped his tool and hurried to assist. A second worker arrived, and they hoisted the mill owner to his feet. One held a hand in front of his face. "How many fingers do you see?"

Tucker batted the hand aside. "I'm okay."

"You sure?" The first man knelt in front of Tucker. "That was a pretty hard knock."

"Stop fussing like a couple of old hens." Tucker sat up, rubbing his shoulder.

Shrinking back, Willow held her breath. Had they seen her? How could she have been so ungainly? Then again, she hadn't known someone had propped lumber against the inside doorframe.

Easing even more into the shadow, she waited until the

hammering resumed, then casually stuck her head around the doorframe and said perkily, "Anyone home?"

Hammering ceased again. Three pairs of male eyes turned to center on her.

Heat bathed her cheeks. She grinned. "Good evening."

Tucker grunted, rubbing his injured shoulder. "I might have known."

Not expecting an invitation, Willow stepped inside the stuffy henhouse. The floors had been swept clean, but feathers stuck here and there to the inside walls. One of the men had a feather plastered to his shirtsleeve. "Ah, I see the work has begun."

"Yeah." Tucker picked up a hammer and drove a nail. "Need something, Miss Madison?"

"Not a thing."

Pausing before the first man, Willow smiled. "My name is Willow Madison."

Quickly rubbing his hand clean on the side of his denim pants, the young man nodded. "Eli Gray, Miss Madison."

"Eli." She accepted his friendly handshake. She wasn't good at guessing ages, but he looked to be in his early to midtwenties, with dark hair, sun-bronzed skin, and blue eyes. "Eli. It's nice to meet you."

"My pleasure." He resumed work, color blotching his cheeks. *Why, he's shy.*

The second man wiped his hands on a work cloth. "You're the new schoolteacher." He extended his hand. "Caleb Gray." Willow accepted his courteous greeting. Tucker drove another nail and answered her unspoken question. "First cousins. Our mothers were sisters."

Willow's gaze touched the dark crease of sweat striping his back; then she quickly looked away. Grasping her hands behind her back, she roamed the gutted structure. "It isn't large."

Tucker bent to pick up a two-by-four. "You'll only have a small number of students the first year. As the town grows, we'll expand."

"I expected a goodly number."

"The war has taken its toll, ma'am." Eli wiped his hands on a cloth. "The fighting broke most families apart. Some of the women and children who survived have moved to be with kinfolks."

The war. Families torn apart, members dead or wounded, homes lost, lives altered forever. Nothing would ever be the same. Yes, the fighting had ended, but could anything so terrible ever be over? The anger and hatred didn't stop because soldiers lay down their weapons. Wounds had been opened that would take generations to heal.

Eli smiled down at her. "I'm sure the families left will be grateful for the opportunity to educate their little ones."

She pushed aside the grim thoughts the war conveyed and grinned up at him. "Of course. Cooped up, being forced to study is probably high on their want list."

Considering the building's former purpose, perhaps *cooped* wasn't the best choice of words.

"Well, they'll appreciate it later when they find that life is easier because they know how to read and write. Cipher, too." Eli drove a nail. Of the three cousins, Eli seemed the most reserved. He didn't smile often and spoke very little, while Caleb was more outgoing and friendly.

Tucker was nothing like the other two cousins; he went about his work in silence, unless he had something to say, which wasn't often anything Willow wanted to hear.

"Yes, cipher too." Willow's eyes roamed the room. "It's very generous of you to spend your nights working on the schoolhouse, particularly since you've already put in a full day of labor at the mill."

Caleb shook his head. "Guess we'd do most anything for the kids. They deserve the best we can provide."

She focused on Tucker. "What about you? Do you enjoy children, Mr. Gray?"

He spared her a paltry glance. "As much as the next man."

Willow stepped past the men, moving to where the roost used to be. The wooden rack had been removed and new boards nailed over the weather-beaten wall along the side. She assumed the men planned to nail fresh boards around the room's perimeter; however, the remodeling needed a woman's touch.

She paused, hands on hips, lips pursed, as she inspected the future schoolhouse. Her desk would be on the north wall, with the children's desks facing hers. The room was under-sized, dark, and rather dismal. They needed more light.

Turning back to Tucker, she asked, "Would it be possible to have a large, sunny window along the east wall? I'm sure the children would love it if the room were filled with the warmth and light of the morning sun."

His hammer never missed a beat. "Where do you think we could get the glass for a large window? We're still trying to get enough panes to replace the old frames."

"No new windows?"

"Miss Madison, as I'm sure you know, there has been a war. We're on the outskirts of civilization. It's hard enough to come by out here in good times, but this is not a good time. There is a shortage of everything, window glass included."

She itched to tell him what he could do with his window glass and his aggravating arrogance. Who did he think he was, talking to her in that tone? She knew about the war. She'd done her part, defending her town and her county. If glass was sparse, then he could simply say so. He didn't need to imply that she didn't have the sense God gave a goose. What was it about this man that set her nerves to twitching? She was a reasonable woman who got along with everyone, but not even a saint—which she wasn't—would be able to endure this Gray.

She moved across the room, farther from him. "We'll need a blackboard."

Caleb interjected. "The Widow Gleeson offered one that will fill that need quite nicely. She's also offered a water bucket and dipper."

"We'll need that, of course." It was a need she had completely overlooked. The children required lots of drinking water. "Is there a well nearby?"

"Two doors down from the church, and it's still got water."

"Very good."

She roamed the room, hands clasped behind her back. "We'll need a heating stove for winter."

"John Franklin is taking care of that." Eli spoke this time.

"Stovepipe too?"

"Stovepipe, too."

"I assume you have made arrangements for desks?"

"Well, there we may have a problem. You might have to get by with tables for a while," Caleb admitted. "They'll work, don't you think? Just until we can come up with something better. We're capable of building desks, but right now, we're a little short of lumber."

"Oh, of course." What remained unsaid, but what she was sure was in the minds of every man there, was that they were short of lumber because of her. She switched subjects. "Are there books and maps? All the teaching tools I need?"

"Not right now. We're hoping to come up with a few things, but you may have to make do with what we can find." Eli said. "Be patient, Miss Madison. We'll get you fixed up as soon as possible."

She sighed. "I'll try. I'm so eager to get started, and I want the room as nice as it can be for the children." It would be difficult, but not impossible, to teach without proper supplies. A blackboard would help a lot. She needed a pointer stick to indicate things she wanted the students to observe. Perhaps the judge would provide books on history and other subjects she could use to prepare lessons.

Silas would provide anything she asked, but she didn't intend to infringe upon his generosity. Tucker Gray might think she was a moneygrubbing female without a brain in her head, but she would prove him wrong. Somehow, regardless of shortages, she would conduct a proper school.

"The school will be fine. Trust us." Caleb said. "But it won't all happen at once."

Willow realized that that was exactly what she wanted. For Tucker Gray to present her with a completed classroom that contained everything she needed. *Forgive me, Father. I'm being unreasonable.* Why couldn't she be submissive and pliable instead of having such grandiose expectations?

Caleb picked up a hammer. "It'll take time, but Thunder Ridge will build back, and having a school is a good start."

Willow noticed that Eli and Caleb were carrying the bulk of the conversation. Tucker was bent to his work, doing what he did best—ignoring her.

She stepped closer to the older Gray. "Building must be tiresome work. May I bring you men a glass of lemonade?"

All three men looked up. Finally Caleb managed. "You have lemons?"

"Why . . . yes. I'm sure I saw some in the pantry earlier."

"Then, indeed." Caleb beamed. "We'd drink a glass of lemonade. Thank you!"

Tucker straightened. "You have lemons?"

Willow lifted her chin. Did he think she was a complete fool? Would she suggest lemonade, if there were no lemons? "We have lemons. Is that so peculiar?"

Shrugging, Tucker turned back to his work. "They're not native to this part of the country. Not many people have access to fresh lemons."

Willow thought back to the truly delicious lemon meringue pie Betsy had served two days ago. Surely the woman hadn't manufactured them out of air.

"I'll be back shortly," she promised, and turned censuring eyes on the arrogant mill owner.

"Oh, do hurry," he mocked. "I'm simply parched, and lem-onade is going to taste so heavenly."

She left to the sound of men's chuckling voices.

The boor. Try to do something nice, and see where it got her?

Up ahead, she caught sight of the judge. She lifted her hand. "Uncle Wallace!"

The older man's eyes turned bright when he spotted her. "There you are. I've been looking for you. Thought I might join you for your walk."

She caught up with him. "Did you need something?"

"No, nothing, just thought a little exercise would do me good."

"Uncle Wallace, do we have lemons?"

"Lemons?" His steps paused. He frowned. "Lemons? Why no, I don't believe so."

Willow's heart sank. "No lemons?" Oh, Tucker Gray would get a good laugh out of this.

"But I know someone who does," he offered.

Her heart leapt. Saved. Saved from another humiliating encounter with Mr. Know-It-All Gray. "Who?"

"Why, Silas Sterling. He has a cellar full of produce brought in every month. Betsy got a few from him just the other day for that lemon pie. If he has any left, I know he'd share with you."

"I don't want to bother Mr. Sterling," Willow murmured.

"Bother him? Why dear, you're going to marry the man! I'm sure if you have a hankering for lemons, Silas would be more than happy to oblige."

"The lemons aren't for me. I promised lemonade to the Gray cousins."

"Oh." Wallace frowned. "Well, I'm sure Silas would comply with your request. The boys are working on the school, are they not?"

"They are."

"And the school is a part of you, so I see no need for alarm. We'll go to Silas's and ask for a few lemons."

"Uncle Wallace, I'd rather not be beholden to Mr. Sterling."

"Nonsense. Soon, you two will be inseparable. I believe Silas would want to provide your every wish, dear."

Lemons. Why had she ever mentioned lemons? If she had a wish, it would not be for a sack of lemons, yet she had promised Tucker Gray a glass of lemonade, and if she failed to show up with one, he would only think her a bigger fool.

When they reached Silas's house, Willow was daunted by the large white two-story home with a third-floor attic, and a large wraparound porch. It reminded her of pictures she had seen of antebellum homes in the south. A maid answered their knock.

Shortly afterward, Silas appeared. "Willow and Wallace. How delightful. What brings you this way?"

Willow tried to gather her thoughts as he ushered them inside a marble-floored foyer more opulent than anything she'd seen before. The floor was highly polished; the walls were covered with a burgundy-and-gold-striped paper. A large gold-framed mirror hung over a long, narrow mahogany table. The judge wiggled his eyebrows, apparently trying to indicate what riches would be hers when she married the tycoon.

Silas ushered them into the parlor, where they sat on chairs upholstered in burgundy brocade. Willow fixed on her purpose, wishing she had not promised the lemonade. However, since she was here, she would have to carry through.

"Now then. To what do I owe the pleasure of your company?"

Willow cleared her throat. "I was wondering if I could have a few fresh lemons."

"Lemons?"

"For lemonade."

"You want lemonade."

"No, I don't want lemonade—it's not for me." She met his inquisitive gaze and decided honesty was in order. "The men repairing the schoolhouse have worked all day on the mill. It's hot, and they are weary, and I thought it would be nice to take them a glass of lemonade. However, if you don't have lemons, that's quite all right."

"No, of course I have lemons. How kind of you to consider the men—would that be the Gray cousins?

"Yes."

"Then, by all means. I'll summon Cook, and you'll have your lemons."

Her eyes locked on his, and she felt her heart sink. This was a very good man. How could she think of marrying him without being able to give him the love he so richly deserved? Was she doing right to even consider the thought?

He summoned a dour-faced woman to fetch the lemons, and while the judge trailed the woman to the root cellar, Silas drew Willow aside. "I know it's very early yet, but I do hope you find me acceptable and well-suited to call on you."

Willow smiled. "You're always a perfect gentleman. Of course you may call on me. I'd be honored."

Judge returned carrying a small basket heaped with yellow lemons. "Here are your lemons, dear."

When the massive front door closed behind them, the judge turned to Willow and grinned. "Didn't I tell you you'd have your lemons?"

The moment she reached home, Willow squeezed lemons and added water and sugar in a large jar. Afterward, she carefully packed three tall glasses in a wicker basket, and then set off for the schoolhouse.

Tucker froze when she breezed in the door. His incredulous expression made every moment of Willow's dilemma utterly worthwhile. *He never expected me to find lemons.* She handed out the drinks, made with fresh, cold well water and turned to leave.

He trailed her to the door. Bending over, he whispered in her ear. "Thank Silas for the lemons."

A blush crept up her cheeks, and she knew that he was smarter than she had suspected. She had a hunch he knew her reservations about marrying Silas for his money, but she would never admit it. She was getting in too deep to change her mind, though being subject to a man as handsome and vital as Tucker gave her pause. She could be good to Silas and in time, grow to love him like a father, but she knew down deep, where it counted, that she would never experience the tingling, breathless reaction she experienced with Tucker, a man who consistently challenged her.

Chapter 19

Willow drew a damp cloth across her flushed face. Outside, thunder rolled in waves. How she wished for a good drenching. *Just one, Lord, and I'll not ask for another.* Thunder Ridge was losing hope. According to Uncle Wallace, more than one hundred and fifty days had passed without a drop of moisture. Talk centered more and more on the mill and the schoolhouse; it was as though folks had forgotten to pray for relief.

Reaching for a board, she passed it to Tucker. "Too bad Eli and Caleb couldn't work tonight. I miss their banter."

Tucker took the piece and nailed it into place. Sweat dampened the back of his cotton shirt.

A jolting boom shook the building. Willow started, though by now she should have been used to the noise. She turned accusing eyes on Tucker when he chuckled. "What? You think it's funny that I jump every time a clap of thunder sounds?"

Laughter lit his features. You'd think a man who worked from sunup to sundown wouldn't be so downright cheerful. She bent, hoisting another two-by-four. "I miss Eli."

"You do? You got a crush on him?"

Willow's cheeks burned. She hated it when he teased her, especially about Eli and Caleb—not that they weren't worthy candidates for a woman's attention. How she wished Audrey and Copper could meet those two men who were nothing like their cousin.

Ignoring his jesting, she picked up a handful of nails and doled them out when needed. "Why haven't two such fine men married before now?"

"Eli was married. His wife died in childbirth a few months after he was conscripted. He didn't see Tate, his baby boy, until he got back from the war. By the time he heard about Genevieve's passing, she was long buried. He came home to find out he was a stranger to Tate. The boy's six now and having trouble adjusting to his father. It's been a struggle for both of them."

She'd seen the child playing near the mill, but she'd never connected Eli and the boy. "I didn't know that. How very sad." Willow handed him a couple of nails. "What about you and Caleb?" She couldn't believe she was so bold as to ask him that question. He'd be itching to set her in her place.

He hammered a nail into place. "No time. We've been off fighting a war, remember? Caleb's looking, if that's what you're asking, but Eli isn't interested in women. Seems that he lost heart when his wife died." He glanced over at her, sweat shiny on his forehead. "Where did you fight?"

"Timber Creek, my hometown. It wasn't that I wanted

to fight—far from it. We had no choice. The Yankee raiders came through and took our horses. And food. What few men were left alive after the fighting were taken prisoner. We never heard what happened to them. Most of the women moved after that, taking their children to kinfolk. A few women and Asa Jeeters, the town drunk, were all that were left, so every time a band of raiders rode through, we fought."

"How did Jeeters manage not to be taken prisoner?"

"He was in a cellar, sleeping off a night on the town when the raiders rode through."

"Wasn't much use to you, was he?"

"Actually, he was. He sobered up real fast when he had to. Thanks to him, we learned how to shoot straight and defend ourselves. We stocked a small cave outside of town with necessities, such as we could find, and we slept in root cellars. I stood lookout many a night, with only the coyotes and owls for company. It was a very lonely, frightening existence, but no more than many others had to endure." Willow handed him another nail.

"It was rough all over," he agreed. "Particularly for the women, but they were tough. I know many of them kept the farms and homes going, in spite of great hardship. I could never figure out why they are considered the weaker sex."

"There are many kinds of strength. I believe we find strength in whatever trial God sends our way, for whatever situation we find ourselves in at the time."

"I suspect you're right. I've found that God always supplies what we need. The problem is, I usually want more than I need." He pounded the nail in with a couple of strong whacks. "What do you think about using a small table for your desk? It will only be until Eli can finish the bigger one he's building for you."

"Eli's building me a desk? How thoughtful of him! But a table will do fine." She'd lowered her sights considerably since the remodeling had started. She'd become a bit more realistic.

Tucker picked up another board and fitted it into place. "He'd already have it done by now if he didn't have the mill work. And Tate takes a lot of his time."

"Tucker . . ."

"Yes?"

She tried to gather her thoughts. A question tormented her day and night, and she had to know the answer. "How . . . where did you get the funds to build back? I know it's really none of my concern—"

He stopped her. "Padget refused to loan me more money, but a few days after he turned me down, the money suddenly showed up. I think Silas is responsible, but I can't say and Padget won't say. I didn't like it, but I can't argue with cash in my situation. Sterling's the only one around here with those kind of funds."

Silas. Willow might have known. Of course he would provide the money if he felt it would benefit her—directly or indirectly. The noose around her neck tightened further.

A peal of thunder shattered the humid night. Startled, Willow dropped a board, and Tucker caught it before it hit the floor. Hands touched. Willow felt the jolt clean to her toes. The encounter was over almost before it started, but her hand tingled.

When she looked up, he was staring at her. What? Had he felt it too? The energy—the sudden surge of responsiveness? He was still staring at her.

She lifted a cloth and blotted her cheeks. "Stop looking at me."

"Why? Because you're a beautiful woman?"

There it was again, the unexplainable drop in her stomach. Should she rise to his bait? Was it bait?

Absently rubbing sawdust off her cheeks, she refused to look at him.

"Do I embarrass you, Miss Madison?"

"If you're serious, then yes. You're being much too forward."

"For what? A woman about to become engaged? You're not spoken for yet, are you?"

He was baiting her, snaring her into a quarrel. Well, tonight, she refused to do battle; tonight, she intended to do her work and return home early enough to take a bath. Water was precious, but she looked forward to splurging in the tub of previously used water. She'd prefer fresh, but she could make do like any other person in Thunder Ridge.

Thunder rattled the ground, immediately following deadly lightning. It sounded like the strike had split a tree-top nearby.

Dropping her hand from her face, Willow collected her thoughts. Why did the man want to torment her? What had she ever done to him—other than burn down his mill and be a constant thorn in his side? Still, he shouldn't taunt her about Silas. She wouldn't be the first woman to marry out of duty, nor the last, if she did carry though with her intent.

Yet heaviness weighed her spirit. Silas was caring. He'd been nothing but a gentleman, and she had enjoyed their walks and talks, but could she really spend a lifetime with this man?

No no no.

A boom shook the ground, and she surged into Tucker Gray's arms.

His arms closed around her, holding her trembling body. How could such wrong feel so right? Willow didn't bother to spring away; she knew she should, but for a moment—this moment—she settled into the fleshly bands of steel as thunder and lightning raged, and not a drop of rain fell from the angry sky.

"You're trembling." Tucker's uneasy voice penetrated her alarm, yet she remained locked in his arms, arms that held her tightly. Possessively. As though she were his, not another man's. *But you're not another man's,* her heart cried out. *You haven't accepted a proposal. You're free! You can stop this nonsense now and . . .*

And what?

She didn't have the answer. Snuggling closer, she surrendered to the moment. *Shame on you, Willow Madison.* Yet her heart could find no fault in this man's embrace.

He met her gaze. "You aren't seriously going to marry Silas Sterling."

"I . . . I don't know. I should . . . he's a good man . . ."

"But a man you don't love."

Her eyes slowly lifted to meet his, and she swam in the warm pools. "I could learn to love him."

"Maybe. But you wouldn't."

"You don't know me . . . I can do anything I set my heart on."

"Oh, I know you."

Thunder rattled the small structure. The racket seemed to shake some sense into her. What was she doing? Had she lost her mind?

Quickly stepping back, she severed the embrace. "You know nothing about me, Mr. Gray. Nothing."

"I know plenty about you, Miss Madison. And women like you. You think you'll marry a man for his money, and that man will provide all your needs, but there's one need man can never provide without your agreement, and that's true happiness." He straightened, a slow grin forming on his handsome features. "You know the feeling, Willow. The kind that makes your insides weak and you question your sanity, yet there it is—this crazy warmness that makes wrong right."

Oh, she knew the feeling. She was experiencing it right now. Because he'd reminded her that she was settling. Settling for a life of luxury for friends and family, but wasn't sacrifice good? Didn't God implore his children to love others as they loved themselves?

He gently placed a finger to close her parted lips, lips ready to deny his charges. "You're fooling yourself, Willow. You'll never carry through with the plan."

"When I set my mind to something, I follow through."

"Not with this plan." He chuckled, and she saw red. How dare he have such complete disregard for her word? And how could she have surrendered to his arms so willingly?

Turning on her heel, she stalked out the front door, oblivious to the storm raging overhead . . . and inside her. Above the thunderous fury, his amused laughter followed her halfway home.

If water wasn't so scarce she'd douse him with a bucket and cool his amusement, but water was sparse, and if it didn't rain soon nobody would be around to laugh.

Tucker stood in the henhouse door, arms crossed, and watched Willow as she flounced toward home. She was a surprising woman, not afraid to get her hands dirty, or to help with the remodeling. She was determined to get the school finished on time for fall session. She had grit. She and her friends had been willing to fight in self-defense, but that wasn't so surprising. Women all over the country, both north and south, had done what they could to hold their world together.

He reached down and picked up a board. Somehow he had to get this job done so he could concentrate on the mill. He was losing money every day it sat idle. He held the board in place and drove home the nails with a few swift blows. So she missed Caleb and Eli, did she? Would she miss him if he weren't here? Why should he care? A woman determined to marry a man for his money wouldn't look twice at Tucker Gray, impoverished male. Not that he wanted her to look at him. He had enough on his plate without getting involved with a high-tempered, volatile female like Willow Madison.

A tap on the door drew his attention. Reverend Cordell stood in the open doorway. "Evening, Tucker. I thought I'd drop by and see how work's progressing."

"Going well, Reverend. Come in and see for yourself."

The good reverend stepped inside, and his gaze roamed the structure. "Well done, Tucker. I'm impressed. What does Miss Madison think of the changes?"

"You'd have to ask her, but seems to me she's lowered her expectations."

Reverend Cordell nodded. "She's a good woman. Been cleaning the church and doing a good job of it. I appreciate her willingness to help. I've heard her playing the piano, too. Even with the instrument out of tune, she can coax the sweetest music from it. A very gifted woman."

Tucker grunted. An irritating woman. What would the reverend say if he knew Miss Madison had her sights set on Silas's fortune? Would he regard her so highly if he were privy to that information?

"How much time do you usually put in here at night?" Reverend Cordell tested a beam with a strong hand. Thunder jarred the ground.

"We try to get in three or four hours. Tonight, Eli and Caleb couldn't be here, but I've been working."

"With Miss Madison?"

"She was here." He knew what the reverend was thinking. It wasn't proper for Willow to be alone with him at night. He should have thought of that earlier, but folks in Thunder Ridge weren't that rigid. Were they? Maybe a few narrow-minded gossips, but surely most would recognize that Willow was intent on helping with the new schoolhouse, and they wouldn't read anything unseemly into her chosen hours. "She was only here for a little while."

"I know. But people will talk."

"I'll be more careful in the future." He would make sure there wasn't anything to stir up gossip. All they needed was Cordelia Padget to get wind of this, and the banker's wife would whip up a rumor storm that would make the thunder overhead seem like a summer shower.

Chapter 20

J udge was out again? Willow walked through the downstairs looking for him. He'd been a busy man today. They'd missed each other at every turn. Allowing for the rising heat, Uncle Wallace might have to be more conservative with activities. She wiped moisture from her cheeks and forehead. It was so sticky. Thunder roiled in the distance as she checked the kitchen, then the side porch. Still no sign of the judge.

Tripping lightly up the stairway, she anticipated the cool bath. Wallace's bedroom door was closed. Pausing, she considered knocking. Most likely he was taking one of his frequent catnaps. Often he would lie down for a few minutes to "study the back of my eyes," he'd say with a chuckle.

She tapped lightly on the heavy oak door and waited for his response. A second and third try produced no answer.

Grasping the porcelain doorknob, she pushed open the

door and peeked inside. The judge was lying atop the bed, eyes closed. Should she disturb him? Perhaps he had retired early and wouldn't welcome company.

He stirred, lifting one hand.

"Sorry," she whispered. "Just checking on you."

When his hand dropped to the mattress, she smiled and softly closed the door. Shortly afterward, she peeled out of her oppressive clothing and sank into the wooden tub. Tepid water closed around her weary bones and she closed her eyes.

Pure heaven.

Betsy had asked for a few days off to look after Mr. Pike, who had complained of indigestion recently, and Willow rose early to fix breakfast. She rather enjoyed the household responsibilities.

Daylight had broken when Willow walked to the bottom of the stairs and called, "Uncle Wallace?" No answer. She called up a second time. "Get up, lazybones! I've made hotcakes."

Hotcakes and fat sausages. Strong black coffee and freshly churned butter. Judge's favorite breakfast these days. Willow returned to the kitchen to set the table and turn the sausages. When five minutes passed, she laid the turner aside and briskly returned to the bottom stair. "Uncle Wallace?"

When he didn't answer, a niggling fear rose in the back of her throat. What was he doing? She grasped the handrail, and hurried up the stairway. Standing in front of her uncle's closed door, she rapped. "Uncle Wallace. Your breakfast is getting cold."

Still no response. She shoved the door open, and her eyes landed on the man in bed. He wasn't moving.

Oh, dear Lord.

She whipped across the floor and knelt beside the bed, searching for a pulse. A faint, thready one met her efforts.

"Uncle Wallace?" She gently tried to rouse him. When all efforts failed, she rose and bolted out of the room, taking the steps two at a time. Her leather heels struck polished wood as she ran downstairs and out the front door, racing toward the mill. When she spotted Tucker's tall form outside the building, she ran faster, overlooking the painful hitch in her left side. She arrived at the sawmill with the velocity of a fired cannon.

Tucker dropped what he was doing and ran to meet her. "What's wrong?"

"It's Uncle Wallace. I can't wake him."

He fell into step with her, and they raced up the path toward the tall green house.

Dear God, let him be all right. He had looked so still and frail lying there, so awful.

Willow bolted through the open front door, and up the narrow stairway, Tucker on her heels. When they approached Wallace's room, she slowed to catch her breath, holding her aching side. Tucker brushed around her, and entered the bedroom. Taking one look at the judge, he called, "Willow? Go get Jolie!"

She turned and raced back down the stairs and toward the outskirts of Thunder Ridge where the Acadian woman lived. Willow found her on the front porch, nursing a young infant.

"It's my uncle. Can you come?"

Jolie quietly handed the baby to a girl who looked to be no more than eight or nine, and buttoned her bodice. She disappeared into the house and came back carrying a bag.

Speech was impractical as they half-ran, half-walked back to the judge's house and started up the steep stairway. The house smelled of burned meat.

"The sausage. I left it on the stove." Whirling, Willow ran back down to the kitchen, while Jolie proceeded up the staircase.

Willow grabbed a hot pad and jerked the skillet off the fire into the cold dish water. Smoke plumed. She fanned the remaining stench out of the kitchen through the open window, heart hammering. Uncle Wallace was all she had. If anything happened to him . . .

She shoved the notion aside, ran out of the kitchen, and scaled the stairs.

Jolie was bent over Uncle Wallace when Willow entered the bedroom. A grim Tucker stood to the side. Willow approached, eyes tracing the figure lying on the bed. "Heart?" she asked softly.

Tucker took her hand and pulled her aside. "It looks like a stroke."

Stroke. Her mind raced back to the night before when she couldn't rouse him. Had he gone to bed early or had he suffered the stroke prior? She had left yesterday morning while he was still sleeping, missed him at dinnertime, then he'd been in his room when she'd returned last night. Her breath caught, and she covered her mouth with her hands. *Dear Lord, have I left him here unattended for over twenty-four hours?* She sank to Tucker's broad chest and he supported her slight weight.

"Jolie can't tell how long he's been like this. He opened his eyes a moment ago, but he's clearly incoherent."

"Oh, Tucker." She briefly explained about yesterday's hectic day, and her fears that the judge might have lain up here unattended. "He could have been this way for hours and hours."

"Don't blame yourself. Anyone would have assumed the same." He eased her to a nearby chair, and made her sit down.

Jolie straightened, her eyes dark with concern. In heavily accented English, she said, "There is nothing more to do. Now we wait."

Wait. Willow shook her head. For what?

"He's going to die?" Life had been nothing but death and suffering the past year. *Why, God? Why would you take my last living relation?*

The Acadian lifted her shoulders. "Wait."

Between Jolie and Willow, they made the judge comfortable. Jolie bathed the older man and slipped him into a clean nightshirt. Willow stripped the sheets, and put on clean, cool ones, smelling of wind and sunshine.

Tucker stood over Wallace's bed, gazing at the stricken man. "I'll be by as often as I can. If you need anything, I'll come."

"Thank you."

Tucker's eye traveled the length of the bed. Drool pooled at the corners of Wallace's mouth. His right hand curved into a claw. "He's a good man. He's helped me out so many times I've lost count."

"Yes, he is." Willow longed to slip her hand into Tucker's, to feel his strength, yet this morning's tragic turn had sealed her fate. Wallace needed care—long-term care, the kind of care that money could acquire. If she had foolishly considered discarding her plan to marry Silas, those thoughts had died the moment of Wallace's stroke. There wasn't anyone to care for him other than Willow.

She excused herself and slipped into the hallway. Tears came, sliding hotly down her cheeks. Jolie came out of the room and paused. Shaking her head, Willow motioned for her to close the door. The woman complied, dark eyes inquiring.

Burying her face in a handkerchief, Willow surrendered to her grief, tremors racking her body. She hated this weakness! She rarely cried. She managed to look up at Jolie, silently conveying her need to keep this private. Somehow the woman understood. She stood in front of the door, blocking Tucker's exit.

The weeping storm passed. Willow wiped her eyes, and blew her nose.

Jolie stared at her. "Mademoiselle?

"I . . . yes, I'm fine." Her heart softened. Women had a way of crossing language barriers. "Thank you."

The woman nodded and stepped aside, clearing the doorway. Willow watched her proceed down the narrow stairway.

Seconds later the door opened, and Tucker appeared. "Everything okay?"

"Fine. Thank you. May I offer you a cup of coffee or something cool before you go back to work?"

"Thanks, no. I need to get back."

She followed him down the staircase. "Thank you for coming."

He caught her hand, preventing her from moving away. She refused to meet his eyes. "You will come for me if you need me." It was a demand, not a question.

"Of course." *Odd that you didn't run for Silas, Willow.*

Not so odd, she decided.

Just discouraging.

Tucker held the door for Jolie. He hated leaving Willow alone with the sick man. What would she do if he took a turn for the worse? She'd been scared tonight and with good reason. The judge was in bad shape. Forgotten were the times Wallace Madison had irritated him. Like Caleb said, Wallace was good. Good to his friends, good to the town. Good, and bullheaded as a billy goat. He cast a glance at the sky. Overcast. Fingers of lightning darted across the western horizon, followed by a sullen rumble of thunder.

Jolie glanced up. "Cloudy. No rain."

"No. No rain."

She smiled up at him. "You a good man, Tucker Gray."

"There are a lot of good men, Jolie. Women too."

"A lot of the other kind, too. Jolie knows."

"Probably so."

"Miss Willow, she a good woman."

"I suppose so. What do you think about the judge? Will he live?"

She shrugged. "Only God can say. If Judge lives, he need much care. Miss Willow, she sees to him."

"I'm sure she will. She's that kind of person."

"Judge needs her." Jolie stopped and looked up at him. "You call me, he gets worse, yes?"

"I will. Thanks for coming, Jolie." He put a coin in her hand.

Tucker walked back to the mill, his mind on Wallace and Willow. Yes, she'd take care of Wallace, but she'd need help. He'd do what he could, but the full responsibility of the judge's care would fall on her shoulders. Tomorrow he'd talk to Reverend Cordell and see what the community could do to ease the situation for her. She'd felt so small and vulnerable in his arms. He had teased her last night, enjoyed provoking her. She was a beautiful woman, full of fire. Now she had a peck of trouble. He'd be there when she needed him. She wasn't alone in this tragedy. But he had no right to help; Silas would see to her care. Like it or not, that's the way it had to be.

Pausing, he turned to stare back at the peculiar green house. Yet, when she'd needed help she'd come to him.

Chapter 21

Dear Copper and Audrey,

I hope this letter finds you well and enjoying the summer weather. Wallace is improving slowly. For weeks, we feared the worst, but now it seems as if he's turned a corner. Last week, he was able to sit up for brief periods, and now it is a part of his day. His right side remains paralyzed, and his speech is difficult to understand, but I'm beginning to detect signs of the old, jovial judge.

I cannot praise Tucker Gray's compassion enough. He stops by on his dinner break every day and reads to Wallace. When I thought to inquire about his noon meal, he assured me he ate on the go. I had to laugh. Eating 'on the go' is surely not the proper meal for a large, hard-working man like Mr. Gray.

The school is progressing nicely, and work should be finished early next month in time for me to prepare for the fall session. The children are happily anticipating school, with the possible exception of Eli Gray's young son, Tate. That boy is plain trouble, even at an early age. Just yesterday, he stopped by the school and planted a "barnyard bomb"—his words, not mine—and who should step in the disgusting mess but Tucker! For a moment, I thought he'd go higher than a kite, but to his credit, he simply stepped outside, scraped the stuff off his boot, and then warned his precocious nephew that he'd best run for his life. Mr. Gray can be downright comical at times, and extremely aggravating at others.

There still appears to be a lot of little boy in this man because the very next day after the barnyard bomb incident, Tate bit into what he thought was Grandma's sausage biscuit only to find roofing tar between the bread. Honestly. You'd think Mr. Gray had better sense. Tate flung the sandwich aside and howled like a banshee. Eli was justifiably put out with Tucker, saying he could have harmed the child, which I can't say since I've never heard of anyone eating roofing tar. Apparently the child only got a taste of the vile concoction, but one thing I do know for certain—there have been no more of those dreadful "bombs" planted.

It is hardly conceivable that I have been in Thunder Ridge all these weeks now. We're planning an Independence Day celebration. There'll be no fireworks this year because of the extreme dryness, but the town children have made colorful streamers and confetti to strew about—not quite as good as aerial works, but the folks of Thunder Ridge manage to cope admirably.

Silas Sterling is fine.

One nice thing happened this week. Mr. Sterling sent a lovely wagon, stating that he knew I was without means of travel. He sent a plain, sturdy wagon, for which I am ever so grateful. His accompanying note gives you an impression of the man's sensitivity and generosity.

The message read: "I would send the finest surrey, but I know your preference for the simpler life."

Even in this short period of time, the man seems to know me better than I know myself.

I am still eagerly awaiting word on whether you will choose to move to Thunder Ridge. Please share your thoughts as soon as possible.

My unending love to each of you,
Willow

Dearest Willow,

Audrey and I look forward to your missives and news of your new life in Thunder Ridge. It's hard to conceive of a town where it thunders and lightnings but produces no rain.

We give thanks to the Lord for Wallace's continuing recovery. For a while, we also feared the worst, but God's plan isn't our plan, and praise be for that certainty.

We are planning a grand celebration for the upcoming Independence holiday. Timber Creek will have fireworks and watermelon this year, though there will be a meager handful to celebrate. There is no lack of rain; in fact, it was

so wet this Sunday past that I ruined a perfectly good pair
of slippers. I should have known better than to wear such
finery on such a wet day, but the shoes went so well with
my gown that I couldn't resist temptation.

Again, we are heartsick that you are wearing dresses
that don't fit you properly. Please allow us to send you garments, Willow. We're poor, but well clothed. My father lav-
ished gowns on me before the fighting touched our lives, and
I have a closet full of lovely dresses begging to be worn.

Audrey sends her best. We've established a business
taking in odds and ends of wash and sewing, so although
our coffers are not overflowing, we are eating well. We're still
very lacking in necessities and new families. We are prayerfully considering your invitation to move there, but Audrey is
hesitant about leaving home. Still, the matter is under deep
consideration. Please thank Wallace for the generous offer to
share his home. It would be heaven to be reunited with you.

Mr. Sterling sounds pleasant.

> Your devoted friend and comrade,
> Copper

Late morning, Willow pinned a nightshirt to the clothes-
line. Wallace's illness had doubled the wash, but she wasn't
complaining. Today, she had put him in a chair beside her
washtub, and he had watched her work, his eyes more alive
than she'd seen in weeks.

He motioned to the sky and the sun's angle.

She nodded, speaking around the clothespin wedged between her teeth. "Yes, it's close to noon."

She pinned a shirt. "Tucker will be here soon." She was not in the least surprised to discover that she looked forward to the mill owner's visits as much as the judge.

The invalid smiled, settling deep in the chair, face lifted to the sun. Judge had come to anticipate Tucker's daily visits. It was kind of him to spend his lunch hours reading the Bible to the stricken man. Willow even sat in on the sessions, enjoying Tucker's deep baritone reading the Old Testament—the battles, the shameless intolerance and disregard of God's word, the force with which God struck or instructed his children to fight.

Hanging the last towel, she turned to Wallace. "It's time to go inside. Dinner is almost ready."

She helped him up from the chair, and he clung to her arm as they entered the house. Betsy was still off, caring for her husband, but things were moving along without a hitch. A huge platter of crispy fried chicken sat on the table. She'd made potatoes and cream gravy to complement the biscuits about to go into the oven. These days, Tucker enjoyed a decent meal instead of a hurried dinner eaten on the run.

After settling Wallace at the table, Willow dished up the potatoes. Tucker's knock at the back door came right on time, and Willow could predict his exact movements and words as he entered the house each day. He'd enter without waiting to be invited—at Willow's insistence—and wash up at the sink. After this, he would say, "Afternoon, Miss Madison." And she would say, "Afternoon, Mr. Gray. It sure is hot."

And he would concur. "You could fry an egg on a rock."

Sure enough, he entered and washed up, then turned from the sink, towel in hand.

"Afternoon, Miss Madison."

"Afternoon, Mr. Gray. It sure is hot."

"You could fry an egg on a rock."

He pulled the chair away from the table and sat down, eyes centering on the judge. "You're looking mighty fit, Wallace."

Nodding, Wallace attempted a laugh that turned into more of a gurgling drool.

Patting her uncle's shoulder with her left hand, Willow poured coffee with her right. "Wallace sat with me while I hung wash this morning."

"Is that right?" Tucker reached for the platter of chicken. "Did you enjoy that, Judge?"

Wallace nodded, and Willow spooned mashed potatoes on his plate, then mashed a few green beans. Setting the bowl aside, she began to feed him.

"How's the mill coming?"

"Good. We're building faster than before, and we're able to add a few essentials we overlooked the first time around."

The corner of her lip twitched with amusement. "Then the accident was a blessing. You'll have a new mill with all the conveniences you forgot to include earlier."

He poured cream gravy on his potatoes. "You should write books, Miss Madison. You have a vivid imagination."

She grinned, relieved that they were finally able to bring the quibble to a mutual understanding. The accident was both their faults. She believed Tucker had conceded the obvious weeks ago, but had he actually accepted it? She nudged green beans between Wallace's lips. "You won't work tomorrow, will you?"

"On the Fourth?" Tucker shrugged. "I'm taking the day off. Wouldn't miss the picnic, and the men's choir will be singing later that evening."

The men's choir. The new organ was only weeks away, and the church had insisted on keeping the men's choir. Silas constantly reminded her how he looked forward to the day she would play in public. Truth is, she could do that now, but she wouldn't, and not just because of the sorely needed tuning. She didn't want to detract from the choir. The men worked hard on their Sunday presentations, and Tucker spared an hour he didn't have for weekly practice. The two older men who hit the discordant notes still sang with the others, because no one wanted to hurt their feelings by urging them to quit.

Willow grinned. "How is choir practice going? I think you sing very well."

Tucker's fork paused in midair. "Well, it's going. Bill and Burk carry their tunes in a bucket, but we manage to work around them."

"They seem to enjoy it." Willow took a bite of potato. "I think it's the high point of their week. It would be a shame to make them quit. And the Bible does say to make a joyful noise."

He laughed. "Well, Bill and Burk are noisy for sure. Can't fault them there."

Willow fed the judge a spoonful of egg custard. "How's the work progressing on the schoolhouse?"

Since her uncle's stroke, she hadn't been able to do much. Uncle Wallace got upset when the housekeeper had tried to assume his personal care.

Willow—with Tucker's help—had the patient's full care.

"As well as expected. Eli finished up the doors, and Caleb plans to hang them tonight. I meant to check at the mercantile to see if they have any supplies you can use. I'll do that tomorrow."

Tucker turned to Wallace. "Do you have spare books she can use? It would help a lot. The town doesn't have many available."

Wallace nodded, and Willow reached over and patted his hand. "That's wonderful. I'll go through your bookcases this afternoon."

His office walls were lined with book-laden shelves, and she was sure she could find something suitable. Just having access to the judge's well-stocked library was a blessing. For the first time since the war began, she would have a chance to sit and read. A bountiful luxury, even if it was one not of her choosing. Now that she had an invalid's care, she was cut off from much opportunity to socialize except for limited church excursions.

After lunch, Willow cleared the table, then hurriedly untied her apron and went into the parlor, where Tucker and Wallace waited. Once she was seated, the mill owner opened the book and began to read where they'd left off in Galatians, chapter five.

Willow picked up her darning and listened to the resonant rise and fall of Tucker's voice. Silas spoke in a gentler timber, sometimes hesitant, but Tucker spoke with authority, rather like King David, she imagined. Or Samson, before the haircut.

Wallace leaned back in his chair, a smile on his face. From

his peaceful expression, it was clear that he enjoyed the time spent with Tucker. Before the stroke, the judge was consistent in his church attendance, seldom missing a service. She had also glimpsed his open Bible, left lying on a table or footstool. How he must miss his daily personal readings.

It was very good of Tucker to take time from his own responsibilities to study the Word with an ailing, lonely man. Her first impression of the mill owner had been misguided. They had gotten off on the wrong track with the mill incident. If they had met under different circumstances, they would have been more civilized, if not outright cordial.

Tucker read until Wallace fell asleep; then he placed a strip of paper in the Bible to mark his place. "Time for his nap, and time I got back to work."

Willow followed him to the door, repeating what she said every day. "I'm so glad you came by. He looks forward to your visits."

He smiled down at her. "And do you look forward to them, too?"

Heat crept up her neck. "I'm sorry I was so contrary when I first met you. And yes, now that I know you better I'm grateful for your company. It can get lonely here with just Uncle Wallace. Mr. Pike hasn't been feeling well, and Betsy has her aging mother to look after as well. So it's very good to have you stop by."

He nodded. "Same time tomorrow."

She watched him stride down the path, thinking that she shouldn't be eyeing the way his broad, muscular shoulders filled the faded blue shirt. Perhaps the daily visits from Tucker weren't that good an idea after all. She closed the door and then checked on the sleeping judge before meandering into his office. The room felt vacant, but the judge's spirit was alive in this room. One by one, she pulled volumes from the shelf and then replaced most of them. There were books on plants with Claudine's name on the flyleaf. Evidently, she had liked to garden.

In the end, she found a history of the world and a world atlas that would do very nicely. She also chose a dictionary, which she would use for spelling lessons and building vocabulary.

She carried the books up to her bedroom, planning to start work on lessons and schedules. By the time the schoolhouse was finished, she would be prepared. The only problem: what to do with Uncle Wallace when she was at work? He was showing slow improvement. Perhaps by fall, Betsy could stay longer, or she could hire someone to check on him throughout the day.

Chapter 22

⤢

July Fourth dawned with a thunderclap that jarred Willow's teeth.

Rolling out of bed, she approached the nightstand and basin of tepid water. Often she used the same water for days on end, so she picked up the lye soap and scrubbed.

Dressed, she walked down the hall and checked on Wallace, who had spent a restful night.

"I'll come and get you when breakfast is ready," she told him, straightening the bedcovers. "Today is Independence Day."

His eyes lit, and he murmured something. She reached for a cloth and wiped the corners of his mouth. "I'll bet you and Claudine loved this holiday?"

He nodded, tears coming to his faded eyes.

She patted his hand. "We all love it and what it represents. How about pancakes this morning? I'll smush 'em up real fine."

He nodded.

She left the room with a dozen trivialities on her mind. Widow Gleeson said the whole area turned out for the noon picnic, and stayed the day and late into the evening. There would be music, watermelon, cakes, pies, and lemonade— the lemons courtesy of Silas, of course.

She'd spent hours with Silas, and yet she felt nothing. He came to visit almost daily, and they'd sit in the parlor with the judge, listening to the ticking mantel clock. There seemed to be little to interest each other. No anticipation twinges. No heady surge of elation when she was in his company. Well, love and devotion didn't happen overnight, and in time she would learn to love this kind, gentle man. She needed to be patient.

Meanwhile, she had chicken to fry, two pies to bake, and had yet to wash and hang another load of laundry. Until it rained, the town's women were now instructed to wash with river water. River water worked all right, especially after she heated it in the large iron kettle and used plenty of Betsy's lye soap, but somehow, she didn't feel it was as clean as water from the cistern or rain barrel.

Please God, just a few drops to bolster our faith.

Later, she slid two blackberry cobblers into the oven and closed the door. The kitchen was hot as blue blazes. Deet Jackson, an elderly neighbor, would be here later to sit with the judge. They would watch what part of the festivities the two men could see from the Madison yard.

She started upstairs to change her dress when she heard a buggy stop in front of the house. Straightening her bodice, she backtracked, waiting for a knock on the door. Who would be calling at this hour? Everyone in town would be getting ready for the day.

Minutes later, she swung the door open, then caught the frame for support as she met Audrey's smiling countenance. Willow squealed. "I can't believe it! Where did you come from?"

"Timber Creek, where else?" The women flew into each other's arms.

Willow drew back. "Where's Copper?"

"Outside with the horse and buggy, and she's dying to see you."

Willow stepped outside and waved. "Around back, there's a shed where you can shelter the horse. It's better to have him inside. The thunder will spook him."

Drawing Audrey inside, Willow shut the door and led her to the kitchen while Copper took care of the horse and buggy. Then the three sat around the table and shared a pot of tea. Willow shook her head. "I can't believe you're here."

"Well, you invited us to visit, so here we are! I assume you still have room for us?" Copper stirred a spoonful of sugar into her tea.

"Fifteen rooms," Willow offered. "You can have your choice. Having you here makes today even more special." How she needed a long talk—and a longer cry with these two women who had shared so much of her life.

Audrey reached for her hand. "Are you all right? I know you've had a difficult time since you arrived."

Willow nodded. "Almost everything has gone wrong. The mill fire, my clashes with Tucker Gray—the judge's stroke."

"Oh, the man is wretched," Copper agreed.

Willow drew a blank. "Who?"

"Tucker Gray. He sounds positively dreadful."

"No." Willow shifted in her chair. "He's not dreadful—a bit hardheaded, and he's a man with strong opinions."

Copper and Audrey exchanged a look.

"What?" Willow prompted.

"You just defended him."

"I did not. I just told you what he's like. Bullheaded and . . . and ornery.

Audrey nodded. "And the schoolhouse is really a henhouse."

"It's taking shape now. Tucker has worked very hard, and I can't find it in me to complain. After all, I've done worse things than teach in a former henhouse."

"How's your uncle Wallace?" Copper asked. "It's so ghastly that this should happen when you two just got reacquainted. Is he making progress?"

"He's doing well, considering. I pray he will eventually regain some of what he's lost. Really, have you decided to take the judge up on his offer to live here? It's wonderful, but completely unexpected."

"Not completely decided," Audrey said. "Letters are good, but we wanted to see for ourselves what Thunder Ridge is like."

"It's a good town. Uncle Wallace has been good to me, and I'm adjusting to life here well. Oh, I do hope you'll love the area as much as I."

A furious thunder blast vibrated the house. Audrey gasped, and both women leaped to their feet. Gradually sinking back to their chairs, they sat, dazed.

"My stars." Copper shook her head. "That was a loud one."

"We get a lot of those." Willow laughed. "It appears we'll have a heavenly display of fireworks after all. The lightning can put on quite a show."

Copper removed a handkerchief from her reticule and fanned. "Does it ever strike anything?"

"Once in a while. Mostly it's too high to do any damage." Willow got to her feet. "I need to finish packing the picnic basket, and then see to Uncle Wallace before I change."

Audrey held up an admonishing hand. "You see to your uncle. Copper and I will take care of things down here."

"Of course." Copper was on her feet in an instant. "Audrey's right. You do what you have to do. We can handle the kitchen and food."

"But you're guests . . ."

Audrey shooed her out of the kitchen. "Go."

Willow grinned. "I'm so glad you're here. It's like coming home!"

She turned to leave when Copper's voice stopped her. "Oh, Willow. I meant to ask. How do you feel about Silas Sterling? Do you still intend to go ahead with this foolish plan?"

"It's not foolish. It's a sensible way to safeguard our future. Silas is very kind, and I'm sure he'll make an agreeable husband."

Audrey shook her head. "But Willow, if your uncle will allow us to live here with him, why must you marry Silas? Once we get jobs, we can care for ourselves."

"Before the judge had this stroke, he mentioned that he would have to sell the house soon. Now, with his illness, his savings are dwindling fast." Willow had ran across the judge's financial ledger, and the shockingly meager balance concerned her. There was barely enough money to last through fall. The house would have to be sold quickly, and Wallace would have to move. In his present condition, he couldn't live alone. Marrying Silas now seemed even more important.

"Oh . . . that's so sad."

"Yes. Please make yourself comfortable while I'm gone." Willow left the room before the two women could comment. She would marry Silas, and he would do everything possible to make Wallace comfortable. Yet she couldn't help wondering if everything he could do would be enough to make her happy.

Around noon, the women left for the picnic, carrying the basket of food between them. Copper turned to look back at the Madison home. "That's quite a house. Not sure I've ever seen another like it."

Willow laughed. "I'm afraid both Uncle Wallace and Aunt Claudine were rather eccentric. It's comfortable, once you get used to climbing all those stairs."

The common area teemed with activity, people enjoying the celebration. Copper and Audrey helped Willow set out plates of fried chicken, green beans, and pies. Betsy and Mr. Pike were there, though Willow thought he looked as though he should be abed. She eyed the man's ghastly pallor, gray and wan. Concern filled her as she introduced her friends.

"I didn't know Miss Willow was expecting company," Betsy said. "I'd never have left her alone with so much to do."

"We surprised her." Audrey patted Betsy's hand. "She's often told us how much she relies on you."

Betsy smiled, her bosom heaving in a satisfied sigh. "She's a good one to talk. Since Wallace's stroke, that girl takes a load of work off my shoulders. We make a good team."

Willow kept an ear on the conversation, but her attention was engaged elsewhere. Not twenty feet away, Tucker Gray sat laughing and talking with that Meredith Johnson from Blackberry Hill. It wasn't any of Willow's business, but he could behave with a shade less adolescent exuberance. Willow could hear their laughter all the way over here. Propriety said Miss Johnson was sitting entirely too close to the mill owner. Not that she cared. Mr. Gray was free to talk or sit by whomever he pleased. She forced her eyes in a different direction, only to see Eli standing aside, but Caleb edged closer, hat in hand.

"Hey, Miss Willow." He grinned. "Why don't you introduce me to your friends?"

Willow glanced at Audrey and Copper, to find them focused on the newcomer. She smothered a grin at the admiring expression on Caleb's face. Expectant, youthful. She made the introductions, and Caleb trailed after Copper, moving wherever she stepped. Willow soon found herself seated in the core of a laughing group, participating in word games.

Suddenly, a baseball rolled to her feet. In the distance, she spotted the banker's son, Junior Padget, eying her. She reached for the ball, thinking she'd get better acquainted with the young lad before school started. Junior started for her, eyes fixed on the orb.

She lightly tossed the ball back and forth in the air.

Junior arrived in a storm. "The ball! Gimme!"

Willow pretended complete ignorance to his demand. "What ball?"

Sweat rolled down his chubby, flushed cheeks. "*My* ball!"

Artfully avoiding his grasping hands, Willow grinned. "How do I know it's your ball? What proof do you have?"

"MAW!" The bellow halted the festive air. Heads swiveled. Willow felt color creep into her cheeks. "MAW! SHE *STOLE* MY BALL!"

Cordelia dropped what she was doing and stalked to the site. "What is going on here?"

Junior sobbed, crocodile tears running down his pudgy, dirt-stained face. "The schoolteacher stole my ball."

"She what?" Cordelia protectively drew the sobbing boy to her chest.

Willow was appalled at the fuss. "I . . . was only teasing him."

"Teasing? Teasing! Taking a baby's ball? You consider that *teasing*?" Cordelia challenged.

"I'm sorry." Willow struggled to her feet. "I was completely out of line." By now, the commotion had drawn Horace's attention, and he was threading his way through the crowd. "What is all this racket?" He glanced at Junior. "Stop sniveling! What's happened?"

"Papa—the schoolteacher stole my ball and wouldn't give it back to me!"

Horace's eyes fixed on Willow.

"I . . . was only teasing." She meekly handed the ball to Junior.

"Of all the . . ." Cordelia mumbled as the parents and child walked away. The crowd melted except for a small girl, maybe six years old, with a front tooth missing. She wore her ball cap jauntily to the side and carried a tattered ball mitt.

"Junior's a crybaby."

"Well, actually I was at fault," Willow admitted. "I'd hoped to make a good impression on him, but it seems my efforts were misguided." She gazed down at the imp. "What's your name?"

"Ralph."

A smile broke. "Ralph?"

"Yep." She gave the center of her glove a hard smack.

"Ralph. That's an unusual girl's name."

She shrugged. "All us young'uns are named Ralph."

"Really." Willow couldn't conceive why.

"Ma says it's easier that way. When she calls Ralph we all come a runnin'. Saves a lot of time and energy, she says." The little girl turned and skipped off to rejoin the baseball game.

Walt Sessions sidled up beside Willow, lighting a smoke. Willow had seen him around the mill on occasion. "That Parnecker girl botherin' you?"

"Oh, no. The little girl was just visiting. She told me her name is Ralph. Can that be right?"

Walt took a long draw off his cigarette. "Yep. There's a herd of them young'un's, boys and girls, but their maw and paw named them all Ralph. You've seen the father around the mill site. Big ole fellow, long black hair, he stands about six-five and weighs close to a full-grown mule. If you ask me it's just pure laziness on the parents' part to name all those kids Ralph."

"Maybe the father wants a lot of namesakes," she suggested.

"Namesakes? Marion Parnecker? Nope, he's just weird as a pear in winter." Chuckling, Walt took another draw. "If you don't know the Parneckers, you will. They got nine young'uns, all school age."

Nine children! Willow blinked back light-headedness.

Nine Ralphs in a henhouse.

Shortly before time to eat, Willow received a light tap on her shoulder. She turned to find Silas looming above her.

"Willow . . . may I have a word with you?"

She sprang to her feet, wiping grass from the back of her skirt. *Silas.* She hadn't thought to look for him. "Of course." Willow followed him to the far edge of the area, away from the crowd, where he paused beneath a spreading oak.

She waited, and when he remained quiet, she wondered if she had angered him. She hadn't introduced Audrey or Copper. Where were her manners?

"Well, it seems as if we have a lot in common," he began.

She smiled, trying to think of an instance, but she came up empty-handed. They liked most things, but on a social, polite level. She didn't feel she yet knew beans about Silas Sterling other than his business interests and that he was most generous with lemons.

"You know I have declared my intentions."

Nodding, she waited for him to continue. *Oh, why did he have to bring this up now?* She didn't want to think about matrimony and serious issues today.

"I am most eager to take a wife."

She smiled. "Yes, I am aware of your search."

He turned, eyes tender with emotion. "I believe I've found the right woman."

She wanted to laugh with joy. All this fuss and bother, and he'd quietly found the woman of his choice, and it wasn't her! Bands of steel snapped from around her heart. The judge would be disappointed, but they'd make do—the good Lord would give them a way to live. Copper and Audrey could move here, and share the judge's house. . . .

Silas's voice came to her from far away. "I'm asking you to marry me, Willow—if you will accept me."

Every ounce of breath left her body. She mentally slumped as his words penetrated.

"Willow?"

Recovering, she drew a cavernous breath, willing her voice to remain steady. "I'm flattered, Silas. It's an honor to be asked, and. . . ." Her mind searched for acceptance, but it wasn't there. It was too soon! "I'll give you my answer soon. There's . . . Uncle Wallace . . . I must consider him."

"Of course I will assume the judge's full care. No expense will be spared, I promise you this."

She nodded. "That's very kind of you." Silas wasn't perfect, but he was close—closer than she would ever be, so why wasn't she pleased? The plan had worked. She'd met her goal. Where was the happiness? All she had was an intensified ache in her heart.

The proposal took the shine off the holiday festivities. Silas escorted her back to her friends, and joined in the conversation. Willow held back, letting the talk and laughter flow around her without contributing. She glanced up once to note that Tucker and Deet had brought Uncle Wallace to the picnic. He sat in a chair, padded with pillows, and appeared to be enjoying the outing.

Before dark, someone mentioned the new school. "Oh, let's go see it," Audrey suggested.

The entire group insisted on trooping to inspect the premises. All except Silas and Eli. Eli hung back with Tate, and Silas had developed indigestion. Willow tried to help by fixing soda water, but when her efforts failed to provide relief, he said, "I have these bouts frequently. The best thing I can do is to go home and let it wear off. You go on and show your friends the schoolhouse. I'll be fine."

Willow reluctantly left Silas behind, allowing Tucker and Caleb to escort them. She hadn't visited the schoolhouse since the night of Wallace's stroke. A lot had been accomplished since then. Audrey and Copper were suitably impressed.

"You'd never know it was a henhouse," Audrey exclaimed. "What wonderful workmanship. And the doors are magnificent."

"Eli's work," Willow said. "And I believe he made that marvelous desk, too."

Audrey ran her hands over the smooth surface. "Impressive. Very impressive. He seems so quiet."

"Eli? Not when you know him," Tucker supplied. "But then again, he's the thinker in the family."

"I haven't seen his wife around."

Willow quietly filled her in on Eli's circumstances.

"How tragic," she remarked.

Judging by her tone of voice, Willow wasn't sure if she meant the circumstances or the man. She had a poignant light in her eyes that had been missing earlier, but then, Audrey was a caretaker. She took in every stray dog and cat, nursed animals back to health, and once mended a butter-fly's wing with a piece of sheer sewing thread. When Audrey turned protector, she was like a dog with a juicy bone—no one deterred her efforts.

Audrey was the first to leave, excusing herself by saying that she was parched, and she hoped there was still lemon-ade in the jugs.

Cicadas sang as the two couples sauntered back to the common area, walking together at first, but soon Copper and Caleb wandered in the opposite direction, leaving Willow and Tucker to continue their stroll.

"Look at that," Willow teased. "Seems those two have taken to each other."

Tucker's eyes traced the couple. "I wish Eli would take an interest in Copper. She seems the type of woman who could pull him out of his shell."

Willow laughed. "She could, indeed. She's a fighter, and she can't abide anyone feeling sorry for himself—not that Eli feels sorry . . ."

"Yes, he does, but with good reason."

"If Copper decides to move here, and he would like to come courting . . ."

"He won't come courting; he's too set in his ways. But I want Eli to find a good woman and settle down. Tate needs a ma."

They strolled in silence before Tucker said, "I saw you talking to Silas."

"Oh?" Did he know the subject of their discussion? Though nothing had been said, Willow expected Silas to maintain integrity regarding the matter. She hadn't accepted the proposal yet so there was no need for the town to be in an uproar.

"He's too old for you."

She flared. "And how is my personal life any of your business? What about Miss Meredith Johnson? You seemed to be enjoying her company. How could you just walk off and leave her alone?"

"I didn't bring her to the celebration. She's here with her family. But Meredith's fun to be with. You need to loosen up, be a little more like her. Get rid of your quirks, like this fool idea of marrying for money. For the record, I'll wager the mill you'll never go through with your plan to marry Silas. You need someone to match you in age, spirit, and pure orneriness."

Willow stopped to confront him. "You don't know the slightest thing about me. Silas has plenty of spirit . . . and an ornery streak, too." Yet she couldn't think of a single instance of Silas's orneriness—he must have outgrown that element twenty years earlier. But he could laugh, and he liked to laugh. He laughed a lot.

"No he doesn't. He tires easily. His bones ache, and spicy food sends him to bed for days."

"That's not true. He seems in very good health for a man . . ."

"His age?"

She resumed walking. "Someday you'll be old and tire easily, and won't be able to eat spicy food or keep your eyes open past eight o'clock."

"Might be, but my wife will most likely share the same miseries. We'll tough it out together. You, on the other hand, will be mixing soda water and wondering how you let life pass you by for the sake of money."

Willow drew herself up to her full height. "I fail to see how it can concern you who I marry, Mr. Gray. And I'll thank you to keep your opinions to yourself."

She strode off, leaving him behind. Why couldn't she enjoy that man's company without coming apart at the seams? He could be so accommodating when he chose to, like the way he helped with Uncle Wallace, but at other times, he was exactly what she had suspected in the beginning—just plain wretched.

Chapter 23

⟨flourish⟩

Avoiding Tucker Gray was more difficult than avoiding a pesky mosquito. Willow admitted it when a week passed, and she had bumped into the man at every possible turn. They were perfectly adult about the coincidences.

Her chin shot up, and she walked in the opposite direction. He did the same.

Yet the community was too small for two warring spirits, and Willow was growing weary of shunning the man. Late morning, she hung her apron on the peg and decided to practice piano. If she followed the path skirting the mill, walked a half mile to the east, and then doubled back to the church, she wouldn't bump into the mill owner.

The plan worked like a charm. Midmorning, she arrived at the church, pulse quickening when she saw Eli's old hound sitting in front of the church. Surely the men weren't having choir practice on a workday morning.

The hound stood up, yawned, stretched, and followed her into the sanctuary. Willow's pulse gathered speed when she saw Eli sitting at the altar, playing a violin—or making a valiant effort. His musical skills appeared to be minimal. The squeak-squawk of the bow sawing across the strings and the unreliable fingering were, at best, the equivalent of running fingernails across a blackboard.

He looked up when she came down the aisle. "Miss Madison. Good morning."

"Good morning, Mr. Gray." She glanced at the instrument. "I didn't know you played." A misnomer to be certain, but he was giving it his all.

Color crept up his ruddy complexion. "Oh . . . I used to play some for the fellows in camp. I'm rusty," he admitted. "Used to play for Ma before the war, but except for the times I've played for my fellow comrades, I haven't touched the instrument."

She smiled. "Will I bother you if I practice piano? I'm a bit rusty, too, and the new organ will arrive any day."

"Not in the least." He beamed. "You play however loud you want. It won't bother me."

"Mill work slow today?" she asked and proceeded to the piano.

"No, we're always busy, but I'm playing Sunday."

Her gaze darted to the violin propped beneath his chin. "The violin?"

He nodded and drew the bow across the strings, producing an ungodly noise.

Willow sat down on the piano bench. "Audrey and Copper decided to drive to Beeder's Cove and explore. They hope to reopen school there soon, and both women are looking for a teaching position." Eli had shown not an inkling of interest in either Copper or Audrey, but Willow had plans—plans Eli might object to.

"They'd have to move here, wouldn't they?"

"They're considering the possibility."

Placing her fingers on the keyboard, she accompanied the sawing squeak-squawk.

Squeak, squawk.

Squeak.

Squawk.

Screech.

"Shall We Gather at the River" had never sounded quite like this . . .

Willow concentrated on the notes, ears tuned to the hound that now lifted his head and howled along.

Periodically she changed music, hoping to persuade the dog to leave, but the hound had a musician's heart. With each new piece, the animal lifted his head and *howwwwwl*ed in harmony.

The whole trying ordeal grated on Willow's nerves.

Screech.

Squawk.

Ahhhwhooooo!

Reverend Cordell stepped out of his study. Willow had to admit the practice session resembled feeding time in the barn lot. She shot Reverend an apologetic shrug and played on. The minister turned and disappeared back into the office, firmly closing the door.

Eli's musical skills failed to improve during the following

half hour. Willow didn't see how he could possibly entertain the notion of playing Sunday morning without disgrac-
ing himself, but he sawed away. *Crescendo, pianissimo*—it all
sounded much the same, the only difference being volume.
The hound had an uncanny knack for vocalizing and undoubtedly enjoyed singing.

The racket went on endlessly until finally the study door
flew open with a resounding *bang*! Revered Cordell stood in
the doorway, features flushed, hair mussed. The man looked
anything but peace-abiding.

"Will you *please* play something that dog doesn't know?"

Willow blinked and quickly shut the piano lid. Sliding off
the seat, she made her exit.

Last she saw of Eli, he was packing his violin away, and the
hound had laid his face in his paws and stared morosely at
the closed study door.

Tracing the same path home, she skirted the mill. It was
hot. She considered the cool riverbank, running in back of
the town, and decided to splash her feet. Betsy had agreed
to sit with Wallace while she did her mending. It would give
them both a break. The housekeeper had been on her feet all
day, and the rest would do her good. Wallace needed company other than his niece and Willow needed to get away for
a while.

The river ran full, fresh and clean. Thank the good Lord,
the land upstream received sufficient rainfall most years to
keep the water flowing, according to Uncle Wallace.

Mid-center the water deepened and formed a fishing hole.
As Willow approached, her footsteps faltered. Standing
knee-deep in the river, Tucker Gray worked a fishing line.

Chapter 24

Willow drew back and watched as he plied the water with the lightweight line—twitching, working the string in the clear stream. Her eyes focused on the strong muscular play beneath his damp shirt, and she warned herself to move on. *Let sleeping dogs lie.*

Yet she lingered in the cool shade of the riverbank. A light breeze rippled the water. Gathering a handful of thick hair, she lifted the mass from the back of her neck to allow the breeze to play over her heated skin.

"Didn't your mommy teach you not to stare, Miss Madison? It isn't polite."

She dropped her hair into place and stiffened. "Do you have eyes in the back of your head?"

"Yes ma'am. And horns, a fire-breathing nose, and fish gills. Ah . . . is *that* why you've been staring at me?"

Color flooded her cheeks. *Of all the unmitigated gall. . . .* She whirled and started off, refusing to sink to his level. *Staring at him.* She wasn't *staring* at him. She had innocently crossed his path, and he wasn't gentleman enough to acknowledge the mistake.

She stamped through the thicket, parting brambly bushes and battling tree limbs out of her hair. The overgrown path and prickly weeds tore at her skin. Burrs snagged her shirt. She wound through the area for over ten minutes. Without realizing it, she had circled the bank and was now on the opposite shore.

He stood in the middle of the stream, chuckling.

Taking a deep breath, she lunged, wading into the water. One swift swing, which he effortlessly ducked, caught her off balance. The next moment, he lost his footing, hitting the water with a noisy splash.

This time *she* laughed.

Latching onto her foot, he yanked her under. Surfacing, she spit water and then flew at him, landing in the middle of his back.

Staggering, he warded off blows. Twice they went under. It occurred to her that she was acting like a hooligan.

Arms flailed and water flew. Sometime during the skirmish, where she gave as good as she got, his fishing rod went under.

The words that flowed fluently from that man's mouth were nothing short of blasphemy.

She surfaced and whacked his left shoulder hard. Gasping for breath, she struggled to the bank and collapsed in a heap. Seconds later he joined her, crumpled flat on his back.

"You. Are. The. *Most* . . . grating woman. God ever . . . put in . . . my path," he gasped.

She had been on the battlefield all those months; she'd fail to retain proper etiquette. "Same to you, mister."

Surging to her feet, she marched off, holding her muddy hem with the last shred of decency she possessed.

Tucker Gray might not smell of mothballs, may be able to keep his eyes open until long after dark, and get out of a chair without snapping bones, but whatever misfortunate soul got that man was in for a pitiful life.

Willow hadn't gone far before shame crept over her. How could she have behaved like that? What would Tucker think of her now? *Hooligan* was the most complimentary word he had chosen. She flushed with the knowledge that he had a point. No woman of upbringing would have behaved as she did. And she planned to teach school in Thunder Ridge? If Tucker Gray, who was on the school board, told anyone what had happened today, she could kiss the teaching position goodbye. How could she have been so rowdy?

Overcome, Willow fell to her knees, right there on the edge of a bramble patch, and did some heavy praying.

Oh, Lord, you know I was extremely out of line, but it's not all my fault. That man brings out the worst in me. Surely you can understand.

She had a prickly feeling God understood her only too well. He knew her innermost thoughts, and some of those thoughts weren't as nice as they could be. Why did she have this problem with Tucker? Why did Silas—nice, nonthreatening Silas—bring out her better qualities? Because *he* was nice, and nonthreatening. So did she find Tucker threatening? Her thoughts were as confused as the weather.

Lord, all I can do is ask you to take away this bizarre attraction for the mill owner. I know my behavior this afternoon wasn't what you would expect from one of your children, and I ask you to forgive me. And if it isn't too much bother, make me a tad more ladylike when I'm around that man.

If the Lord would just give her a sign that everything would be all right.

A blast of thunder rent the air. Willow froze. Was that message for her? If so, she wasn't sure she should wait around for the translation.

She yanked her muddy skirt free from a bramble, and strode down the path for home. Hopefully she wouldn't meet anyone before she reached the shelter of the house. She couldn't bear to be seen like this. She rounded a corner of the path and came face-to-face with Tucker Gray. He loomed over her, and she slid to a halt.

"Miss Madison."

"Mr. Gray."

"That little encounter got a bit out of hand."

"It did, at that."

"You best squelch that temper. It's going to get you in trouble."

Willow gasped. "My temper? I believe you started it."

"Me?" Tucker's brows rose at an alarming rate. "If you will remember, I was standing in the river fishing when you pushed me under."

"I did no such thing. You slipped and fell."

"After you took a swing at me! And you know that's the truth."

Well, yes, she did, but she wasn't about to admit anything

to him. She drew a deep breath. "Will you step aside, sir? I wish to get home and change out of these wet clothes."

"You should do exactly that. Are you aware of how snugly the Willow Gleeson's dresses fit you?"

Willow glanced down in horror to see the wet clothing clinging to her in a most unladylike manner. "Oh . . . you! Why are you so despicable? Go away and leave me alone. I never want to see you again." She pushed him aside and walked on.

"That can be arranged. Give my apologies to Wallace and tell him why I won't be coming by anymore," he called.

"Fine. Just stay away from me!"

"Fine. I will."

He strode off, leaving Willow to stare after him. How could she have been so thoughtless? Uncle Wallace enjoyed visits with Tucker, and now she had deprived him of those. Why did everything related to this man seem to backfire?

Chapter 25

Willow wearily climbed the stairs to her room. Thirty minutes later, dressed in clean clothing and her wet hair combed into some semblance of order, she descended the stairs to Wallace's second-story bedroom. Deet Jackson was seated in a chair by the bed.

"Good afternoon, Deet. Where's Betsy?"

"Betsy got some bad news and had to leave." Deet never used an overabundance of words to get his message across, and he didn't this afternoon.

"What happened?"

"Leonidas dropped dead while he was walking into the mercantile. Just stepped in the door, and fell like he'd been struck by lightning."

"Was he?"

"Was he what?"

"Struck by lightning?"

"Land, no, least that wasn't my understanding. His heart just stopped."

She'd never heard Deet string together that many words at one time in all the weeks she'd known him. Evidently, the event had shaken him and loosened his tongue.

"Who's Leonidas?"

"Leonidas Pike. Betsy's husband."

"Mr. *Pike* died? Betsy's Mr. Pike! How horrible!"

Deet stared at her like she was a couple of eggs short of a dozen. "Didn't I just say that?"

"Sorry, but I've never heard his first name. Betsy always referred to him as Mr. Pike." He had looked gray and sickly at the Sunday picnic, but Willow never realized his illness was a grave one.

"Betsy respected him that way. Woman knew her place."

Knew her place? For a moment Willow wondered if he had heard about the water fight, then reason prevailed. News couldn't have traveled that fast . . . or had Tucker said something? Never. The prideful mill owner would never admit a woman had gotten the best of him, so there was no way Deet could have heard about anything that happened on the riverbank.

She forced her thoughts back to Betsy. "I need to fix something to take to Betsy. Maybe a pie." The widow wouldn't want pie, but she felt a need to do something.

"That would be real helpful, Miss Willow. She ain't going to feel much like cooking today."

"No, of course not. I'll get started right away. Thank you for staying in Betsy's place, Deet. I'll make a second pie, just for you."

"That would be right nice of you, Miss Willow. Make mine raisin."

Willow descended the stairs and headed for the kitchen. Betsy would have more food than she could use, but it was the only thing she could do to show condolences. She'd take it over to the Pikes' house while it was still light and offer her sympathies. Betsy would be lost without Mr. Pike.

An hour later, the pie sat cooling on the windowsill. Deet had taken his raisin one and left. Uncle Wallace was asleep. A rattling buggy announced Audrey and Copper's return from Beeder's Cove. The two women came in the back door, chattering like magpies.

"Oh, Willow." Audrey pressed a hand to her chest. "I love Blackberry Hill. It's all I ever hoped for. The people are so nice, and they were interested in me as a teacher."

"I thought you visited Beeder's Cove"

"We visited both Beeder's Cove and Blackberry Hill." Audrey peeled off her bonnet. "We adore both areas."

"That *is* good news. If God wills, and the two towns reopen their schools, we'll be close enough to visit."

Audrey sighed. "Oh, Willow, they just *have* to hire the both of us as teachers. It would be wonderful to be together again. Even though we wouldn't live in the same town, we could stay in touch. We wouldn't be but less than an hour apart."

"I'm so glad you both applied for the positions. I don't see how they can find anyone better qualified."

A thunderous boom rattled windows. Copper yelped, while Audrey clasped her heart and turned white. Willow hastened to reassure the women. "It's all right. Don't worry. Thunder here is just noise, for the most part." She lifted the curtain and peered out musingly. "But it could rain—some say we get a shower every now and then, but I haven't seen one."

"That's hardly reassuring." Audrey patted her heart. "The very noise is enough to frighten a body into a spasm. I've been told Blackberry Hill doesn't have this problem. Oh, they can hear the thunder, but it's rather muted—more of a rumble than an explosion."

"I made sure to inquire about the noise at Beeder's Cove, also." Copper pulled out a chair and sat down. "It's really most disconcerting." She indicated the cooling pie. "Been baking? It looks scrumptious."

Willow sighed, recalled to the day's tragic event. "It's for Betsy. It seems her husband dropped dead in the mercantile this morning. I thought I'd take the pie by later."

"Oh, I'm so sorry." Audrey shook her head. "How tragic . . . wasn't he the man with Betsy on Sunday? He seemed very ill. When is the funeral?"

"I haven't heard, but it will be in Blackberry Hill. Right away, I'm sure. I'd like to go, but I'll need someone to stay with Uncle Wallace."

"Problem solved." Copper reached to take Willow's hand. "I'll stay with Wallace. Audrey can go to the funeral with you. That way you won't have to go alone."

"I can't ask you to do that," Willow protested. "You don't know my uncle that well."

"It doesn't matter. Perhaps I can read to him or find something that will pass the time."

"He does like to hear the Bible read. Perhaps he wouldn't mind your staying." Especially since Tucker wouldn't be coming anymore. How could she explain that to the judge? He had enjoyed the younger man's company so much. Now it had come to an end because of her temper. She couldn't even tell her best friends about her encounter with the mill owner because she was so ashamed of her behavior. They would have been astounded at her lack of civility.

Willow fixed a skimpy meal, which they ate with little enthusiasm. Uncle Wallace refused the evening respite. Afterward, she and Audrey carried the pie to the buggy.

Later, the new widow hugged them, tears streaming from her eyes.

"Such a shock. I knew he wasn't feeling well, but we thought it would pass. Who could ever expect something like this to happen?"

Willow held the grieving woman close. "I know it's hard."

She didn't know that. Death had touched her all around, but other than her parents passing, she'd never suffered this incapacitating grief—never loved someone as much as Betsy loved her husband.

Betsy caught back a sob and nodded. "I keep telling myself that Mr. Pike was a good man, and he loved the Lord. I know he's all right, but I'm not. I don't know what I'll do without him."

"Take as much time as you need to get through this, Betsy. Don't be in a hurry to come back to work."

"That's another thing," Betsy said. "I won't be able to work anymore. I've got my eighty-year-old Mum to take care of. She's not sick—in fact, she gets around better than I do—but she wanders off. Mr. Pike watched over her, but now she's my responsibility. I have to put her needs first."

"Of course you do, and I fully understand. Anything I can do to help, let me know."

"That's good of you, Miss Willow. It surely is. I'll drop by and visit the judge when I'm able, and I appreciate you coming by tonight. It means a lot to me, and it would have to Mr. Pike. He liked you, he did."

A woman carrying a covered dish approached, and Willow and Audrey took their leave.

They returned to the buggy in silence. Willow's mind whirled with the day's events. Without Betsy's help, how would she assume the judge's full care, indefinitely? Could she ask Audrey and Copper to stay—take advantage of their friendship? She couldn't do that. If they stayed, it would be because they insisted.

But would they insist?

Chapter 26

M r. Pike picked a fine day for burying. Willow and Audrey dressed for the funeral. Copper had followed through on her offer to bring dresses, shoes, and other garments—a welcome gift. Willow had about burst off all the buttons from the Widow Gleeson's offerings.

Able now to take a deep breath without worrying about the consequences, she appraised her mirrored image. Amazing what a proper-fitting garment could accomplish.

"Such a pretty day," Audrey fretted. "And Mr. Pike doesn't know."

"Mr. Pike doesn't care," Willow assured her friend. "His worries are over."

Blackberry Hill was draped in mourning when Willow's buggy pulled into Betsy's yard. Mr. Pike had many friends.

Chairs lined the yard, and several mourners were already seated under the spreading oak. Willow noticed the three

Gray men sitting together, toward the front. She and Audrey were lucky to find seats in the back row. Latecomers had to stand. A dark-suited pastor rose to read the obituary, then led the mourners in prayer.

A fly buzzed the netting on Willow's hat. She brushed it aside, noticed Audrey eyeing Eli, and wondered if her friend was attracted to the young man. He'd shown absolutely no interest in her or Copper, but then maybe in time. . . . Tate would be a handful to tame. He'd been the apple of his grandmother's eye for far too long, and the lack of discipline showed all too often.

Willow spotted Silas in the crowd and instantly filled with horror. She hadn't consulted him about the services—or thought to invite him to accompany her. It wasn't fair to keep him waiting—promising an answer and failing to give one. Why couldn't she just say yes and get it over with? She knew what she must do, but a personal demon intervened, and she couldn't bring herself to do it.

"Lovely attendance," Audrey said later. "The Pikes are well loved by the community."

"Yes, so it seems. The Gray cousins were there."

"I noticed."

"The child you've seen with Eli—that's his son. His name is Tate."

"You mentioned Tate in your letters. He's quite a handsome lad—like his father."

And every bit as hard to reach as Eli, too, Willow fretted.

The following Sunday, the church hosted the last watermelon feed of the season. Deet volunteered to sit with the judge again. Willow had a hunch Deet's generosity was born more of his love of meat loaf than community activities, so she left plenty of food for their dinner.

Long tables sat in white-tableclothed rows under the trees, and the fragrance of freshly cut watermelon scented the air. Willow intercepted several curious glances sent her way, and she knew the gossip that floated about. Somehow word had spread that Silas asked for her hand. The rumor mill thought this would be the day she would accept Silas Sterling's hand in marriage. The rumor mill was erroneous. Today, Willow had nothing more than a cold piece of watermelon on her mind.

Cordelia Padget approached, her bird-like eyes alight with speculation. "Willow, dear. I understand there will be an announcement tonight?"

Willow reached for a piece of juicy watermelon. "Oh? Regarding what?"

"Silas's upcoming nuptials? I must say, the committee is a bit upset that you accepted the teaching position when you weren't planning to fulfill the terms of your contract."

Willow bit into the fruit, catching the sudden spurt of sweet juice in her mouth. "I have every intention of serving out my contract. Why would you think otherwise?"

"Once you're married to the richest man in town? I hardly think so." Cordelia shook her head knowingly.

Willow took another bite of melon. That woman was purely maddening.

She caught a glimpse of Tucker Gray from the corner of her eye. He was sitting with Meredith and apparently having a grand time. Others around the couple laughed and talked so heartily they made the rest of the picnickers look stuffy.

Willow's mouth pulled into a pucker when Meredith cut the heart out of her slice of melon and fed it to Tucker. He ate from her juice-dripping fingers, laughing as she forced the whole piece into his mouth.

Eli had moved over to sit beside Copper. Their heads bent close, engaged in conversation. Willow shoved her plate of melon aside. The lump in her throat was too big to eat around. Not that she cared what Tucker Gray did.

Cordelia Padget's probing expression deepened when Willow left shortly after, making certain the banker's wife knew she was leaving with no forthcoming wedding announcement.

Silas hadn't approached her today, and she knew either his patience must be growing thin or he was biding his time, confident that eventually she would accept his hand in marriage.

If only she shared the same conviction.

Chapter 27

Thunder tolled in the distance as Willow set off in the wagon for Blackberry Hill two days later. She hadn't seen or had word from Betsy since the funeral, and this morning, she rose with a compulsion to check on the newly widowed housekeeper. Willow knew the woman would have a hard time dealing with her loss. A fresh apple pie and a crusty loaf of white bread nestled in the wicker hamper at her feet.

She didn't bother to bring an umbrella. She wouldn't need it. Fresh air filled her lungs—at least as fresh as it got in Thunder Ridge this time of year.

Threatening clouds hung in the west, heralding the coming onslaught of thunder and lightning, but the mare had grown accustomed to the earsplitting barrage and appeared to barely notice anymore. The horse stepped lively this morning, seeming to have fully recuperated from the panic brought on by the mill episode. For days after they'd first arrived, she'd had a tendency to tremble uncontrollably at the slightest noise, but now she had developed a resistance to thunderous discharge. Willow giggled. Either that, or the poor thing had gone deaf.

Once she paid her respects to Betsy, Willow planned to spend the day exploring Blackberry Hill. If the best happened and Copper and Audrey were able to secure the new area schoolmarm positions, she would be making this journey often, and she wanted to know the families. Older children here could make the ride to Thunder Ridge until their school opened, weather permitting. She'd heard there were two boys in their teens who planned to attend her classes during winter months.

Did it snow in Thunder Ridge? And did it thunder and lightning then, too? Thunder-snows, she'd heard them called.

Ha. Lightning streaked the sky. Snow meant moisture, and it was as dry here as a drunk's mouth on Sunday morning.

Willow, you really shouldn't practice the salty phrases like the ones you've encountered on the battlefront. It is quite unbecoming. Yet, phrases like the latter were usually the ones that popped first into her mind these days. Definitely impolite— like the water fight she was still trying to forget. She could say one thing for Tucker Gray—apparently, he hadn't talked about the episode. At least, word of the encounter hadn't gotten back to her. Cordelia and her sidekick, Pansy Henderson, would have been sure to reveal Willow's behavior to the rest of the community.

Halfway between Thunder Ridge and Blackberry Hill, she felt a sudden sway. And a jolt. Then she watched a wagon wheel roll down the hillside into dense thicket. The wagon bed dropped onto one corner with a terrible groaning and creaking. The horse stopped short in the road.

Willow managed to salvage the wicker basket containing the pie and bread before it slid over the side.

Climbing off the seat, she moved to the back and took a look at the broken axle. Silas would be concerned if he knew she'd had trouble with the buggy, but any buggy could lose a wheel. Bending low, hands clasped on her knees, she studied the calamity. Crouching lower, she peered at the wagon's bottom, aware of approaching hoofbeats.

Relief filled her. *Thank you, God. At least I'll have help.* Heat was already building, and in another hour, it would be unbearable.

The approaching wagon slowed. Willow realized her backside was sticking up in midair, but why move when she would just have to get back down and show the broken axle to whomever was driving the wagon?

"Trouble?"

She jerked upright when she recognized the traveler's voice. Eli Gray. Whirling, she smiled, but the greeting died a frosty death when she saw Tucker sitting on the buckboard, piled high with wood shingles. Tipping his hat, the mill owner grinned.

Eli handed the reins to Tucker and sprang off the wagon. He bent to study the broken axle. "Looks like you've got trouble."

Ignoring Tucker, she explained her dilemma. "The wheel came loose and rolled into the thicket. . . . I was on my way to Blackberry Hill to visit Betsy."

Eli's gaze roamed the wagon. "She'll be glad to see you.

Hear she's not faring well." His eyes skimmed the buckboard. "Where're your friends?"

"Copper and Audrey are keeping the judge company."

Together, they walked around the wagon. Tucker perched on the seat, eating an apple.

Well, what did she expect from him?

A quick search of the wagon bed turned up nothing helpful. Eli took off his hat and ran his hand through a head of damp dark curly hair. "We'll have to leave your wagon here and come back. The axle will have to be replaced."

Willow glanced at the apple-eating mule sitting in the buckboard and supposed her thoughts were plain. Wasn't he going to have the decency to help?

He met her eyes and shrugged. "I would help, but you've asked me not to come near you."

"Tucker, you're going to hurt the lady's feelings." Eli shook his head. "Don't mind him. He likes to tease you."

"Tell your cousin I don't find him particularly amusing."

"Tell Miss Madison I am only following her wishes." Hazel-colored eyes crinkled with amusement as Tucker took another bite of apple.

She turned to Eli. "Will the wagon be safe here, unattended?"

"With a broken axle? I imagine. I doubt anyone could move it. It won't take us long to deliver those shingles. A couple of hours, and we'll see what we can do. As soon as we get through here, I'll go back to the mill and see if we can come up with something to use for a new axle."

She nodded. "Thanks."

Eli unhitched the mare, lashed her to the back of his wagon, and loaded the wicker hamper into the space behind the seat. He then assisted Willow in climbing on board. She eased as far to the middle as she could without crowding Eli, but when he climbed aboard, he barely had room to position his large frame. Her skirt brushed the blue fabric of Mr. Know-It-All's trousers. Tucker gave a sharp whistle, and the buckboard surged forward.

Eli kept up a friendly stream of conversation. "Good party last Sunday afternoon. Notice you left early."

"I promised Deet I wouldn't stay long. He was good enough to sit with the judge." Willow scooted closer to Eli. Tucker's eyes remained fixed on the road. He had a small speck of apple on the front of his shirt, and she resisted the urge to brush it away.

Eli glanced at Willow. "Did you get any of Pansy Henderson's buttermilk pie?"

"No, I missed that."

"She makes the best buttermilk pie in the state."

"How nice." Her heart hammered in her throat. The nearness of Tucker Gray disturbed her. The warmth of his denim-clad leg through her gingham gave her goose bumps. *Why didn't he shift closer to the side?* He just sat there, oblivious to her distress. She reached to retie her bonnet strings.

"You get any of that buttermilk pie?" Eli asked Tucker.

"Couple of slices."

"A *couple of* slices?" Eli flashed strong white teeth. "No wonder it was gone when I went back."

"She brought four pies."

The grin widened. "Like I said, no wonder the pies were gone when I went back."

They rode in silence, the wagon creaking over potholes.

Then Eli spoke up again. "Tucker, why don't you ask Miss Madison about Mr. Sterling?"

Tucker's features tightened. "I'm not supposed to speak to Miss Madison."

"Sure enough?" Eli was being nothing but a scalawag now.

Willow stiffened. "You may tell Mr. Gray that in social circumstances, he is free to express his opinion. And I am free to ignore it."

"Tucker, in social circumstances you are free to express your opinions."

"Tell Miss Madison I don't have an opinion."

"Tucker says he doesn't have an opinion."

"Oh, but surely he must." She stared straight ahead. "He knows simply everything."

"You know everything, Tucker." Eli clearly enjoyed the sparring, though it gnarled Willow's nerves into an ugly knot.

"Wrong," Tucker said. "For instance, tell the lady I don't know why she failed to announce her upcoming marriage Sunday afternoon, especially since it was widely rumored that she would."

Willow's lips twitched.

"Tucker says—"

"I know what he says, and you tell Mr. Gray that my business is none of his affair."

"She says—"

"I heard her. You tell Miss Madison it's not nice to tease. If she's going to marry the man, then for heaven's sake, put him out of his misery—or confirm it." He switched the reins. "Either dive in, or towel off and go home, lady."

"Well, I never . . ." She scooted so close to Eli, she forced him onto the passenger rail. Blackberry Hill loomed up ahead, and Willow breathed a grateful prayer. One more second with Tucker Gray and she would wring his neck like a Sunday pullet.

Eli chuckled as the wagon rolled into town. Willow gritted her teeth when he made no effort to hide his mirth. "Do you find this amusing, Eli?"

"Very," he admitted. "God must have made you two in the same day."

Perish the thought. She was nothing like this hardheaded . . . mule.

The wagon rolled to a halt in front of Betsy's house. Eli helped her down.

Betsy met them at the door. "Miss Willow. I declare, if you're not a welcome sight! And Tucker and Eli. Well, well. What brings the three of you out this way?"

"Willow's wagon lost an axle, and we happened along," Eli explained. "She's going to visit with you while we deliver a load of shingles, then we'll head back and see what we can do about that axle."

Betsy's eyes rounded. "You don't say. Well, what a blessing you happened along. The good Lord must have sent you."

Willow sighed. If the Lord had been behind the Gray cousin showing up in her hour of need, he might be a tad put out at her obvious lack of gratitude. She did, indeed, need to work on her social skills.

Betsy motioned them toward the open door. "Why don't you come in for a cool drink? I'm anxious to hear the news from Thunder Ridge. It seems like I've been gone for a long time."

"We'd sure like to come in, Betsy," Tucker said. "But we've got these shingles to deliver. We'll stop by one day next week."

"I'll hold you to that, Tucker Gray."

Tucker and Eli paid their respects, and then returned to the wagon. Willow trailed behind to get the pie and bread.

Eli moved to the back of the wagon to retie a loose bundle, while Tucker handed the wicker to Willow. Their hands briefly brushed. Willow looked away. The sudden silence intimidated her. When he and she were alone, she felt as if a coiled snake were in her stomach.

Suddenly he spoke, his tone as sober as a judge. "Would it do any good to try and talk sense into you?"

Lifting her chin, she asked. "In what regard?"

"Regarding this insane notion to marry Silas."

"You don't care for Mr. Sterling?"

"Sterling's fine. He deserves more than a loveless marriage."

"You're quite right, he does. But I will love him, and besides, he's the one who initiated the search for a wife."

"Love him? Ha!"

She kicked dirt on his boots. "You are undoubtedly the most exasperating man I've ever met."

"Yeah, well, you're the most obstinate woman I've ever met. I'm trying to do you a favor, Willow. Why won't you listen?"

"Perhaps I have my family in mind. Uncle Wallace. How am I supposed to properly care for him if I don't marry Mr. Sterling?"

"You marry a man you love, and the two of you take care of Wallace."

"Copper and Audrey need me."

"Copper and Audrey are two lovely women who'll marry one of these days, and you'll be on your own, with a man old enough to be your father." He gently grasped her shoulders. "Someday Wallace will die. We all die, Willow. When he's gone, you'll be left with an empty life."

"Silas is a decent man."

"That he is."

"Then why are you so set against me marrying him? If it were any other woman, you would be happy that he desires a mate and children."

Shifting, Tucker looked down. "Maybe I would."

His stark admission startled her. Her tone softened. "Then why are you so dead set against me marrying him?"

His head lifted, his eyes focusing on hers. "I ask myself that question a hundred times a day."

Her heart whacked her ribs. Was he saying . . . could it be? She dashed the thought. He loathed her. They'd done nothing but clash from the moment they met. Her eyes searched his.

Eli called out, "I'm ready when you are."

Gaze still locked, Tucker asked, "Would it do any good to ask you not to marry him?"

Her legs threatened to buckle. Why would he ask such a thing? "I . . . I haven't accepted Silas's proposal."

"Yet."

"Yet," she acknowledged.

"Let's go, Tucker. You two can argue later. We got to get this load delivered and that axle repaired before dark."

Stepping aside, Tucker acknowledged the summons. "Have a good afternoon."

She nodded. "You also. And Tucker?"

He turned.

"If I do marry Silas, I promise you that I will be a devoted wife."

He nodded, grim now.

She watched the buckboard rattle away, her emotions as irregular as a hummingbird's flight.

Betsy called from the porch. "Let's sit out here and have a good visit. Mum is asleep, and we can talk without being interrupted. She's a spot of trouble sometimes when we have company."

Willow turned and walked back to the porch. "I'm not company. I'm a friend."

"That you are, and a blessing. I'll fetch us a cup of coffee and a slice of angel food cake, then we'll sit and talk."

Betsy disappeared, and Willow sat down in one of the cane-bottom rockers and tried to compose herself. Why would Tucker behave so strangely? It was as though he had a personal interest in whether or not she married Silas, but surely the man didn't care a twit about her. She was crowding his patience. Most likely, he didn't think she was good enough for Silas. The thought produced a slow burn. How dare he entertain such a notion?

Betsy returned, carrying a tray holding two cups of fragrant coffee and a plate loaded with slices of angel food cake. She handed Willow a saucer and a fork. "Help yourself to the cake. The neighbors have brought in so much food, some will go to waste." Willow took a slice of the cake and cut off a bite. She closed her eyes and the let the sweetness calm her. "It's very good, Betsy."

The housekeeper's smile faded. "Mr. Pike always loved angel food cake, God rest his soul. I sure do miss him."

"I know you do, and I'm so sorry. He would understand if you're sad."

"I know he's in heaven, walking those streets of gold, but I'm down here, and there isn't much that's golden in my life anymore."

Willow hesitated. "Are you all right financially?" Not that she had anything to give that would help, but if Betsy had a need, she could talk to Reverend Cordell and Silas to see if something could be done.

Betsy shook her head. "I have all I need. Mr. Pike was a good provider, and the judge always paid me well. We have money put back, and I can bring in something by selling eggs and taking in washing and ironing. And I've always got baking to fall back on."

The last was said with an air of pride. Betsy smoothed her skirt and smiled at Willow. "I'd already started doing some baking for the women in town. They pay good money for my cakes and pies. Even cookies and fruit bread go well, and I've developed quite a following for fresh loaves of white bread."

Willow thought of the pie and bread she had brought from home. "Then I suppose my offerings won't be needed. I had no idea you were so resourceful."

"Don't you think it," Betsy said. "It will be a rare treat to eat someone else's cooking. I do get weary of my own."

Willow's eyes softened. "I'm really proud of you, Betsy. You're becoming quite the businesswoman."

"It's something I can do and still keep an eye on Mum. She

does tend to wander off when she's left unattended. Not that she'd bother anything, but I worry she might get hurt."

"I'm glad you can be here for her and still have an income. You're amazing. I miss you and the talks we used to have."

"And I miss you, too. How's the judge today?"

"About the same."

"And you and Tucker? Still spittin' at each other like ole cats?"

Willow sniffed and shook her head. How indeed? On par with the Yankees and Johnny Rebs—war from the beginning, and the daily skirmishes continued. She pitied the woman who ended up with that contrary, frustrating, uncivil man.

Tucker rode in silence. Was there no way to make that stubborn woman see the light? Getting her to admit she was wrong was like trying to lead a mule in the opposite direction. Both woman and animal were too contrary and hardheaded for their own good. Why couldn't Willow be as easy to get along with as Meredith? Now there was a woman who enjoyed life, and she didn't keep a man stirred up all the time, with one fuss after another. Willow could take lessons from Meredith on how to get along with people. She was blind to everything except her own opinion.

Eli interrupted his thoughts. "Willow's some woman, don't you think?"

"If you say so."

Eli threw back his head and laughed. "If I say so? You looked at her lately? She's more than an 'if you say so.'"

"I thought women didn't interest you."

"I'm thinking of you."

"Well, don't." Tucker grunted. He knew what Eli was getting at. There weren't many single women in town—weren't all that many women in the area, period. A lumber town didn't attract families, and several women whose husbands had been killed in the war had moved closer to civilization. He couldn't fault them for that. There weren't many ways to make a living in Thunder Ridge, not to mention the inhospitable climate.

His thoughts turned back to Willow, and the stubborn tilt of her chin, the glare of independence in her eyes. That one could take care of herself. Why, the way she had picked a fight with him at the river was evil. What well-brought-up young woman would have acted like that? His lips quirked in a grin. She was feisty, he'd give her that. Didn't know when to quit. She had a fire that was missing in every other woman he knew.

Tucker shook off his thoughts. "You think we can get that wagon repaired today?" He turned to Eli. "If we can't, maybe we'd better stop by Betsy's and make arrangements for Willow to spend the night. Betsy would welcome the company."

"No need to do that. Let them visit. We can go back to the mill and get a new axle. It won't take long to get it in place and reattach the wheel."

Tucker nodded. "We'll deliver these shingles and get on that axle."

Willow and Betsy rocked companionably. "So tell me, what's been going on in Thunder Ridge since I've been gone?"

"We had a watermelon feed. That was rather nice." At least Tucker had seemed to enjoy it. Sitting there, eating watermelon, talking and laughing with that Meredith. Created a real stir, in her opinion. Not that he would have cared what she thought about who he courted. He'd made that plain enough.

"Was Silas there?"

"He was there, but we didn't visit. He and his men friends were playing horseshoes."

"Has he asked for your hand yet?"

Tears sprang to Willow's eyes. What was wrong with her? When she was within reach of security and freedom from want, and the ability to help those she loved, why was she behaving in such a wishy-washy manner? Marrying Silas was why she had come to Thunder Ridge in the first place.

"Willow?"

She nodded, miserable. "He has, yes."

"And have you given him your answer?"

"Not yet. I told him I would—soon." She had to stop daw-dling. Silas deserved better treatment. She had to tell him, one way or the other. The judge was determined that she become Mrs. Silas Sterling. How could she disappoint him, in his weakened condition?

Betsy's question penetrated. "What do you plan to tell him?"

Willow forced the truth, the honest truth, from her soul. "I haven't decided."

"Oh, honey. You see. You just don't want to recognize."

"Silas is a good man."

She seemed to be saying that a lot. And he was. Silas was well-liked in the town. No one ever said a harmful word about Silas Sterling. His wife could hold her head high, knowing she would be treated with respect—not only by her husband, but by the townspeople too.

Betsy swayed with a distant look in her eye. "I remember the day I married Mr. Pike. Seemed like my heart would fairly burst with happiness. It was like every dream I'd ever dreamed came true that day."

The admission infiltrated Willow's weary soul. There was no mistaking the love shining in Betsy's eyes. She had adored Mr. Pike. Loved him with heart and soul. Words from the Bible flitted through Willow's mind. *Therefore shall a man leave his father and mother, and shall cleave unto his wife: and they shall be one flesh.* Those words meant something to Betsy and Leonidas Pike. They had been rich in ways that counted.

Betsy's eyes glistened, but her voice was steady. "No matter how bad things got, I knew I wasn't alone. I had God, and I had the love of a good man. In all the years we were married, I never had a single regret. Oh, we had our times, but they were just minor spats. I'd marry him again in a second if I had the opportunity. I miss him, yes, but I'd not take anything for the years we had together, or the memories he left behind."

Willow swallowed, threatening to choke on the lump in her throat. She searched for something meaningful to say, but words escaped her. Betsy was speaking of something she'd never known—never would know, if she married Silas. Yet, how could she hurt that good man by refusing him?

"Do you read your Bible, Willow?"

"Not as often as I should." She was beginning to realize that her father's teachings had gone by the wayside. Once, she could recite scripture with admirable skill; now, she barely picked up the Good Book. Maybe that's why the world was so confusing.

"But Judge said your daddy was a stickler for memorizing verses, so I'd say you're familiar with the book of Second Corinthians. It's been my solace. I know I was one of the fortunate ones. I found true love on earth, and now I'm waiting to be reunited with my husband one day. I know the day is coming, just as sure as I'm sitting here."

An approaching wagon interrupted her. Tucker pulled up at the yard gate, seated in the rental wagon from the livery stable and driving the mare. He jumped down lightly and tied the animal to a post. Willow watched as he walked to the porch with a young man's gait. Strong, virile . . .

She pulled her thoughts away. Silas. She was going to marry Silas. She had no right to be looking at Tucker like this.

"So you got it fixed," Betsy said. "Didn't take you boys all that long."

"Eli knows his business. Axle's fixed. It must have been weak, because it looked brand-new. Shouldn't be any more trouble."

Willow pushed out of the rocker and extended open arms to Betsy. "I have to go now, but I've enjoyed our visit so much."

"So have I, young'un. It's lonely around here these days. But before you go, I have something for you." Betsy walked to the side of the porch, where several pots of flowers sat along the railing. She picked up one filled with small blue flowers, and held it out. "I want you to have this."

Willow took the pot, marveling at the soft, sky-blue flowers and black soil. "What is it?"

"Forget-me-not. The flower of true love. I have a feeling you need to be reminded of what's important. And maybe this little pot of flowers will help."

"Oh, Betsy, they're wonderful, but I haven't the spare water to feed them."

"You'll find it," Betsy promised. "Just like you'll find true love. It's there. All you have to do is reach deep and grasp it."

Reach deep and grasp it. Willow fingered the delicate plant, wondering if her arms were long enough to reach for what she really wanted, or more to the point, if she had the courage to water her emotions.

They'd been dry for a long spell now.

Chapter 28

"I can't bear for you to leave." Willow clung to Audrey's neck, tears coursing down her cheeks. The visit had been too short, and now Audrey and Copper had to go home—or what was left of home. Her heart ached with the thought of the lonely weeks to come without their daily encouragements. In their company, the load she bore seemed lighter. Now the burden descended full force, all the more wearisome for the brief respite she had been given. There must be some incentive she could offer to hold them here.

"Stay," she urged. "Uncle Wallace doesn't mind, and I can use help."

"I'd stay in a moment." Audrey lifted a handkerchief to her nose. "But I can't, Willow. You know that. We have responsibilities in Timber Creek, and we've stayed much longer than we anticipated."

"Two weeks hasn't been long! And there's nothing left of the town."

"We only planned to stay a few days," Audrey argued. "Our few patrons will think we've left for good."

Copper crowded in for a mutual hug. "You know we want to, but if we close our business before we find teaching jobs, we'll have no income." The women formed a three-hold embrace and clung to one another.

"We'll be back soon," Audrey promised.

"It will take months, maybe years for other communities to reopen schools." Realistically, and that's as far as Willow would allow her thoughts to wander these days, it might be a year before Blackberry Hill or Beeder's Cove reopened a school because of the war economy.

Copper patted Willow's back. "We'll try to come sooner. Maybe we can close the business."

Audrey protested.

"Soon," Copper promised. "And we'll move here for a while, at least to help you."

"Thunder Ridge is a three-day ride," Willow said.

"Well, we'll just have to adjust until circumstances change." Copper broke the embrace, smiling through tears. "Perhaps Silas will provide an escort to bring you to Timber Creek when we can't make it here."

Yes, Silas would do that for her. He would do anything to please her. Willow knew this, but the knowledge didn't make parting any easier. With Copper and Audrey here, the situation was manageable. Now Willow didn't know how she would make it through the engagement period.

Audrey dried her eyes. "Most assuredly, we'll visit over

the Christmas holidays, and they'll be here before you can say fruitcake!" Gathering a hatbox, Audrey climbed into the buggy. "Come visit us the moment you can get away. We can't wait to show you the sewing room."

"It's small and barely adequate, but it allows us a roof over our heads and sewing space, though business is meager." Copper settled on the padded seat. "Now stop, or you're going to make me cry again."

Willow took a deep breath and dropped her argument. *I'd love anywhere away from thunder and this pressing responsibility.*

Audrey cocked her head. "You're sure you'll be okay? I know the town is good to help with Wallace's care."

Willow nodded. Without Deet's help, she would be in a real fix.

"I am sending more gowns," Copper announced. "Argue all you like, but I'm sending more garments that fit you. With the ones we brought, you should be able to dress comfortably."

Sighing, Willow accepted the offer. "And while you're at it, please send a few chemises." She squirmed, trying to loosen the tight drawers she endured on a daily basis. Copper had forgotten those all-important articles.

Audrey picked up the reins. "Willow."

"I know. 'Willow, please reconsider and come back home with us.'"

"Well, you must. I know life appears momentarily bleak and without compromise, but God can work miracles."

Could he restore Wallace's health? Willow knew that he was able, but would he? She'd thought her problems worrisome a few weeks ago; now, they were insurmountable.

"Please consider coming here to live."

Copper nodded. "We will pray about it, Willow. Promise."

She smiled up at her friend. "Don't worry about me; just come visit as often as you can."

Copper's gaze meandered to the mill, where the men hammered and sawed. "I'd rather hoped that Caleb would come to see us off." The words had no sooner left her mouth than the women saw the cousin glance up, apparently realize that the women were leaving, and depart his post to hasten up the hill. Swiping his hat aside, his eyes sought Copper. "I'm sorry to see you leave."

The young lady turned three shades of red, cheeks blazing. "We plan to visit often."

He bent and tweaked her nose. "See that you do." Giving the other women a wink, he returned to work.

"Oh, Copper," Audrey murmured. "I think he's smitten with you."

A schoolgirlish giggle escaped the schoolmarm. Willow swapped looks with Audrey. She'd have given a pot of gold if Eli had come to bid Audrey good-bye. Instead, she saw him planing lumber, unmindful of the departure. What sort of woman would win that man's heart—could one ever accomplish that feat again?

Copper settled on the buggy seat. "Caleb is a wonderful man, but his coming to say good-bye means nothing." Her eyes followed the tall figure striding downhill. "I'm just looking for a small ray of hope that someday I'll meet the right man—the man God created for me."

Willow watched the buggy roll away.

Weren't they all?

Chapter 29

Days and weeks started to blur. Willow had still not accepted Sterling's proposal. What was she waiting on? Silas was not openly pressing for an answer, but she saw confusion and hurt in his eyes as the days passed and no word came regarding his formal request for her hand. She couldn't delay forever—or could she? Maybe suggest a winter courting period . . . maybe a late-fall wedding next year. . .

Early one morning, a carriage arrived. The big black hansom cab rolled to the front of the Madison house. Who on earth would come here in such a fine means of transportation? Willow knew for a fact that no one in Thunder Ridge, other than Silas, owned anything so elaborate.

She turned and approached the visitor. She hadn't seen the carriage before, and the driver didn't look familiar. "Good morning."

A thin man wearing austere black tipped his tall hat made of fine beaver skin. "Top of the morning to you, Mrs."

"Miss," Willow corrected. Irish, she decided. The thick brogue was always pleasant to encounter.

"Fine day it is." He stepped from the carriage and secured the reins to a post before turning to face her. "Might this be Wallace Madison's place of residence?"

"It is."

Willow paused as the man approached. He extended a skeleton hand. "Elliot O'Malley, at your service."

What could Elliot O'Malley want so early in the day? The man was dressed like an undertaker, although she'd never seen anything this fancy in Thunder Ridge. Kirkland Burying was the local mortician, and ran the burying parlor.

Willow accepted O'Malley's warm handshake. "Willow Madison."

"Oh. I understood you to say Miss. Are you not Wallace Madison's spouse?"

"Niece."

"My pleasure." He lightly touched his lips to the top of her hand. Lifting his head, he smiled. "Might the good Mr. Madison be in this morning?"

She felt a bristle of apprehension. Why would this man be here to see Uncle Wallace? In all the time she'd been in Thunder Ridge, no one like this stranger had ever shown up on the doorstep.

"My uncle had a stroke a few weeks past. It has affected his speaking and motor skills."

O'Malley's features softened. "A burden, to be sure."

"May I help you?"

He took a snow-white handkerchief out of his pocket, folded it in a neat square, and mopped his perspiring brow. "I wonder if I might have a glass of cool water."

"Of course. Come inside." Willow led the way up the walk. Behind her, she could feel O'Malley gawking at the unconventional house. It did appear rather like a large birdhouse without a proper tree. In time, the home would probably have to be sold to have money enough for Wallace's care, but where would they live? She'd been homeless after the war and didn't want to experience that again.

She knew the answer.

Silas.

Yes, with . . . him. She sighed and opened the front door. Silas would freely accept Uncle Wallace into his home, but perhaps if the house were to sell quickly, Willow could find a small private accommodation to suit the two of them.

In a few minutes, she carried a glass of water into the parlor, where O'Malley sat stiffly, satchel resting on his bony knees.

"Thank you, my good woman." He downed the water in moments, Adam's apple bobbing as he thirstily sucked down the life-giving substance. Little did he know how difficult it was to find a cool drink in Thunder Ridge. Even the water tower at the edge of town now stood guarded, in case some enterprising citizen decided to raid the emergency water supply.

Willow lifted a handkerchief to her temple and wiped moisture. It wasn't yet seven in the morning, and already the room was as hot as Hades.

"Much better." He set the glass on a crocheted doily, and

then leaned back. Clasping both hands on his knees, he smiled. "I am here to collect the funds."

What a funny, odd man. He resembled a well-to-do scarecrow.

"Funds?"

"Yes. Today is the signature date of amount due."

She couldn't connect the significance of the date.

"And . . ." He lifted thick black brows that sprouted in fifty directions.

"And?" she repeated.

His jovial demeanor started to droop. "And . . . the bank has sent me to collect monies due on Mr. Madison's loan."

"Loan," Willow whispered. Her stomach knotted. "What loan? Uncle Wallace owns the house, free and clear."

"Ah . . . no, I don't believe your information is correct." He hastily snapped the lock on the satchel and opened it. Picking up a paper, he read. "Your uncle took out a note some five years ago. The full amount is due today." He extended the paper as though he needed proof to back up the assertion.

Willow reached for the legal-looking document and read it, her heart sinking to the floor. "Five thousand dollars." An enormous amount. Her eyes skimmed the document securing Wallace's home by a large Amarillo banking establishment. The judge had apparently gone outside the community for financial help without anyone's knowledge. And now the payment was due. Had the judge known someone—been associated with someone at this bank who would forfeit policy and make such a highly irregular business contract? That could be the only answer.

"Yes . . . that would be correct. Five thousand." The representative sobered. "Is there a problem?"

She bit back rising hysteria. Was there a problem? No, there were five thousand problems! Suddenly everything fell into place—Aunt Claudine's extravagances, Wallace's frantic pleas for Willow to meet and woo Thunder Ridge's wealthy Silas Sterling. For the past two years, Wallace had forged a path of deceit, using Willow for bait. He had tried to give Claudine anything she wanted . . . including this spectacle of a house, which he could not afford. When she fell ill, he must have panicked and borrowed against the house to make it larger, grander. More hideous. Willow's fingers closed around the legal note, crushing the paper. O'Malley quickly reached for the document.

"Miss Madison! This is a legal and binding agreement!"

Snapping to her senses, Willow apologized for her impropriety. "I'm sorry. So clumsy of me." She retrieved the paper and smoothed it out on her knee, her mind reeling. Where would she get five thousand dollars? She didn't have five dollars. And it was due today?

O'Malley sank back in the chair. "I gather you were not aware of your uncle's commitment?"

"I wasn't," she admitted, barely able to speak around the bile forming in the back of her throat. *Please don't let me be sick in front of this gentleman.*

"I see . . . it would be highly irregular, but I could delay my departure until tomorrow morning . . . if that would help. The amount must be paid in full, or the bank will foreclose on the property."

I'm going under, Lord. You must help, or I'm going under.

"No, that won't be necessary, Mr. O'Malley." She cleared her throat, returning the note. "I don't have the money. Not today, nor tomorrow, nor ever." And no chance of getting it without going to Silas and accepting his proposal today.

"Oh dear."

Yes. Oh dear. How perfectly, unthinkably dreadful. Yes, she could go to Silas, and yes, he would pay the note, but she refused to use the man this way.

Then why are you marrying him, Willow? The voice was so physically powerful, she looked up. "Beg pardon?"

Mr. O'Malley scribbled in his notebook. He glanced up. "Beg pardon?"

"Did you say something?"

"No. I'm afraid there isn't anything to say. I merely work for the bank. I don't make decisions." His features remained calm, almost expressionless.

It meant nothing to him that he had just dealt a fatal blow to her heart. Her future.

"Oh." Who had said, 'Then why are you marrying him, Willow'? The words had been so clear and direct that even now she could still hear them ringing in her mind.

Mr. O'Malley closed the notebook. "You have my deepest sympathy. I know life is often cruel, my dear, but I am old enough to know that one never knows God's workings. What looks to be beyond our comprehension is often God in his finest hour."

All right, then. Maybe he wasn't as detached as she supposed. Perhaps he fully trusted on the Lord. Perhaps nothing had ever dealt him a blow like the ones she'd been getting all too often lately.

If it weren't for the sensation that she was drowning in troubles, she would agree, but right now it looked as though

God had left his throne, and all this talk about mercy and love was just that—talk. She had almost never failed to serve him—to honor and to trust him—but where was God now? Certainly not in the parlor of this hideous, mortgaged house with its owner lying upstairs, his heart pumping life through a shell of a man—a man who would sacrifice his flesh and blood for a wife's demanding whims.

It hardly seemed like God had his eye on Willow Madison.

Rising, Mr. O'Malley extended his hand. "I am so sorry."

Willow looked at the soft hand, not the hard flesh of a workingman. Tucker's sun-darkened, calloused hands came to mind. Tucker Gray. She was in love with that man. Hopelessly, ill-fatedly in love. Why had she not recognized it sooner? Before this awful morning, when her last hope of not marrying Silas was dashed?

"If you change your mind—if God sends a way for you to meet this obligation by morning—this disaster can be averted. I'll stop by before I leave early tomorrow—perhaps you can make arrangements?"

"I can't." She hated to shatter his staunch belief in the Almighty, but she wouldn't have the money tomorrow, or the next day, or next year.

He proceeded to the door, then turned. "You know, Miss Madison, I've found that when life is at its worst, only then are we forced to look within ourselves and see if perhaps we've created the problem."

She lifted lifeless eyes. "I didn't borrow money I didn't have. I didn't start a war and tear families apart. I'm not to blame for folks going hungry at night, and friends needing a decent roof over their head."

The collector's eyes softened. "That you didn't, but I sense you're very troubled. I know the news I bring is distressing, but might I ask why you take it upon your shoulders to fulfill the Good Shepherd's promises? If he can give life, then he can most surely sustain life without our help. Doesn't his word tell us, 'For the Kingdom of God is not meat and drink, but righteousness, and peace, and joy in the Holy Ghost'? I urge you to hold fast in your faith, Miss Madison. Without hindrance, permit God to do his work."

Tipping his hat, he said, "I bid you a fine day, Miss Madison. One filled with renewed hope."

Willow listened to the front door close, then sank back in the chair and stared at the ceiling.

I bid you a fine day, Miss Madison.

When was the last fine day Willow had experienced? Life was about hope, wasn't it? Clearing a path so God could walk through the rubble? Times spent with Tucker flashed through her mind. The care he'd taken with the schoolhouse remodeling, the hours he'd read the Bible to Uncle Wallace while she sat close by, listening.

Even the day they'd had the water fight. She remembered the way he'd tried to talk her out of marrying Silas, and how she went home and couldn't sleep a wink that night, his arguments racing around in her head. Was he the least bit interested in her? Or was his concern for Silas? She was a stranger to town, and townsfolk looked after each other.

Words from Matthew filtered through her mind. God's promise. *Take my yoke upon you and learn of me, for I am meek and lowly in heart: and ye shall find rest unto your souls.*

Willow leaned her head against the chair's softly quilted

back. How had she gotten herself into this mess? Oh, she knew all right. Uncle Wallace had used her for his own purposes. Although she yearned to be angry at the man, she couldn't. He had loved Claudine. There it was, that word again.

Love.

The pot of blue forget-me-nots in a shady spot on the porch mocked her. Betsy gave them to her to remind her of the importance of love, but Betsy didn't understand. No one did. She was responsible for Uncle Wallace. He had no one else. She could not allow the man to be set out in the road with no place to go. All the bank would care about was its money. No sympathy would be spared for a helpless old man.

As much as Willow wanted to walk away from it all, she couldn't. She was trapped, and she had walked into it with her eyes open. She knew it was wrong to marry a man for his money. No stranger to what her Bible said, she had deliberately set out to do something that was contrary to God's will. Now she had no way to escape the consequences.

Sunday, she would accept Silas's proposal. Mr. O'Malley had agreed to delay his departure to collect the money. The long-anticipated announcement would come during lunch in the town common and perhaps, if she were candid, the announcement would go something like this:

Miss Willow Madison does hesitantly and with dread announce her engagement to the very nice—but not the man she loves—Silas Sterling.

Chapter 30

Willow sat on the front stoop trying to make sense of her world. She had gone through the motions of preparing food, cleaning the house, and seeing to Uncle Wallace's needs. Now drained, she sat in the quietness and let her mind wander. *Lord, if there's some way out of this maze, please show me.*

Not even thunder answered tonight. What did she expect? She had gone into this plan willingly. Now she would have to pay the price. Tears blinded her. Nothing had gone right for her since the Yankees had overrun Timber Creek. How could life go wrong for so long? Didn't God care anything about her anymore?

Tears rolled unheeded. Her shoulders shook with sobs. Suddenly, the front door swung open, and Wallace awkwardly made his way outside, gripping his cane. His lined features carried worry. His mouth moved, but only a jumble of sound emerged. He shuffled close enough that his arms could encircle her.

She leaned against him, trying to nurse her earlier impatience with his choices. He had acted out of love. She didn't want to forgive him, but how could she hold it against him? She'd had time to absorb the shocking news about the mortgage, enough time to realize that if she didn't marry Silas, Wallace would lose his home. She sniffed, and wiped her eyes.

Wallace's worried eyes searched hers. She patted his shoulder. "It's all right. I'm just missing Copper and Audrey."

His lips jerked in what passed for a smile, and he nodded. Appeased. Willow gazed out across the sun-baked yard. Her uncle had meant well. Yes, he had tried to use her, but she sensed now that he had been desperate. He was old, lonely, and ill. She couldn't turn her back on him, and she wouldn't. Regardless of how she felt about Tucker, she had to accept Silas's help.

Down the hill, Tucker sat at his desk, staring at the column of numbers. No matter how many times he added them, he arrived at the same figure. If the mill didn't start operating soon, they were going under. The new contract with the town to reinforce the supports on the water tower wouldn't come in time.

The squat receptacle sat on the outskirts of Thunder Ridge. Powered by a windmill, it held the town water reserve to be used in case of emergencies. The windmill sat over a deep well, and kept the tower tank full, but in a drought, the town well, like others in Thunder Ridge, could become dangerously low. But as long as the water tower tank remained full, the population could survive until supplies could be hauled in from neighboring towns.

An inspection had shown that one of the supports had weakened. Tucker had been called in assess the problem, and work would begin on the tower as soon as the new saw arrived, but not in time to stop the money hemorrhage. For now, the repair was the only job on his list. Not enough to meet payroll.

Caleb entered the mill office, a smile on his face. "It's here."

Tucker looked up, frowning. "What's here?"

"The new saw. It finally got here, weeks late, but it's here. They're unloading it right now."

Tucker shook his head. "You're serious? I had given up." Elation raced through him. They could start trimming and cutting the logs piled up in the mill yard into boards and rafters. They were back in business!

He grinned at Caleb. "It's about time. Let's get those logs out of the pond and get to work."

"The men are ready to go. Pete's in charge, and in another hour, we'll be up and running. Come on, Tuck, let's go look over the operation."

Tucker followed him out, to find the men working together like a well-oiled machine. They had the saw uncrated, and were fitting it into place. They worked in a satisfied silence, their smiles expressing their moods. The mill would be operating again—the lifeblood of the town, flowing once more.

Tucker glanced up to see Eli rushing down the path. "I heard the muley finally got here."

Caleb motioned toward the men. "It's here and will soon be working. We're ready to start cutting."

Eli laughed, slapping Caleb on the back. "We made it. Praise God. We made it."

"Yes, God came through for us," Caleb said. "He always does."

Tucker agreed. The saw's arrival was an answer to prayer. For a while, he had lost faith, not sure if life would ever be the same. Now shame washed over him.

The men attached the saw blade and rolled a log into place. Then chips flew as the water mill powered the logs.

Eli grinned. "Been a long time since we heard that particular music, eh, Tuck?"

Tucker smiled wryly. "A very long time."

The sharp smell of fresh-cut lumber filled the air. Tucker breathed deeply. He'd waited so long for this hour. His thoughts turned to Willow. He needed to apologize to the Lord for more than lack of faith.

Reverend Cordell dropped by toward dusk. Men worked late tonight, eager to catch up after a long delay. Willow visited with the pastor, while Wallace nodded and smiled. The reverend crossed one leg over the other, leaning back against the step. "I hear the schoolhouse is about finished."

"Yes, I believe so. The men have worked very hard to restore the building." A week ago, that would have been a matter of great rejoicing, but recent events had crowded the teaching position to the back of her mind. Wallace's needs must come first.

"Your friends were a charming addition to our community. I was sorry to see them leave."

"They were sorry to go. They have a small business in Timber Creek—you'll recall that was my home until a few months ago. I, too, miss them." Her former home might as well have been thousands of miles away this afternoon. Events had left her wholly detached from her previous life.

"Well, perhaps they'll return soon. Blackberry Hill and Beeder's Cove will surely be reopening schools soon."

Willow pushed a lock of hair out of her eyes. "I'm hoping they will be accepted. It would be comforting to have them close." She needed her friends more than ever, considering that after tomorrow, she would be a promised bride. Perhaps a mother within the year . . .

"I see no obstacles to their being hired. Surely they are suited for the positions." Reverend Cordell smiled. "It will be good to have schools operating in all three towns. We've been without teachers since the war began."

Log hitting ground split the air. Willow jerked around, staring at the mill. Beside her, Wallace gave a strangled laugh. Reverend Cordell grinned. "Praise the Lord. The mill is working again. I heard the saw came today."

Her gaze shifted to the work site. She seemed to spend a lot of time gazing at it lately. "The mill is running again? That's wonderful." Tucker had waited so long for this day. Now that the mill was operational, the load of guilt she had carried since the fire lifted.

Good news in the midst of bad news was a reminder that God did provide, in both the good and bad times.

Chapter 31

⁓

A shout went up outside early Saturday morning, and Willow's gaze switched to the window. A flatbed wagon approached the outskirts of town, drawn by two sturdy oxen. Her gaze focused on the load securely lashed to the frame.

The new organ.

She whirled and skittered out of the room and downstairs. Finally, the instrument had arrived. She couldn't wait to feel organ keys beneath her fingers again and hear the soaring notes that only a fine instrument could produce.

Racing outside, she met the oncoming vehicle, her eyes skimming the tightly bound instrument. Endless time passed before the wagon stopped at the church, and sturdy men stripped away heavy ropes and canvas to reveal a fine mahogany organ. An *Adler*. Intricate carving and decorative work framed a mirror on the upper back. The top bore elaborately formed finials and raised flowers and vines. On either side of the high front were decorative shelves for vases or bric-a-brac. What a wonderful addition it would make to the church.

Willow clasped her hands to her heart. "It's lovely!"

The driver nodded and waved her aside. She watched the unloading process, her eyes fixed to the instrument. Silas was right; the organ would greatly enhance the worship service.

By now, the arrival had attracted gawkers. Men and women formed a long line as the instrument gleamed in the morning sunlight. An excited chatter rose.

Men dropped their work and climbed the hill to view the spectacle. Willow spotted Tucker's tall frame in the oncoming crowd. How would he feel about the new arrival? He'd been quiet on the subject—at least in her hearing—but she was sure he had an opinion.

"Stand back!" the driver ordered. "Don't anyone touch anything!"

The crowds melted back a safe distance as the driver and attendant swung aboard the wagon bed. One grasped a heavy rope, and tugged. The rope held secure.

Tucker came to stand behind Willow. She glanced up. "Isn't it beautiful?"

He grunted.

"Oh, admit it. It's lovely, and I can accompany the choir."

"Very good of you."

"I didn't order the instrument," she reminded.

"And it's not your decision who does what."

Workers began to scale the wagon in preparation for unloading. Reverend Cordell stepped out the front door, face beaming. Like everyone else, his attention was on the wagon's contents.

"Ah! It's here."

"Stand back, Reverend," the driver cautioned. "This thing is heavy, and once we start to unload we won't be able to stop until it's firmly on the ground."

The minister cleared the door, allowing workers access. His eyes roamed over the fine instrument. "Breathtaking!"

By now, excitement had spread, and Silas hurriedly approached. He paused beside Willow. "Finest money can buy—and it is superlative, even better than I had hoped." He glanced at Willow and grinned. "What do you think?"

"It's perfect," she agreed.

"Christmas Eve, you'll play Schubert's *Ave Maria*. Oh, the joy! I can hardly wait to hear you . . . here! Careful, my good man," Silas called when a worker carelessly bounded aboard the wagon bed.

An hour went by before the workers secured the heavy object enough so they could lift it from the wagon bed to the walk. A huge wooden pallet awaited the instrument. Then, the job of laboriously moving the organ into the sanctuary, down the long aisle, and to the side of the left altar would begin.

Two men shoved the old piano aside. Willow's protective side wanted to shield the old from the new, yet she knew exactly how the new instrument would sound. Her first presentation must be exceptional. Her thoughts centered on Handel—or perhaps one of the older hymns. Folks who had hovered nearby all morning dispersed for home and later returned with the noon meal. Fragrant smells rose from the various covered dishes. Pies and cakes of every variety filled the dessert table. A platter of fried chicken sat at one end of the main table, flanked by a huge beef roast and a pot of chicken and noodles. No one would go away hungry today.

Willow frowned when she handed a worker a glass of tea. Tucker had abandoned the site and gone back to the mill. Why wasn't he taking part in the celebration? She knew orders for lumber would be pouring in when word spread that the mill was working again, but surely he could take off long enough to eat and help move the organ.

"How will you ever get the instrument into the church?" she worried out loud as she poured coffee for one of the movers.

"Don't worry, ma'am. There's enough manpower to get the organ inside the church."

True, almost every man in Thunder Ridge, aside from the immediate choir members, had assembled to help. Was that the reason Tucker hung back? Around one o'clock, the workers set their drinks aside, and pulled on heavy work gloves. By now, Tucker had returned to watch the activities, and Willow had to grin. He pretended indifference, but he was curious as a cat. He stood to one side as the townsmen gathered to help move the instrument into the church. Silas bustled about, giving orders. Willow thought he really should keep silent. Purchasing an organ was different than moving an organ, and it was obvious Silas had moved very few, if any, large pieces in his day.

"Over here! Shove it this way, men!"

"No! The opposite way!"

"Now to the right!"

"No—the other right!"

The driver paused, removed his gloves, and said, "Mr. Sterling, If you'll step back, I believe we'll get this job done sooner."

Silas's cheeks flamed. "Sorry, my good man. I just thought . . ." He stepped back.

Compassion filled Willow, but she knew the driver was correct. Silas wanted to help, but he was underfoot. Only a few men were needed. Too many would hinder the operation.

A worker tested a rope pulley and nodded. The crowd pressed closer.

Willow turned to find Tucker beside her. He took a sip from his glass. "That thing must weigh a ton."

"It's an Adler—the finest money can buy."

He took another sip. "No doubt."

She bit her lip. How impolite of her. She knew his sensitivity to Silas's wealth. She only meant . . . oh, drat. Did it matter? He found fault with everything.

Four men took opposite corners, and three men manned the rope pulley. A hush fell over the crowd when the pulley tightened and then slowly began to lift the mammoth object.

Willow lifted her eyes heavenward. *Please don't let it thunder.*

The deafening sound might startle the workers and cause them to drop the rope. Images of the lovely organ smashed to smithereens sickened her.

Overhead, a blue sky promised nothing but fair weather.

Tension grew among the spectators. The pulley creaked. Hemp rope stretched tight. The instrument lifted, gyrating to the middle inch by inch.

Tucker took another sip of his drink, dark eyes focused on the work.

"You're not going to be cordial about the organ, are you?" Willow accused softly.

"No, ma'am. That money could have been used elsewhere."

"Like where?"

"Like the Seabo family. They were burned out earlier this year. The young couple has two young'uns, and a third on the way. They're living in a tent, and Old Man Winter's right around the corner. Money spent on that organ could have put a roof over their head."

"Does Silas know?" She was certain that if he knew he would provide a place for the family to live.

He shrugged and took another sip.

Willow put her hands on her hips. "It doesn't matter, you know. The Lord must surely want the church to have the organ, or he wouldn't have sent us one."

There. The man would argue with a brick wall, but she presented sound reasoning. Yes, most assuredly the Seabo family needed a home, and this very day Willow would form a committee to see that they had proper shelter before winter set in, but the organ would greatly enhance the Sunday worship experience. Greatly . . . no matter what Tucker believed.

The pulley slowly eased the organ upward. Ropes creaked but held firm.

Three notches.

Two notches.

The instrument now dangled atop the wagon bed. Men jumped down to man the side ropes.

One more crank and the lovely instrument reached the summit.

A collective "*Ooh*" rushed over the crowd.

Then, snap!

The organ fell like an anchor, shattering the wagon bed amid a thunderous wheeze and billowless tune. Pieces of frayed mahogany pelted the walkway.

Willow's jaw dropped.

Tucker took another long sip of tea. Lowering the glass, he said, "Oops. The Lord changed his mind."

Chapter 32

Losing that organ upset Willow. Tucker had no doubt about her emotions. To tell the truth, most of the towns-people were upset, and Tucker supposed he should be, too, but he meant what he had said. The money spent on the organ, wasted now, could have been used more wisely. The Seabos weren't the only ones in serious financial straits. They were just the worst off. They'd lost everything, and while Reverend Cordell was making an effort to find them a place to live, they still had only the bare necessities, and that was what others in town could spare. No one in Thunder Ridge had more than they needed. Except Sterling. It was a poor town, with poor people, but the sawmill could help. If he and his cousins could build up their operation, the mill could expand, hire more workers, and bring new business to Thunder Ridge.

A few men were sweeping up the organ remains. He noticed Tate holding one of the finials belonging to the top of the organ. Caleb stopped beside him, eyeing the organ. "That's a shame. We could have used that instrument. I imagine Willow could play real pretty."

"Well, we'll never know now."

His cousin eyed him. "You don't sound all that sorry."

"I don't guess I am. The organ would have been nice, but I can think of better uses for Silas's money."

Caleb nodded. "'For ye have the poor always with you,' Believe the Maker said that, and there's always folk going to need help. And it's right and good to help them, but there's a need for beauty in the world too. And that organ music would have been beautiful, you got to admit it."

His cousin was right, and he knew why he was so set against the organ. Because Silas had bought it for Willow. He'd tried to accept the fact that she would marry the rich man, but his heart couldn't accept the truth. By all that was holy, he'd fallen for the troublesome female.

Pieces of the organ had been swept up and piled off to the side of the church. Reverend Cordell's expression looked as if there had been a death in the family, and some women were wiping tears. Tucker sighed. He sure wasn't behaving like a follower of Christ. He couldn't imagine the Lord taking pleasure in the destruction of something so obviously impor-tant to the church. Caleb was right; losing that organ meant something more than money to the town. The folks had few pleasures. Why did he want to take away a vessel of praise?

The crowd wandered back to the common area, but Tucker knew their earlier buoyancy was gone. Tate carried his piece of the organ, resisting Eli's attempts to take it from him.

"No. I'm gonna keep it."

"Why would you want it?"

Tate stared up at his father, eyes solemn. "It's pretty." His features threatened to corkscrew. "I wanted to hear Miss Willow play!"

Eli patted his shoulder. "We all wanted to hear Miss Willow, didn't we, Tucker?"

His cousin's eyes were all too communicative. Tucker glanced at the child and nodded. "Yes, we were all looking forward to hearing Miss Willow, Tate. But we'll manage without it. God will send another blessing."

Tate's expression grew pensive before heaving a sigh. "All right, but I'm keeping this." He held up the finial, the sunlight gleaming off its polished surface.

"That's fine, son," Eli said. "It's yours. You can keep it."

"I want some watermelon."

Eli placed his hand on the boy's shoulder. "We'll get you a slice."

Tate looked up at his father. "When's Miss Audrey coming back?"

Eli's expression sobered. "I don't know, son. Audrey's home isn't here. She has a business to run in Timber Creek."

"But she's going to be a teacher, ain't she?"

"She is, and sounds to me like you're going to need a few lessons. The right way to say what you said is, 'isn't she.'"

"Isn't she what?"

"That's the proper way to talk. You said, 'ain't she.'"

"Ain't she what?"

Eli sighed.

"I want to go to her school."

He drew a deep breath. "We'd have to move to Blackberry Hill."

"Okay."

Eli laid his hand on his son's right shoulder. "Why don't we go get that watermelon?"

Tucker silently chuckled, watching son and father walk away. Audrey would be good for Eli, but the two hadn't hit it off—not like Caleb and Copper. But Tate had taken to Audrey in a big way. The boy needed a mother. Maybe he could fix Eli up with Meredith. She'd make a good mother and wife, but her incessant good humor was beginning to wear on him.

Chapter 33

Willow gathered a knot of hair, twisted it up, and inserted a hairpin. Miserably hot weather greeted the last day of August. The air was so humid, you could wring it dry. Strange, given the fact that it didn't rain.

There'd been no further word from Mr. O'Malley. She assumed he'd left Thunder Ridge early, as promised. How soon would the bank serve the eviction notice? And where would they go? The answer was as simple as "Yes, I will marry you, Silas."

Slipping into yellow sprigged cotton, courtesy of Copper, Willow turned to the mirror. The dress fit perfectly, nipped tightly at the waist, puffed lightly at the sleeves. Her friend sewed a flawless seam. She pirouetted in front of the mirror, studying the way the skirt flared. Copper had chosen well. The dress was most becoming, and a welcome addition to her limited wardrobe. Comfortable, too. That was an added blessing.

Willow heard the town common area stirring. The last official Sterling summer picnic was about to begin. She'd been
told the celebration was nearly as large and boisterous as
Fourth of July. In a matter of weeks now the long summer of
heat and lack of rain would give way to cooling temperatures
and, prayerfully, fall rains. Local women would be setting
up long tables with pretty white tablecloths. Massive jars of
lemonade would sit nearby, prepared with Silas Sterling's
contribution. Women dressed in white uniforms with the
Sterling Enterprise emblem emblazoned on starched pockets
would be bustling about the area.

Silas's swift-piloted ships had a heart-shaped midsection,
a short keel with very raking stern-and-stem outline, and a
low-sided and sharp-bowed hull.

She enjoyed this about the town. Poor, dependent on the
sawmill to survive, and dry—endlessly dry—but the spirit
of life was strong and contagious here. She'd taken pleasure
in the fellowship that was evident during Thunder Ridge's
celebrations.

Her thoughts turned to Tucker and Meredith. No doubt
they would be there today, talking and laughing. Well, it was
no concern of hers. She had other things to occupy her mind.
If Tucker wanted to spend his time with Meredith, he had
a right to do so. He needn't turn up his nose at her, though,
for trying to enhance Wallace, Audrey, and Copper's lives. It
wasn't as if she had the freedom to make the choice. Sometimes, circumstances dictated an action that was in direct
contrast to the desirable.

Arranging an errant lock of hair, Willow peered into the
mirror. *Today you will accept Silas Sterling's proposal.*

No!

Yes.

No!

Yes. She turned away from her image before she lost the argument.

On the way downstairs, she checked on Wallace, who was dozing. What a dark, bleak world he lived in—confused, helpless. Why had God left him to struggle through the maze? Was not his work here on earth finished? Sometimes death could be a blessing. Willow shuddered. She never wanted to go through the nightmare Wallace was living.

She lifted the light sheet and folded it over his bare feet. The bedroom was like a stovetop. How could the man sleep in all this heat? Her skin was clammy with perspiration. Perhaps there would be a breeze in the common area. She'd wake the judge later and see if Deet would take him to watch the festivities. Wallace was becoming a recluse. Only too aware of how he looked, and of his own limitations, he preferred to stay home and see only a few close friends. Perhaps she would feel the same in his condition.

Late Sunday afternoon, the picnic was in full swing. The townspeople had begun to accept the loss of the organ, and take the accident in stride as they did the lack of rain. God had a reason, they consoled one another, though no one could think of a single reason why having an organ would be wrong.

Willow rounded the corner where the band was playing and came face-to-face with Tucker. He veered in the opposite direction, but she blocked his escape.

"Tucker. I need to speak to you."

He turned to face her. "If it's about that organ, I didn't have a thing to do with the accident."

"No." She smiled, giving in to her fundamental instinct. The man was hopeless, but she enjoyed his company. Far too much. "About this pointless feud between us. Don't you think it's about time to lay it to rest?" If she married Silas, this man would always be in her life. Her heart. At the least, they could become friends.

Varying expressions crossed his rugged features—skepticism, curiosity, hope. She held her breath. Whatever their future held, she prayed they could peacefully coincide. She wanted—needed—him in her life. Not that she would ever entertain romantic notions of this man once she became Silas's wife, but a future without Tucker Gray would be very bleak.

He nodded. "I'd like that."

When he smiled, she felt her heart contract. The man didn't have a thought of how he affected her. She understood too late the meaning behind all of Betsy's endless discourses on love.

He reached to take her hand. His touch made her weak. "The rumor mill says you're going to accept Silas's proposal today."

The question cut straight to her heart. Yes, she was going to accept Silas's proposal. The enormity of what she was about to do hit hard.

Tucker met her eyes. "I'm begging you to reconsider."

Her gaze met his and her heart was breaking. She took in every line of his face, knowing he could never be hers.

"I can't."

He placed his hands on her shoulders. "If money controls your decision, then I guess you've run out of options. If love is the deciding factor, then you have many. Including me."

Oh, how she had wanted to hear those words, but they came too late. He must understand her situation. What would she do about Uncle Wallace? What about the five-thousand-dollar loan and Mr. O'Malley? Did he even know about the stranger in town? Surely he did. It had been her experience that everyone in town knew everything about everyone else. By the next morning, it would be whispered in every house, business, and gathering place. Shouted from the housetops. Just witness the expectation of Silas's announcement of their engagement. Every man, woman, and child appeared to know as much, if not more, about the matter as she did.

She looked away, furious. How dare he say these things now? He had to know it only made her decision to marry Silas all the more difficult. She'd known for weeks their attraction was more than ordinary. He knew it, too. And she understood how he felt, but why couldn't he support her in this, instead of throwing up roadblocks? Doing her duty was hard enough without him leading her into further temptation.

Her eyes lifted to meet his. "What about Meredith?"

He drew back. "Meredith's a friend."

"Very friendly, from all appearances." Jealousy intervened. "From my observation, she's closer than a friend, and I have a feeling she expects more than friendship from you."

His expression hardened. "From my observation, you don't love Silas."

"We're speaking of you now, not me."

"Who made those rules?"

When she didn't immediately answer, he sighed and released her. The warmth of his hands lingered on her shoulders, as if it had been imprinted there. His manner changed, he withdrew, and suddenly loneliness swept her. *This will be your life after tonight.*

His gaze fixed on her, distant now. "Your mind is made up. Nothing I can say will make a difference. Have a good life, Willow Madison, but don't expect me to stay around and listen to this insanity."

He left her standing, empty and drained, watching everything that mattered to her walk away.

Tucker was so intent on leaving the common area he didn't notice Caleb moving to intercept him until he called, "Hey, Tuck. Wait up."

He paused and turned. He didn't want to face either Caleb or Eli right now. They knew his moods too well, and he was sporting a foul one.

Caleb met his warning look with compassion. "You all right? Where you headed in such a hurry?"

"I've had about all the excitement I can handle for one afternoon."

His cousin nodded. "I hear Silas is going to have an announcement some time later."

Tucker's jaw firmed. "I hear the same."

"That have anything to do with your sudden craving for peace?"

"Not a thing." Tucker kept his voice even and cool. "I just have a hankering for a mess of fresh fish."

"Going fishing, huh? Well, that should be quiet enough. Give a man time to think."

"Yeah. Did you want anything in particular?"

Caleb lowered his voice. "You ever tell her how you feel?"

Tucker turned away. "She knows. It doesn't make any difference to her. She's determined to marry Silas so she can take care of Wallace and her friends."

"That's right noble."

"The fish are biting."

Caleb blocked his path. "You're just going to walk away without a fight?"

Tucker gave him an icy stare. "What's the point of a fight, if you know you're outnumbered?"

"I think the two of you made a good pair."

"It seems you're wrong."

Caleb shrugged. "You want some company?"

"Not now, but thanks."

"You won't be there for the announcement?"

"No." Tucker walked away, aware of his cousin's eyes following him. The whole town knew how he felt and knew why he would be absent. Sometimes it took a wise man to know when to cut his losses.

Chapter 34

Willow found Silas chatting with a group of older men. She hesitated, wary of interrupting the conversation. Finally, he glanced in her direction. "Willow. Did you want to see me?"

"Yes, if you have a moment."

"My time is your time." He winked at the others. "This lovely lady wants a word with me."

Willow knew without asking that he'd heard the speculation that she would accept his proposal. With a heavy heart, she led him to a secluded area of the common grounds, stopping under the spreading branches of a large oak tree. He smiled down at her, his expression one of pure joy.

"Before I hear your good news, may I offer some of my own?"

"Yes, certainly." Yet she wanted nothing more than to confront the moment and get it behind them.

"Just now, Frank Rivers—you do know Frank?"

"Isn't he Blackberry's town official?"

"That he is, my dear, and he's brought most welcome news. I was about to come after you." Silas fairly beamed. "The town has been so impressed by how smoothly our plans have run, it's willing to restart its school late fall. Audrey is being offered the schoolteacher's position in Blackberry Hill."

"She is!" The news was so joyful and welcome, Willow threw her arms around Silas's neck. "I can't believe it!"

Silas returned the affection. "Believe it, and with a little persuasion I'm confident that I can convince Beeder's Cove to follow suit. That would mean that Copper could join you and Audrey no later than next fall."

"Next fall!" Willow squeezed his neck warmly. He was so good—so very good—and she knew none of this would be possible without his assurances of financial support. That's why what she had to say seemed even more hurtful. She broke the embrace, and stepped back. "Oh, Silas."

He nodded encouragement. "Yes, dear Willow?"

She swallowed, and closed her eyes against the pain her words would bring to both her and this man. "I'm so sorry. I know the speculation is running wild, and I am so deeply sorry, but I cannot marry you." There. She'd said it and it felt like a giant weight had lifted from her shoulders. Immensely painful to her and Silas, but sometimes pain was better than lies. Lies she could never fulfill.

He focused on her. "I . . ." He appeared to grapple for words. Then, very quietly, "I understand."

"You do?"

"No, I fear I don't really, Willow, but in many ways, this comes as no surprise." His tone gentled. "I am, indeed, sorry that you cannot commit. I may be years older than you, but I have not forgotten the ways of love."

"Silas . . . I intended to marry you for very selfish reasons. In the end, I find I can't do it because I think so highly of you."

He chuckled lightly. "But more of the strapping young Tucker Gray, I wager?"

Heat flushed her already warm cheeks. "I came here, convinced this was my mission in life—to marry you, protect the judge and my friends—and after meeting you, I found that I loved you . . . but in a completely different way than you deserve."

"I know that, Willow. I suppose I've known it all along. But my daily prayers were that, in time, we would come to love each other."

Her tone gentled. "I didn't need time to love you. I loved you the first day we met in Reverend Cordell's office, but I didn't fall in love with you the way you deserve. At one time, I had convinced myself that I could love you that way, but now I know it's not possible."

She lifted her eyes to meet his. "I love another. Not intentionally, and he has never once encouraged my affection, but nonetheless it's there, and I can no longer ignore it. It wouldn't be fair to you to enter a sacred agreement when my heart could never be yours."

When she saw the light in his eyes dim, she hastened to add. "It's not as sudden as it seems. I've known all along, I just couldn't bring myself to admit the obvious."

"And Tucker. Does he share this love?"

Willow was never one to hedge, and she didn't plan to start now. "He's loved me from the moment I burned down his mill, only I wasn't certain he knew it."

She sighed. "I can't think of two less likely people who should fall in love. Uncle Wallace's house needs to sell to pay a mortgage he took out five years ago. Tucker's strapped for funds; I have nothing. Nothing but love." She squeezed his hands. "I love you, Silas. I want you in my life, but I can't marry you. I pray you will find the same kind of love I feel for Tucker."

Regret filled his eyes, but he smiled. "I admire your courage, Willow. If you change your mind, I'll be there. And I'll send someone forthright to repay the judge's loan, no strings attached."

She protested.

He stopped her. "God has blessed me richly, and in return, I believe he wants me to bless others. So you see, my dear, my giving is between me and the Lord."

Catching her breath on a sob, she whispered, "You're very kind. I do wish my answer could be different, but . . ."

"I understand." Giving her hand an affectionate squeeze, he released her. "Now run along and compose yourself." He used one finger to brush back a stray lock that had fallen across her forehead. "Apparently God has bigger plans for us than we had for ourselves. Now, let's go give those biddies something to really jar their bustles."

Willow surrendered to her emotions, weak in the knees. She had no idea what the future held, but she knew the one who held it. It was high time God had his say in the matter.

She wiped her eyes and glanced heavenward. She had full confidence that somehow He would see her through whatever happened. In time, Uncle Wallace would understand that love can't be purchased, that devotion stems from the heart. After all, he had loved Aunt Claudine. He knew the power of love.

"You go ahead, Silas. I'll be along shortly."

She had a few choice things to say to Tucker Gray.

Chapter 35

Love was many things, but it was not a crutch to uphold a mockery. Silas Sterling deserved love. And devotion. And a woman who would be his soul mate, the love of his life. That sort of mind-reeling intimacy didn't bind her and Silas. Money could buy a lot of things, and it could defeat more. If she married Silas, his loss would be far greater than monetary; it would be a loss of friendship—the kind only a man and a woman in love shared. Stolen glances, wispy touches. Knowing that one didn't have to utter a single word—that love was just there.

Sunlight faded as Willow threaded her way through the merry revelers. Bonfires weren't allowed this year because of the dryness. Kerosene lanterns glowed now, again, courtesy of Silas Sterling—and the fuel had arrived with much less fanfare than the barrels she'd brought earlier.

Children played along the riverbank, catching frogs and fireflies. The scent of perking coffee permeated the hot air. No one would sleep tonight, least of all Willow. She'd faced many a hardship on the battlefield, but none as great as the one she was about to confront. She'd wagered all on love. Would the price be worth the risk?

She cut across the picnic grounds and headed downstream of the activity. What was the old saying? "Hell hath no fury like a woman scorned?"

In truth, Tucker hadn't exactly scorned her today, but he had certainly gotten his point across. His laughter, his devotion to Meredith—it cut to the bone. She relived the sound of his deep baritone, the thrill of Meredith's voice as they hooted and played games. Would he eventually marry her? He'd claimed they were merely friends, but she wondered. His undivided attention to the pretty young woman from Blackberry Hill looked to be more than just friendship to her. Willow had made her own odious stew; now she was forced to simmer in it.

She spotted her destination, some two hundred feet beyond, and she quickened her pace, anger seething. If it wasn't for this man, she could have lived a peaceful life in Thunder Ridge. Wife to Silas Sterling, in want of nothing. Instead, she was cast adrift like a . . . like a . . .

At the moment, she couldn't think of anything except one of Silas's ships, and that hardly seemed fitting for the snit she was in.

Her footfall quickened. There he was, Mr. Know-It-All— he had known from the beginning of this whole disastrous issue. Tucker Gray brought on a dichotomy of emotions, but he was a smart man. So smart that he'd taken one look at Willow Madison and known that she was a woman who needed love. True love, as Betsy's forget-me-nots proclaimed, and he was the man God intended to impart that love.

He glanced up when she strode to the edge of the riverbank. Fading sunlight hit her back. She must make a ferocious sight, eyes snapping fire, hands on hips. Prissy.

Mad as a wet hornet.

"Tucker Gray!"

He casually whipped fishing line over his back, then into the water. "You don't need to shout. I can hear you."

"I want to talk to you."

He flipped the line over his shoulder. "Seems like we've said all there is to say."

"Not yet, we haven't. Do you know where I've been?"

He carefully worked the line, dragging it through the still water. "No ma'am. I don't keep up with your activities."

She rolled her eyes. "Oh please. You know everything I do."

"Not everything. I don't want to know everything you do." He reeled in the line and whipped a snarl free. "Aren't you supposed to be with your fiancé, Miss Madison?"

Willow stepped into the water, ignoring her good shoes. Copper would swoon if she saw the satin slippers going under. Wading out to him, she repeated. "My fiancé. And who might that be, Mr. Gray?"

His eyes followed her unorthodox approach. She reached him, gazing up into his stormy features. "Who might that be?"

"Last I heard, it be Silas Sterling." He eased her aside. "Do you mind? You're scaring the fish. Step out—of—the—way, Miss Madison."

Moving back into his way, she reached out and brought his mouth down to meet hers. For a scandalously long minute, she kissed him, releasing weeks of pent-up emotion.

Staggering beneath her clench, he struggled for balance. When the kiss only intensified, he lost the fight. Both went down in a raucous splash.

"Miss Madison!" he bellowed. "Your fiancé is not going to be happy with your conduct!"

"My fiancé, my foot. You know perfectly well I can't marry Silas." She brought his mouth back to meet hers. Willow Madison had fought plenty of battles, but this front had been the most aggravating, and the most gratifying. She knew that now, and she wasn't likely to forget the lesson.

Drawing back, Tucker's restrained gaze met hers. "Are you telling me that you aren't going to marry Silas?"

She nodded. "I can't. I tried to convince myself that I could, but then you came along and. . . ." She sighed. "I told Silas I couldn't marry him."

A grin started at the corners of his mouth and then quickly slackened. "What did he say?"

"He understood. He's a very nice man. Something you know nothing about."

"Oh, you think not?"

"I know not."

Pulling her back, he kissed her. And kissed her again. "Are you going to take that back?"

"Never." He could kiss her into a stupor, but she'd stand by her vow.

Or at least for a while longer.

"What about me?" Willow tried to interject between embraces.

"You're stubborn as a mule and ornerier than a polecat, but I figure with a little time, I can tame you."

"You oaf." She smacked his arm. "I'm serious. Now that I'm not marrying Silas, what will happen to me?"

"You'll marry me."

Willow kept spouting, the words rushing out like a hard

rain. "What will happen to me, and Uncle Wallace? And Audrey and Copper? I promised to help care for each of them. Of course, they'll have the teaching positions. Silas just told me that Blackberry Hill and Beeder's Cove have decided to reopen schools by next fall. Isn't that wonderful? Audrey and Copper will be close by and . . ."

His words finally registered. She fell silent for a moment. "I'll what?"

He stopped her fretting with a forefinger to her lips. "You'll marry me, and we'll take care of whoever needs help."

"We will?"

"Willow Madison. You're not blind. Can't you see that I'm in love with you . . . bald-facedly in love with you?"

Her gaze softened, and she ran her fingers lightly through wet curly hair. "Bald-facedly? Couldn't you think of a word a little more romantic?"

"Don't need to. Look at the way I've dogged you for all these weeks, argued with you at every turn of the road."

"And that's your way of courting a woman?"

"No ma'am, but that's the only way I could keep your attention. If I had been nice to you, you wouldn't have given me the time of day."

"Oh, you're so wrong." She kissed the tip of his nose. "I'm the one who is shameless. You've been on my mind, day and night from the moment I came to Thunder Ridge."

"And burned down my mill."

"Because your wagon was blocking the road."

"You can't miss an object that big?"

"You really don't want to get into this again, do you?"

"No ma'am." He grinned. "I can think of more interesting pursuits to occupy my time."

"Good," she said. "I'm glad you've finally come to your senses."

She sobered. "Tucker, I can bring nothing to a marriage but love—deep and lasting love, and the willingness to be a helpmate. For the longest time I thought if God didn't want me to marry Silas, he would stop me. Then as each day passed, I realized God will allow me to do whatever I want, but that didn't mean he'd bless the decision."

"Free will," Tucker agreed. "But free will carries a heavy price."

"In the past few months, my life has turned upside down. When I came here on that thunderous night, I had no idea I was walking straight into love. I thought I was walking straight into a noose. And the best thing? Silas understands—truly understands—my decision." She snuggled closer in his arms. "When Audrey and Copper move to this area, my life will be nearly perfect."

His features turned as solemn as a hanging judge. "Willow, I can't offer you anything but a strong back, undying love, and the willingness to believe that God holds our future, and whatever he brings our way is good enough for me."

She held him tighter. "It's good enough for me, too."

"Miss Madison?"

She drew a bottomless breath. Miss Madison. She loved the way he spoke her name, all manly yet gentled by love. "Yes, Mr. Gray?'

"I believe we are drawing a crowd."

Willow glanced to the bank to see a group of children, hands to their mouths, holding back giggles.

"I do believe you're right, Mr. Gray."

Tucker extended an arm, and they regally sauntered out of the river, dripping water.

Thunder shook the ground.

Willow glanced up as the first raindrop hit her head. First, one fat plop. Then two. Then the sky opened up and poured, steam rising from the scorched earth.

"I thought you said it never rained in Thunder Ridge," she challenged above the sudden driving downpour.

"I said you'd never marry me either. God changed his mind again."

Children squealed and danced in circles, catching raindrops on their tongues. Shouts went up at the picnic site, men and women's voices praising God for the long-awaited moisture.

Slipping her arm through Tucker's, Willow walked up the hill, never more confident of her future. Never more convinced of love, the joys it could bring, and God's wisdom.

Peace settled around her like a worn shawl. She couldn't take her eyes off the handsome mill owner. "I wish Audrey and Copper could have been here today."

He grinned. "They were expecting a wedding announcement."

Color touched her cheeks. "Yes, but not the sort that's come." She bit back a grin when she thought of the expressions on the women's faces when she informed them that she had accepted Tucker Gray's proposal—

She paused. "You did propose, didn't you?"

He affected a mock frown. "Matrimony? A man as disagreeable, mulish, and downright aggravating as I am?"

She boxed his shoulder. He grabbed her hand and held it tightly. Thunder and lightning licked across a sullen sky. Rain fell. Dark eyes fastened on her, and he dropped to his knees in the middle of the grounds. "Willow Madison. Will you do me the honor of becoming my wife? I'm a poor but humble man who will love you until I draw my last breath."

Grasping his hand, Willow smiled. "I will, Mr. Gray. Thank you for asking. "

Straightening, he kissed her again as sounds of an approaching wagon heralded newcomers. "Maybe we can find a wife for Silas."

"But who?" Willow would like nothing better, but there were so few available options for Silas.

"What about Audrey?"

"Maybe, but she didn't seem impressed when I was thinking of marrying Silas. Maybe Eli?"

"Eli's set in his ways, and I doubt he'll ever marry again."

"But they would be so right for each other. Three times blessed, Audrey would say. Well, there's always Copper. Who knows if Caleb is really interested in her, or just fascinated with a new woman in the area. She's rather contagious once she's been around someone, and she does like the life Silas could provide for her." Willow suddenly stopped in the middle of the road. "Look at us. Playing matchmaker when we know how disastrous that can turn out to be. Look at poor Uncle Wallace's efforts."

Tucker focused on the road and the sound of a fast-approaching wagon. "Whoever that is is in a big hurry." Pounding hooves overrode the sudden downpour.

Willow frowned. "Maybe the thunder frightened the horse."

She glanced at him and they burst into laughter.

A wagon careened around the corner, heading straight for Thunder Ridge. A bay bore down on the couple standing in the middle of the road, the animal's eyes wide, ears pinned to his head.

Lunging, Tucker seized Willow by the waist and took her with him into the ditch. The horse and wagon flashed past. Willow heard Audrey's familiar tone shouting at the horse. "Whoa! Stop this instant!"

"Stop him!" Copper yelled, holding firm to her hat. "We're going to be killed!"

Willow rolled to a sitting position, unable to believe her ears. "Audrey? Copper? They're here!" They'd come to surprise her!

Female screams filled the air as the wild-eyed bay sprinted out of control.

Willow and Tucker spoke in unison. "Water tower!"

When Willow saw the horse racing straight for the reservoir, she threw a hand over her face. *Not the water tower.*

Blat!

Boards shot into the air. Columns buckled, the platform lunged. Water sprayed, mingling with a virtual downpour. For the first time in a long time, Thunder Ridge was wet.

Shifting a finger, Willow peered through her hand at the disaster site. Rain fell in sheets. Timber lay scattered about like abandoned toy sticks.

Clearing his throat, Tucker said matter-of-factly, "You know, on second thought, I believe Copper *is* the more likely candidate to marry Sterling."

The couple turned in unison and shook on it.

A grin split Willow's features. "Thunder Ridge might be a quaint little town, but nobody—absolutely nobody—could accuse it of being a humdrum community."

Dear Reader,

As I write this letter, I am looking out on a beautiful, late-summer landscape. A hint of fall is in the air; overhead, an endless, inconceivably blue sky stretches as far as the eye can see. Temperatures are in the midseventies. Today, I study the sky, wondering what my brother, Dan, and my sister, Luanna, are doing up there. Both siblings have gone to be with the Lord in a matter of months. My sister in January, and yesterday, we buried my older brother in a full-honors veteran's ceremony. The crisp snap of Old Glory suspended high above a bed of radiant yellow marigolds. Three clear, symbolic rifle shots echo in my mind.

Often I am asked why I choose to write the sort of books I write—lighter in subject, yet stories that endure and—I hope—teach. I love all sorts of writing, but I confess my heart leans toward the old west historicals—a time when life was simpler. Values were absolute. Life was based on a matter of choices, not desires. Even now when I watch a nostalgic movie it will be one similar to *Support Your Local Gunfighter*. (If you haven't seen this old flick, be sure and rent it; it will make your day.) I write my historicals for entertainment value, and always with the prayer that the story will reach the person who needs a chuckle or a reminder that we're in this life together. We face problems, joy, sadness, and a deeper understanding of faith. Those are the principles that I hope my readers garner from my stories.

My grandchildren are growing like weeds. The oldest one, James, got married this summer. Welcome to the family, Abi! What a joy to witness these young lives going about their daily business serving the Lord. James is a youth pastor; Abi will join him in this vital ministry. In May, Joseph returned from working near the Russian border. He's involved in YWAM (Youth with a Mission). Josh worked as a landscaper this summer. He'll complete his senior year in '08. Gage is nine and heavily caught up in football. Audrey is six and just caught up—in everything! I've had the privilege of honoring my grandchildren with devotions in the new *Grandmother's Bible* (Zondervan) coming out this spring. All you Gramps and Grams, pick up a copy for your morning devotions.

I hope sometime during the year you'll find time to "refuel" your spiritual journey. What a joy it was to look death in the eye twice this year and ask: where is your victory? Tears are inevitable, but God's grace keeps us anchored.

Until we meet again, I pray that He will hold tightly to your hand through the storms.

Lori Copeland

Discussion Questions

1. Willow is determined to marry Silas, even though it goes against her idea of integrity, because she thinks it will help her friends. What do you think is most important—holding to your convictions, no matter what, or doing something you believe is wrong in order to bring about good?

2. Audrey and Copper don't want Willow to sacrifice herself for them, but she thinks she knows what must be done. Have you ever been determined to do something because you thought it was the right thing to do, even though others have tried to warn you against it? How can we know the difference between God's will and our own opinion of right and wrong?

3. Tucker held a grudge against Willow because she set fire to his mill. Have you ever held a grudge against someone?

How did it affect the relationship? How did you resolve the issue?

4. Wallace put himself in financial difficulties because he couldn't deny his wife anything. Do you have trouble saying no to someone you love? Is it a good thing for anyone to get her way all the time?

5. Willow has a dream of teaching children in Thunder Ridge. Her schoolhouse turns out to be a henhouse. The world tells us to dream big, but sometimes those dreams have to be modified to fit reality. Have you ever had to change your plans from what you want to what you can have? How easy was it?

6. Cordelia and Pansy try to tell Willow how to do her job. What is the best way to handle people who insist on giving advice, whether it is wanted or not?

7. It seldom rains in Thunder Ridge—just thunder and lightning. Still, the townspeople won't move away. They prefer to stay and trust in God to send rain. Have you ever been in a position where all you could do was pray and trust? Did God come through for you?

8. Silas knows Willow doesn't love him, but he's trying to believe she will change. Can we make someone love us? Why or why not? Does God try to force us to love him?

9. Audrey and Copper are resourceful young women who would rather make their own way. They don't want Willow to marry Silas in order to help them. Do you think we sometimes force help on people who would rather get by on their own?

10. Willow and Tucker each tried to blame the other for the destruction of the mill. Is it human nature to blame others instead of taking responsibility for our actions? If you say yes, why do you think this is so?

11. Wallace plotted to use Willow to save himself from financial difficulty. Have you ever had someone try to use you? How did you feel about that person? Have you tried to use others for your own gain?

12. Tucker and Willow had trouble forgiving each other. The Bible says we are to forgive our brother his trespasses. How easy is it to obey this commandment? Do you have trouble practicing forgiveness? How can we learn to be more forgiving in our daily life?

Three Times Blessed

The next book in the Belles of Timber Creek series

by Lori Copeland

Coming soon from

AVON

INSPIRE

Chapter 1

Audrey Pride knew one thing for certain: life had no certainty. Thunder Ridge had been as dry as a bone for the last two years, and now it was raining. Raining so hard Audrey couldn't see. She had planned to enter the community with a little more decorum than her friend and fellow comrade, Willow Madison. When she'd left Timber Creek three days ago with everything she owned tucked in a leather satchel, she'd intended to make a grand entrance into Thunder Ridge. She'd even told Copper Wilson—her second-best friend (now sitting on the wagon seat beside her) that she wasn't about to bring disgrace down on her head the way Willow had—not that Willow had been given a choice. She didn't mean to burn down the sawmill. That was a shared blunder with the mill owner, Tucker Gray.

When officials from Blackberry Hill recently wired to inform her that she'd been accepted as the new schoolmarm, Audrey had had every intention of reentering this town with dignity. Why, only scant weeks ago she'd spent time here with Willow and her stricken uncle, Judge Wallace Madison, getting to know the people and the area, and she'd fallen in love with the three close-knit communities: Thunder Ridge, Blackberry Hill, and Beeder's Cove. Decorum and ladylike finesse. That's how she'd intended to return.

Instead—if she could believe her eyes—she'd just demolished the town's water supply.

A strong hand latched onto the bridle and brought the horse and wagon under control. Copper had swooned and was now lying halfway across Audrey's lap and the wagon bench. When the buckboard jolted to a halt, she spotted Eli Gray, running to meet the new arrivals. And if the thunderous scowl on his face was any indication of his feelings, he wasn't exactly doing handsprings over her return.

Quickly adjusting her bonnet, she whirled to greet him. "Eli! How nice to see you again!" She extended a hand, which he ignored. The snub didn't surprise her. When she'd visited Willow and the judge last, Eli had remained aloof and detached, unlike his outgoing cousin, Caleb, with whom Copper had formed a promising friendship.

"Is anyone hurt?"

Her gaze shifted to Copper draped across the seat. "Just a wee bit shaken."

My lands! Copper's usually rosy complexion was as white as a snowball. She looked almost as shaken as the time the three women had helped hold the fort at Timber Ridge against a marauding band of Yankees who'd have loved nothing better than to annihilate the town and its remaining survivors. What a glorious day that had been! Copper, Willow, and herself fighting side by side had driven those men back so far they'd finally turned tail and run like frightened hens.

Rain fell in sheets. "Audrey! Copper!" Willow Madison raced toward the wagon, shouting their names. Handsome mill owner, Tucker Gray, trailed in her wake. "Oh, my goodness. Is anyone hurt?" Arriving breathlessly, Willow's gaze sought hers.

Accepting Eli's hand, Audrey stepped lightly from the wagon. "I believe Copper might need some help."

Bystanders turned to accommodate Copper as Audrey stepped into Willow's waiting arms. The women burst into excited chatter, shouting above the din of the rain. "Oh it's so *good* to see you again!"

"I had no idea you were coming until earlier this afternoon. Why didn't you write and tell me!"

"Everything happened so quickly. First the wire saying that Blackberry Hill had decided to open school again, and then on its heel, the wire confirming that Beeder's Cove wanted Copper's services right away. We threw everything we owned into the wagon, closed the shop, and were on our way within hours. We knew we'd be here before a letter could reach you."

The two women shared a warm hug.

Eli and Tucker bent to study the wagon wheels. "Can you believe this?" Eli muttered under his breath. "These are the most *destructive* women I've ever met."

"Watch what you say—you're about to insult my future wife."

His cousin's jaw dropped and a slow grin formed on Eli's lips. "Well, you ole dog. When did this happen?"

"Ten minutes ago," Tucker confirmed.

"You been drinking?"

"You know I don't drink."

Eli good-naturedly slapped his cousin on the back. "You got a good woman—clumsy, maybe, but a good one. Congratulations. What about Silas Sterling?"

"He's okay with it."

Returning the grin, Tucker straightened. "Wipe that smirk off your face. The ladies need our help."

Audrey turned toward Copper. The unconscious woman stirred, beginning to come around. She lifted her head. "Where . . . what?"

"You're fine," Audrey soothed. "We've had a bit of a jar."

Copper's eyes widened. "A bit of a jar? Are we dead?"

Sighing, Audrey murmured, "Dead—really Copper. Look around you. Is this your perception of heaven?"

The young lady's eyes roamed her surroundings. Audrey traced her gaze. Water running in puddle streams. Scorched grass. Rain-soaked, wide-eyed strangers peering at them.

"No . . . I suppose not."

Caleb Gray, cousin to Tucker and Eli, arrived. He jumped from his horse and removed his hat, his eyes fixed on Copper. "Miss Wilson! What are you doing here?"

"Mr. Gray! How nice to see you again." Copper perked up at the sight of him.

Grinning, he took her extended hand. "I didn't expect you back so soon. What's the source of my pleasure?"

Color flooded her cheeks as their hands locked. "I'm going to be teaching in Beeder's Cove soon."

"Is that a fact?" His grin widened. "Well, praise the Lord." The trickle of running water apparently distracted him. He turned to look at the collapsed water tower and the grin slowly dissolved. "What happened?"

"Accident," Audrey murmured. "Thunder spooked the horse."

Here she'd vowed to enter the town with more respectability than Willow, but in essence she'd caused a bigger stir. Willow might have inadvertently burned the mill, but Audrey had destroyed the town water supply. Over and over Willow had stressed the community's pathetic lack of rainfall of years past. Thunder Ridge was a place where it thundered continuously but rarely rained. She held out an open palm to catch a handful of water falling from the sky. Apparently the town's luck had changed.

Caleb turned back to stare at her.

She lifted her shoulders. "Quite a coincidence, huh? Willow, then me disrupting so . . . much?"

"Quite." His eyes traveled to Eli and Tucker, who still stood beside the wagon wheel, conversing in low tones.

Willow helped Copper down from the wagon seat. "Let's get you back to the judge's house." Tucker stepped closer to accept Copper's slight weight, and headed for Wallace Madison's home.

Audrey waited, uncertain about her next move. A tall man dressed in denim and plaid shirt eased to the front of the crowd, clearing his throat. "Miss Pride?"

Audrey turned. "Yes?"

"You are Miss Pride—from Timber Creek?"

"I am."

"I'm sorry, ma'am. I've been waiting for your arrival. I fear there's been a mistake. We've met—I'm mayor of Blackberry Hill, and while we thought we'd be able to reopen the school, it seems our excitement superseded our finances. It will be next fall before we can open the school."

Audrey's jaw dropped.

"I understand your dismay, and we're prepared to pay your

expenses back to Timber Creek." He removed his hat. "We're most sorry, ma'am. We sent a second telegraph right away."

Which by now was sitting in a deserted shack in Timber Creek. She and Copper had left so quickly the wire wouldn't have had time to reach them.

Nodding, the man threaded his way back through the crowd.

An elderly lady stepped up. "Pardon, dear, but I overheard your conversation, and I just wanted to say that there's no need to fret. I hear the undertaker is looking for an assistant."

"Undertaker?"

"Joe Burying."

"Joe Burying?" That's the undertaker's name?

The woman nodded and smiled. "Place belongs to Hank and Marian Burying, but their older son, Kirkland, runs it. The Buryings have been in business for as long as anyone can remember."

I have no job. Audrey stood, trying to absorb the shocking news. She had no job. Copper would be teaching in Beeder's Cove, Willow would be here in Thunder Ridge. She couldn't go back to ~~Thunder~~ Timber Ridge. She couldn't be apart from the only family that she had now: Willow and Copper.

But she didn't know a thing about burying.

Caleb led the horse and buggy up to her. "I'll get your wagon to the judge's house."

"Thank you." Numb, she fell into step behind him. No job? How would she manage?

Her eye caught the mill site, and she noticed that Eli had headed back to work with not even a simple welcome, though logic told her the recluse widower with a six-year-old son had never been the chatty sort. Not even particularly friendly to either her or Copper. Still, she had a stubborn streak that rose to challenges, and Eli was sure to be a challenge, but not for a moment did she doubt that given time, she could melt his reservations toward strangers—if she remained here. This was a big "if." Willow said that he'd lost his wife in childbirth when he'd been off fighting the war. He'd returned to a child who basically didn't know him, and the father and son had struggled to find a common bond. Seems Eli still grieved the baby's mother, and that grief had erected an impenetrable barrier.

One thing could always be said about Audrey Pride: cranky people never bothered her. She'd cared for her older brother before his death for too long to let a little testiness ruin her sunny disposition.

Could she claim the same about dead folk? They wouldn't be apt to argue back. She shook the thought away.

Eli Gray didn't faze her. She could take—and wearing a beaming smile—anything a difficult man could dish out. Mr. Gray was no exception.

Casting a final glance at the mill site, Audrey followed Caleb up to the hill where the judge's towering ugly green home sat. What was it the good book warned, "don't worry about tomorrow, today has enough trouble of its own"? Yet if tomorrow was as bad as today, she was in for a bumpy ride. Without that teaching position, she had a pound of problems to keep her awake nights.

Gathering her muddy hem, she trailed Caleb Gray up the hill in a driving rain to stable the startled horse.

Photo courtesy Picture People

LORI COPELAND is the author of more than ninety titles, including both historical and contemporary fiction. Lori began her writing career in 1982, writing for the secular book market. In 1998, after many years of writing, Lori sensed that God was calling her to use her gift of writing to honor Him. It was at that time Lori began writing for the Christian book market.

In 2000, Lori was inducted into the Missouri Writers Hall of Fame and in 2007 was a finalist for the Christy Award. She lives in the beautiful Ozarks with her husband, Lance, their three children, and five grandchildren. Lance and Lori are involved in their church and active in supporting mission work in Mali, West Africa.

Lori Copeland

Now and Always

Lori Copeland

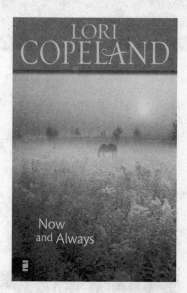

Very few things distract Katie Addison
when she's on a mission, whether it's
opening her home to abused women,
rehabilitating injured horses, or helping
tall, gorgeous Warren Tate mend his
broken heart. But when financial difficulties pile up for her, Katie hesitantly
admits she herself may need help.

Since his fiancée left him, Warren is done
with women—especially independent
women, which he'd guess describes
Katie Addison to a tee. Reluctantly he agrees to help Katie with her financial
troubles. But when his budget doesn't include Katie's daily lattes, Warren
realizes he may have a challenging client on his hands.

Meanwhile, Sheriff Ben O'Keefe can't seem to get Katie's attention. Everyone
in town knows he has had a longstanding crush on her. But to Katie, Ben is
just Ben. When mysterious events turn Katie to him for help, is it the chance
Ben has been waiting for?

Softcover: 978-0-310-26351-7

Pick up a copy at your favorite bookstore!

Introducing

AVON
INSPIRE

Celebrate the grace and power of Love

Discover Avon Inspire, a new imprint from Avon Books. Avon Inspire is Avon's line of uplifting women's fiction that focuses on what matters most: family, community, faith, and love. These are entertaining novels Christian readers can trust, with storylines that will be welcome to readers of any faith background. Rest assured, each book will have enough excitement and intrigue to keep readers riveted to the end and breathlessly awaiting the next installment.

Look for more riveting historical and contemporary fiction to come from beloved authors Lori Copeland, Kristin Billerbeck, Tracey Bateman, Linda Windsor, Lyn Cote, DiAnn Mills, and more!

AVON INSPIRE

An Imprint of HarperCollinsPublishers
www.avoninspire.com

E-mail us at AvonInspire@HarperCollins.com

AVI 1107